MOJAVE
ROCK

MOJAVE
ROCK

BOOK 3 *of the* **ARCPOINT SERIES**

J.W. Gilbert

MOJAVE ROCK

OTHER WORKS BY J.W. GILBERT

Mojave Man
Published by J.W. Gilbert

Mojave Rift
Published by J.W. Gilbert

The Moment
Published by Outskirts Press

Not Your Ordinary Praise and Worship
Published by Elisha Records

Escaping Ignorance – Pursuing Wisdom
Published by Inkwater Press

CHAPTER ONE

The ArcPoint Facility was a cacophony of conversation. Jarden stepped out of the large Quonset hut style building and into the quiet of the sunny south courtyard. His nerves could still feel the disruption that had shattered the peace in this place only an hour ago. No one had ever seen a machine that could fly, let alone one that hovered like an enormous hummingbird—its spinning propellers scattering dust and frightened residents everywhere. Everyone in the Community had seen pictures in the library's old books and magazines, but the real thing had been absolutely exhilarating. And terrifying. Then, to watch Arcon step out of its innards … *this is not a normal day for the laid-back people of ArcPoint.*

Jarden shook his head and surveyed the forest. It's towering trees and impenetrable thorns had created a protective cocoon around ArcPoint—like a shelter in a storm. Until the outsiders stormed in from above. Even now, with the helicopter gone, many people still hid behind trees, some clutching their children.

Those brave enough to come to the Facility after this intrusion were being rewarded with news of their family in the outside world—relatives they hadn't known existed. Arcon had recruited three of his peers, Chad, Tawny, and Raymo, to deliver the bulky envelopes of letters and pictures into the hands of their rightful owners.

Where had Arcon run off to

1

Jarden stepped back in and rescanned the crowd, but didn't see the young man he considered a son. He couldn't help but smile with pride at the sight of Arcon's recruits working side-by-side. *Less than an hour ago they'd been fighting over the gun Raymo fi ed at Arcon. These men truly know how to forgive.*

By his estimates, over half of the families had received one of those blue envelopes. He'd gotten his, plus an unexpected bonus—the arrival of a distant cousin. Victor Merrick, stocky, square-jawed, and with a receding hairline, was the spitting image of himself in his thirties. He was pleased to see that Victor was visiting and getting along well with people but it was time for them to shift gears. Jarden sent a youngster over to retrieve him.

Soon Jarden and Victor were sauntering out of the Facility like old friends. His youngest hunter, Tawny, joined them. "Have either of you seen Arcon?" asked Jarden.

Tawny pointed toward the forest. "There he is," said Tawny. "He's under a tree near the goat trail. See the vest?"

Jarden shaded his eyes from the high noon sun. "Okay. Yeah, I see him." He waved his arm to get Arcon's attention. Arcon saw it and nodded. "Let's go see how he's doing."

Arcon stood, pulled Elaina to her feet, and asked, "Did everyone get their envelopes?"

"There's a few dozen left," said Tawny. "Chad has people searching for the stragglers."

Jarden chuckled. "They need to check behind trees. So why are you and Elaina out here all alone?"

"Aahh, you know I don't like to be the center of attention," said Arcon.

"You won't escape that," piped in Tawny. "You wander away to the outside world, then fly in here on a big noisy machine with two outsiders? Don't expect us to ignore you."

"Well, right now, I just want people to know they have connections on the outside. Sorry I couldn't find some for you."

"That's okay," said Tawny. "You might be able to later on though, right?"

"Yeah, but I need old names from the Founder days. Arcon turned and asked Jarden, "Can you get the word out for families to scrounge up some information about other relatives that didn't come here? That'd help, too."

"I'll let *you* orchestrate that. You've probably got other things to discuss with the leaders anyway." Jarden saw Arcon's countenance fall as he looked toward Elaina.

Elaina gave Arcon's hunter's vest a tug, interrupting. "When do we get to go swinging?"

Tawny heard that and asked excitedly, "Are you going to take her to one of the swingways?"

"We were talking about it," said Arcon.

Tawny couldn't contain himself. "Let's go to the new one. I want to show you what I did to it."

"Maybe someday. Beginners have to start out on the Sunset trainer." He pointed west and when Elaina looked away, put his finger to his lips to tell Tawny to keep quiet. "It's tradition. Besides, that's the first one that Jarden made, and it's where he taught me."

"That sounds perfect then," said Elaina. "But can't we at least just go in the forest? I can't wait to be in there. To walk and climb among those flowers. They smell so good."

"I want to, but we have so much to discuss with Jarden, and people are bound to be confused. We should have a talk with the leaders."

Jarden spoke up. "How about if I arrange a meeting for tomorrow morning? That way, you kids can spend some time together. But I'd like to tag along with you to the trainer. You know … for safety reasons."

"Safety reasons?" asked Elaina.

"It's just protocol," said Arcon. "On a person's first jump, we always err on the side of caution."

3

"Can I come too?" begged Tawny.

"I suppose," said Arcon reluctantly. "At least until she gets comfortable with it. Then we'll swing away from you both. Maybe all the way to the Sunset outpost."

"Really? Has a girl ever been to an outpost?" asked Tawny.

"It's a whole new world out there," said Arcon. "You won't believe what girls can do." Then he hugged Elaina and said, "Especially this one. She can go farther in one day than you have in your entire life."

Tawny turned to go and said, "Wow, then let's get going. This'll be fun."

"We can't go out there right now," said Jarden. "We need to get back to helping Chad and Raymo empty those boxes. We should at least let them know before we go."

"Okay, I'll hurry them up," said Tawny.

"And Tawny," added Jarden, "open the roll-up doors. It's getting stuffy in there."

"Yes, sir," said Tawny. He ran off like a hunter chasing a rabbit.

When he was out of earshot, Jarden grinned and said to Elaina, "I think you've lit a little fire under that boy."

"How so?" asked Arcon.

"Well, think about it. You go away for a few weeks and come back with the perfect girl for you. He's at that age. I bet it won't be long before he'll want to see what might be out there for him."

"I understand," said Arcon, and pointed at Elaina. "I'll explain to him it took me eight years to find this one."

Victor, content to listen like a spectator, added, "I still haven't found the right one for me."

"Well, ArcPoint isn't necessarily the best hunting grounds for that sort of thing," said Jarden. "Anyway, if you three would like to get started toward the trainer swingway, Tawny and I'll meet you there in a bit."

"Okay," said Arcon.

Jarden was halfway across the south courtyard when he glanced back and saw that Arcon was jogging to catch up to him. He yelled, "I need to explain about a couple of the supplies that came in the box."

Jarden stopped. "You said something about technical papers if I remember right."

Arcon came alongside and the two of them walked on together. "I wanted to say that Victor's not as comfortable being off the ground as we are, so I don't think he really wants to go to the swingway. But he likes machinery, so can someone show him what's been done to keep this place going?"

"Sure. Who do you have in mind?"

"How about Luther? He's familiar with the mechanical things. Plus, I don't think I have any family stuff for him. It'll distract him from that disappointment."

"Understood," said Jarden. He whistled toward Elaina and Victor while Arcon waved for them to join him and Jarden.

"Anyway, about the boxes of technical papers—there's one marked Medical. It contains research the outsiders did on the infertility problem. They need more information from us to know for sure what's happening, but it sounds promising. Someone needs to run those papers over to Minda Polk at the Med Shack and tell her to look them over. She'll have questions—she needs to know we'll link her up with the outsiders later."

"I should probably handle this myself," said Jarden.

Arcon agreed. When Elaina and Victor arrived he said, "Slight change of plans, we've one quick stop to make before we go swinging—and Jarden, there's another box marked 'Trees.' It seems the infertility problem comes from the ArcPoint trees. They're pulling certain minerals out of the ground, and we're eating them. That's the *bad* news. The good news is those minerals are valuable to the outsiders. They're working on a plan to extract those minerals and rid us of the needle-brush as well."

Jarden's eyes got big. "Are you saying they can solve the infertility issue, and take away that cursed needle-brush at the same time?"

"Well, yeah, sort of," said Arcon. He walked over to the roll-up doorway and scanned the crowd who were still milling around.

Elaina added, "It's a lot more complicated than that, but that's the end result they're hoping for."

"I think I like you outsiders already," said Jarden.

Arcon spotted who he was looking for. "I see Luther. Let's have him take the tree information to the shop people. It's mostly mechanical stuff, anyway. Maybe Victor can go with him. He understands what it's about, right, Victor?"

Victor shrugged in response and said, "Mostly. You just need them to look it over anyway, right? They don't need to act on anything right now."

"No. Yeah. They only need to try to figure it out. I need to meet with the leaders of the Community before we do anything. This is all just information. I'll go get Luther."

As Arcon jogged off to the other side of the Facility, Jarden said, "Victor, would you like to join us in swinging through the trees, or can I have Luther show you around our Facility? You'll see a lot of worn-out machinery that's been creatively kept running. Arcon tells me you like machinery."

"That sounds like fun, the machinery that is," replied Victor. "The authorities wanted me to find out what you folks may need in your shops. I might as well get started."

"I'll talk to Luther and have him give you a tour of our shops."

"Sounds great," said Victor with a sigh of relief.

Arcon searched until he located a muscular, middle-aged man wearing an oil-stained leather vest. As he got closer to Luther, he noticed Brina standing with her grandfather, away from everyone. As their eyes met, he nodded to her, but she looked away. His heart sank. Besides Jarden, no one in the Community had been a better friend to him. *She always cared about my well-being, and I betrayed her friendship. I need to talk to her soon, but now is not the time.*

"Hey, Luther! Are you busy?"

Luther spun around to look at Arcon, then held out his empty hands. "Wish I had one of those blue envelopes, but you didn't bring me anything."

"Sorry about that. If you tell us names of some of your relatives, I'll see if the outsiders can find something."

"That'd be righteous. How can I help you?"

"I want to introduce you to Jarden's distant cousin, Victor. Would you have time to walk him around the Facility? He's mechanical. Knows all sorts of stuff. You'll like him."

"Sounds like it."

"Then follow me."

When they got back to Jarden, Tawny had rejoined their group. Victor was holding the box marked Trees. "I see you found it," said Arcon. "Victor, I'd like you to meet Luther. He's one of the main reasons a lot of our machinery still works. Luther, this is Jarden's cousin."

"I see the resemblance," said Luther. "Glad to meet you."

As they shook hands, Arcon said, "By the way, there are some papers in this box I'd like you to give to Firsten for the shop people to look at. It's a design for a machine to chew up the needle-brush. See if they can figure out how it works. If they have questions, they can ask Victor."

"What if I don't know the answer?" asked Victor.

"Then fake it," said Arcon. "That's what Luther does." He laughed and added, "We both learned that from Jarden."

"Time for you boys to leave," said Jarden jokingly. He turned to Arcon. "I see Minda over by the kitchen. I'll take her this medical information and meet you at the Sunset trainer. Are you going with them, Tawny?"

"For sure. If he's going to teach her to swing, I gotta see it."

Arcon saw Brina and her grandfather go into the Franklin meeting room. He said to Elaina, "Could you and Tawny wait outside for a few minutes? There's something I need to do."

"Sure, of course. We'll wait for you by the woods where we were before."

Arcon gave Elaina's hand a squeeze. "Great. I won't be long."

Arcon walked across the Facility until he saw Tawny open the south man-door for Elaina. When she was out of the building, he stopped, opened up his backpack, and pulled out a bulky blue envelope. In the Franklin room he found Brina talking with her Grandpa Lars at one end of the conference table. Standard ArcPoint behavior was to let a private conversation run its course before interrupting, but he couldn't wait. He walked into the room. "Can I show you two something?"

"Sure, you can," said Brina, gesturing for Arcon to take a chair. "Grandpa just needed to sit down for a few minutes."

"Hi, Lars. I think you'll want to look at this." Arcon sat and handed Lars the envelope.

"What is it?"

"It's information about some of the Ashford family in the outside world."

"Really? I didn't think there was one for us," said Brina.

"I had it. I wanted to give it to you myself. I don't know everything that's in here, but I know there are letters and pictures from some of your family members. I've even met a few of them. They're all good people, and they're happy to know that we are too—and that we're still alive. Go ahead and open it."

Lars Ashford slowly opened the envelope and carefully pulled out a sheet of paper. He saw a picture of a smiling young man and started reading aloud what was written with it. "Dear Ashford Family. My name is David Bryzinski." He looked at Arcon. "Who is David Bryzinski?"

"I met him. He's the grandson of an Ashford that is related to your father, Norm. He really wants to hear about all the things Norm did for our Community."

Lars set that letter aside and slowly reached into the envelope again. Brina said to him, "Grandpa, can I do that for you?" He handed her the envelope, and she dumped the contents out on the conference table.

Arcon stood and said, "I should let you two look this over on your own. I'm leaving now."

He was two steps away when he heard Brina say his name. He turned just in time to see her wipe a tear from her cheek as she said, "Thank you."

"For the letters?"

"For coming back."

"I had to," he said, as his chin quivered. "This is my home." He had to look away from them. He hadn't planned to make that confession, and wasn't really sure where his ultimate home would be. But he knew ArcPoint would always be one.

His thoughts were interrupted when he heard Lars say, "Is it true what they're saying? Is Jesus ruling in Jerusalem?"

He turned to face him. "Yes. Jesus is on earth again and ruling from Jerusalem. I haven't seen him, but he appeared to someone I know just a couple of weeks ago. He has a whole network of judges and authorities governing the world. Things have changed a lot out there since the evil times. Like the Bible says, there are no more wars or lawlessness."

"That's good to hear, Arcon."

Lars went back to looking at some pictures, so Arcon smiled at Brina. "I really need to go now. I have things to attend to."

"I want to meet her," she said, matter-of-factly. They both knew who she meant.

"She'd like to meet you. But right now, I promised to show her the Sunset swingway. She'd like to try swinging."

"Uh-oh. Maybe I should meet her before you leave, and give her fair warning. You know, just in case something happens."

That statement confused Arcon, but then he saw a smile creep across her face and said, "You promised not to tell anyone."

"I haven't," said Brina. "And I won't. But as soon as you get back, I'll ask her how the training went."

Lars perked up. "What training?" he asked. "What are you two talking about?"

"It's nothing, Grandpa. Arcon's just going to give his girlfriend a few swinging lessons."

"Sounds mighty unwise, if you ask me," mumbled Lars.

Brina smiled at Arcon. "You'll probably be back in an hour or so?"

"Maybe a little longer."

"I'll be watching the trail and praying for her."

Arcon laughed. "I'm sure she'd appreciate that, but I'm not going to tell her why you're doing it." He winked at her and said, "Thanks for understanding. I'm leaving now."

There was a buzz of conversations in the Facility, especially near the dining area. Arcon assumed they'd want to find a private place to browse the family material. Instead, they were excitedly sharing their discoveries with each other.

He stopped for a moment to take in the scene and feel the relief—glad those who didn't receive envelopes weren't upset. He'd not been able to recall the last names of more than half of the ArcPoint Community. Compounding his guilt was knowing every single person knew who he was. None of that seemed to matter at this moment.

As Arcon worked his way through the Facility, several people held up their blue envelopes and smiled at him. *What made me think returning to this place would be unpleasant?*

Arcon looked away from everyone and hustled to get back to Elaina and Tawny. As he approached them, Tawny was grinning ear to ear. "Is she going to get the full training?"

"That'll be up to Jarden," said Arcon. As soon as Elaina wasn't watching, he whacked Tawny on the shoulder and motioned him to keep quiet.

Tawny just smiled.

CHAPTER TWO

Elaina would've preferred to be walking alone with Arcon, but Tawny just had to tag along. She got a sense the ArcPoint people might be uncomfortable with a young unmarried couple going off into the woods alone. She hoped Jarden would catch up with them soon. As they made their way down the Sunset trail, she marveled at the log homes randomly scattered in the forest and asked. "You say they built these without power tools?"

"I said they built *most* of these without chain saws," responded Arcon. "Quite a few without power tools at all on site. We have one big saw at the Facility, but we were never able to make fuel for gasoline engines, only diesel. That meant we had no electric generators except the big ones for the main buildings. We ran power to some of the closer log homes by scavenging wire from abandoned houses."

"So some of these homes have no power?"

"Nothing."

"What about lights and cooking?"

"All done with oil from the ArcPoint trees. When the Community understood we might be here indefinitely, they became very careful with the electrical tools. Jarden told me we lost the last electric saw when he was in his late twenties."

"How long ago was that?"

"Well, let's see. Over fifty years ago."

"Wait, are you saying Jarden is almost eighty years old?"

"Yeah, why? Does he seem older?"

"No, no. For some reason, I thought he was my dad's age, or maybe a little older than him. But not *that* old."

"How old is your dad?"

"Fifty-six."

"Oh. Just a little older than Tawny here."

Elaina looked closely at Tawny and then said, "No way."

Arcon laughed. "Just kidding. Tawny's still a teenager."

"Just barely," countered Tawny. "I'll be twenty next month. How about you, Elaina? Are you still a teenager?"

"My dad thinks so," said Elaina. "But I'll be twenty-two in three months."

"Wow. Do you have any younger sisters?"

Elaina smiled nervously. "No, sorry. I'm an only child."

"Yeah, so am I," said Tawny.

Arcon added, "Almost all of us are an only child. But Elaina knows about that problem." He changed the subject. "Here you can see the ArcPoint River. Your maps call it the Mojave River. It's just muddy now, but it flows after any good rain. They planted a lot of our first trees along this river, but we cut most of those down for the homes you see. When the trees grew up, the seeds were scattered downstream by the river—to the east— and by animals toward the Rift."

"Why toward the Rift?"

"See these hills in front of us? A lot of the rain that falls on them flows northwest toward the Rift and the I-15. Then it turns this direction and flows past the Facility. What we get here is old, mineral laden water. The fresh rainwater is on the other side of the hills. Animals like it there better—but they come to our side for the seeds."

"I can see the trees ahead of us are huge. Are they some of the oldest?"

"And the biggest," said Arcon. "They get a lot of water from the river. That's why Jarden used these trees to build the first swingway. Do you see how the branches grow large and horizontal? The trees fight each other for sunlight by growing sideways rather than getting taller. Our horticulturists say that's typical for an Acacia tree. But these aren't normal Acacias. Jarden figured out how to walk on the branches from tree to tree and was able to get beyond a lot of the patches of needle-brush."

"And then he invented swinging," added Tawny.

Elaina remarked, "I think Edgar Rice Burrows did that."

"Who's that?" asked Arcon and Tawny in unison.

"The guy who wrote the Tarzan books."

"I don't get it," said Tawny.

"She's joking with you," said Arcon. "Ask Jarden about it. Oh, and ask him to show you who Tarzan is. Somewhere in the stuff we brought you is a working disc player!"

"Ask me about what?" asked Jarden as he stepped out from behind a tree.

They all jumped when they heard him, and Elaina blurted out, "How'd you get ahead of us?"

"I walked right past you when you were at the river. I'm going to need to have a talk with these two young men. Their skills at perception are slipping. I could have been a coyote."

"You don't smell like a coyote," joked Arcon.

"I take that as a compliment." Jarden turned to Elaina and asked, "Are you ready for this? Training ground is just ahead."

"More ready than you'd expect," quipped Elaina.

"Alright then, follow me."

After walking past a few large trees, Elaina was now looking at a huge one, with a handwritten plaque at its base that read, *JARDEN'S FIRST SWING*. "I made that," she heard Arcon say as he passed it by and started climbing the tree. She looked at the other two comrades, but they both motioned for her to go ahead. She assumed they wanted to see if she could actually climb it, so she did her best to stay on Arcon's heels, just to impress them.

When she got to what she thought was about ten meters off the ground, she stepped onto a crudely built platform of bare branches laid across two other branches. "This looks like your nest," she said to Arcon, "but without the greenery."

Tawny started to ask, "How did she——"

Arcon interrupted him. "Don't ask. It's a long story." Then he reached over and grabbed one of the two ropes hanging near the platform. "Usually, we just grab a rope and jump, and we swing to a platform in that tree over there. It takes a while to get the strength to hold on."

"Arcon found that out the hard way," added Jarden.

"I told her that."

"And he showed me the scars," added Elaina.

Jarden shook his head. "I got quite a tongue lashing from his parents for letting him use my swingway, although I never actually gave him that permission."

"Yeah, okay," said Arcon, "Let's get back to the training. We developed a trick for the novice. Here, I'll show you." Arcon picked up the end of the rope and tied a loop into it. "Okay, put your foot in this loop, and then, when you're swinging, you're supported by your legs instead of your arms. Here, I'll hold the rope, and you stand with one foot in the loop and hold on tight with your hands."

Elaina eagerly complied, placing her right foot in the loop. As Arcon held the rope, she grabbed it and put her full weight on the loop. She said, "It pinches on my ankle a bit, but I see how it works."

"Just lift up with your arms to get the weight off your ankle," said Arcon, "but don't let your foot slip out of the loop."

Jarden encouraged her to put more distance between her hands. "Eyes ahead, not down," he coached.

"You're okay?" asked Arcon, "and holding on tight?"

"Of course," she answered, looking down at the needle-brush between the two platforms. Elaina's heart was beating like a drum and she was holding her breath but she nodded and said, with as much confidence as she could muster, "I'm good. I can—"

Arcon let go of the rope.

Elaina went flying through the air, screaming all the way. She sailed toward the other platform, then back in their direction, still screaming. As she flew closer, she yelled, "I can't believe you let go of me!"

"You're doing great!" said Jarden, sending her away with a push. "Round two!"

When she came flying back, Arcon gave her another push.

Tawny said, "She's squealing more than screaming now, that's good, right?"

"Sure is," said Jarden. He cupped his hands and yelled, "Straighten your support leg! Stand straight!" Elaina followed his instructions.

"Now she's getting the hang of it," said Arcon. Tawny laughed. Jarden groaned.

Before her fourth approach, Arcon grabbed the companion rope to Elaina's. He reversed, and just when she'd swung closer, ran and jumped. He flew past her as she closed in on the platform. Jarden gave her a push.

Arcon jumped onto the second platform, slung his rope over a branch stub, and when Elaina came sailing towards him, caught hold of her rope and shuttled her safely onto the platform. "You can hang onto me now if you'd like."

"Why would I want to do that?" she joked. "That was amazing."

"*You're* amazing. How are your hands?"

"They're fine, ankle too," she said, presenting both. "I can't imagine doing any of that without the loop though."

"Scary, huh? Ready for more?"

She bobbed her head and tucked her foot back in the loop. "I was just starting to like it."

"Then hold tight—we'll go together." She grinned, got ready, and they jumped off the platform, Arcon holding her rope in one hand and his in the other. The pair sailed through the air together, back to Jarden and Tawny. Arcon swung Elaina ahead and Jarden grabbed her rope. Arcon jumped onto the platform and stowed his rope.

"I think she's a natural," said Jarden, as he helped her step out of the loop. "We'll have her out there hunting rabbits before you know it."

"As long as her screaming doesn't scare them all away," joked Tawny.

"I didn't scream," said Elaina.

"You sure did," said Arcon.

Jarden laughed and said, "Sorry, Elaina, I have to agree with them. You screamed just like Arcon did when I pushed *him* out of the tree."

"And like Tawny did when I pushed him out of the tree," said Arcon. "But be honest, it was fun, right?"

Elaina put her hands on her hips and scowled, then laughed and said, "It was a blast. When do I get to try running branches?"

Tawny's mouth dropped open. "Wow. How in the world did you find her?"

Arcon smiled. "Technically, she found me over eight years ago. But that's a long story." He turned to Elaina. "Want to try it again?"

"Can I try landing by myself?" she asked, looking across at the other tree.

"Sure, but Jarden is here, so we have to abide by the safety rules. He'll help you get your foot into the loop. Then you can jump whenever you want. He'll explain how to jump off at the other end, and I'll be waiting there to help, just in case. We can try the same thing coming back this way."

Elaina swung like a breeze through the trees, back and forth between the platforms. Arcon was occasionally alongside her, and even Jarden joined her twice. When one foot got tired, she just switched it out for the other and kept going.

After a while Jarden said, "I need to return to the Facility,"and Elaina used the interruption to counteract Tawny's non-stop encouragement to keep going.

Arcon begged for permission. "Before you leave, do you mind if I show her the next training step?"

"Tell you what," said Jarden, "you can let her see it but not try it. If you agree to those terms, you two can go ahead on your own." Tawny grumbled in opposition.

"I agree to those terms," said Arcon.

"Okay, I'll meet you back at the Facility. Tawny, you're with me." Jarden climbed down the tree with a reluctant young man following him.

"Are you ready to try a different swing?" Arcon asked Elaina as he stepped over to a new area of the platform.

"But Jarden said we could only look at it."

"He was talking about the next training step," said Arcon. "We need to swing over to this other platform first, and you can do that. Let's go." He swung away from her, and she quickly followed. When they got to the second platform again, he walked to the other side. He grabbed another rope and put a loop in it. "Here's yours. I'll swing first on mine, and you follow. Don't worry; this is an easy one." He handed her the rope and then pointed to another tree platform a short distance away. "I'll meet you over there." Then he grabbed his rope and jumped, leaving her alone on the platform.

19

Elaina quickly put her foot in the loop and, holding on tight, jumped off the platform herself. This swing went much faster, traveling only half the distance of the last one. She was on the next platform and in Arcon's arms before she knew it. As he was helping her step out of the loop, her eyes glimpsed something strangely familiar. "Is that a ... super-rope?"

"Sure is. It's been rebuilt and improved a few times, but this is where Jarden built his first. It's easier to build than a swing, but not as much fun to use."

Elaina walked across the platform and stared at it. "I wondered where you got the idea. All this time, I thought you were brilliant."

Arcon laughed. "You probably thought I was brave, too. To be honest, I was petrified. I'd never tried a super-rope that long before. Or one made out of something I'd never stood on. Over something I've never fallen into. See that needle-brush down there? It breaks your fall, so the only injury you have is from being scratched by the thorns. That's no big deal if you wear enough skins. But thinking about falling into the Rift ..." Arcon went silent for a moment and then said, "I almost couldn't do it."

Elaina wrapped her arms around him. "I'm glad you did." Then she laughed and confessed, "It scared me so bad I almost couldn't watch."

Arcon looked her in the eyes. "I'm glad you could." Then he pulled her close and kissed her. This wasn't the first, but it was certainly the first spontaneous one. Other times, it'd been more like an experiment, both of them testing the idea. She never expected it to happen in *this* place, in this private community, where he said people rarely kissed on the lips in public.

At this moment, she knew she was at home wherever she was with him.

CHAPTER THREE

Roberto rubbed his brow with relief. He was very glad to see that his daughter, Elaina, had finally stopped swinging through the trees. He knew what she'd been up to because she'd snapped Arcon's camera onto her lapel for safekeeping—but hadn't turned it *off*.

Roberto had been nervous watching her climb the tree. Angry when Arcon just let her go flying off that platform. Then he'd grown dizzy watching the blur of trees and other obstacles fly by as she spun around.

But Jarden was there. *Thank goodness.* Elaina looked like she was having the time of her life. He couldn't bring himself to shut off her video feed until this moment. He decided they needed some privacy, so he told Sam, the videographer, to stop monitoring them and focus on Victor. Then he heard Victor's voice over the radio. "Mr. Gonzales, are you still there?"

"I'm here, Victor. What do you need?"

"I'm in the generator shed, and I think we need to help them get one more generator running. I'll get some shots of the nameplate on it and have Luther give you a list of parts they need."

"Sounds good, Victor. I'll continue recording on this end. Ranger Dan will have some folks track down information and parts. By the way, if you see Elaina, tell her to turn off Arcon's camera. I'd tell her myself, but nobody has their earpiece on."

21

"Okay, I'll tell her. Do you see the nameplate?"

"Get a little closer to it. Okay, got it. Now, if you could, hand the camera to Luther so he can give us a tour of the unit while he's telling us what they need."

"Okay," said Victor. He handed the camera to Luther and explained how to use it.

"Hi Mr. Gonzales, this is Luther. I think our needs are extensive on this generator. One of the heads is pretty much useless. It's warped and cracked, so the ..."

Roberto listened as Luther explained in detail the problems with the generator, but didn't care, since an expert in that field would handle those issues. He motioned to the videographer to watch the monitor for him and to let him know if he was needed again. He briefly risked turning on Elaina's video feed and saw they were walking back through the woods. It appeared to him they were respecting his request not to stay away from the Community too long.

He said his goodbyes to Victor and Luther and then walked to the break room to join Ranger Dan. It'd been a busy day, at the end of a long weekend. He needed to find some comfort food that wouldn't ruin his appetite for dinner. He could see Dan was staring at a chocolate muffin and nursing a glass of milk. "Mind if I join you?"

"Not at all. Would you like a muffin?" asked Dan.

"Aren't you going to eat it?"

"I thought I was, but I'm not really hungry. I was just trying to find something to keep me busy. If you'll agree to keep me busy, you can have it. My treat."

Roberto smiled. "I accept your terms."

Dan laughed. "I see the boy is affecting you, too."

Roberto nodded. "I haven't had a normal moment since he arrived."

"But you're okay with it, right?"

Roberto didn't respond, but just took a bite of the muffin. Once he'd swallowed it, he said, "How can I be? The person I care about more than anyone in the world is rarely around to talk to anymore."

"But you're okay with it, right?" Dan repeated.

He looked directly at Dan and said, "Absolutely. I've never seen her so happy. If I care so much for her, how could I not be okay with it?"

"You sound conflicted."

"I do, don't I?" Roberto picked up the muffin, then set it back down and wiped his hands with a napkin. "It's funny. After her mom died, I was aware Elaina was watching me. It made me nervous at first, but I figured out she needed to learn from me. As a child, she'd join me on rescues but had to stay at base camp. Even there, she'd watch me on the drone monitors. Now I see that same attention focused on Arcon. In one way, it sets me free; in another, it makes me lonely. It hasn't been easy, but I'm determined to place her in God's hands and get over it."

"So, how are the two lovebirds doing in their new nest?" asked Dan, changing the subject.

"Well, they're out of the woods now, literally."

"Oh, good. She was making my head swim."

"So, you watched some of that footage?"

"Sure did. Can you imagine those ropes holding up under my frame?" Dan gestured, drawing attention to his own girth.

"No comment," said Roberto. "By the way, I think it was a good idea to send Victor. He sure knows his stuff."

"I agree. I knew we wanted to send a technical expert along, but using a relative of one of the ArcPoint folks was brilliant. I'm glad I thought of it."

"I think it was Arcon's idea."

"Maybe. But he's not here, so I'll take credit for it."

Roberto just smiled. "I agree to your terms."

23

Elaina felt privileged. Every year, thousands of people flocked to the edge of the Rift to admire these acacia trees. Most wanted to see them up close. Right now, she's the only one of those thousands to do so in person. She reached down and picked up a fallen leaf. "These are so delicate. The fragrance is so unbelievably strong, it's almost over-powering."

"At times, it's too potent for some people," said Arcon. "Hunters have quit because the odor made them nauseous. But you get used to it."

"Is it unique to this forest?"

"They say the tree is unique, which is why its official name is the Arcacia tree. But the leaves and flowers are just like Acacia farnesiana, or Sweet Acacia. Lars tells me it first came from a place called Santo Domingo, which is in the Caribbean. You want to know what the Australian name is for it?"

"What?"

"Needle bush."

"You're kidding."

"Nope. Would you like to hear a strange story about one of these leaves?"

"Sure."

Arcon held the leaf in the air. "One day I was walking to the swinging platform, and I saw one of these leaves floating about thirty feet up in the air. I assumed it was caught on a spider web, but I couldn't see one. I spent the day hunting, and when I came back through, it was still floating there. Strangest thing. The next day, it was still there. This time, when I came back from the Outpost, I brought nocs with me."

"Binoculars, right?"

"Uhh, yeah, right. Anyway, the leaf was still floating in the same spot. I looked at it with the nocs, and I saw a spider web glistening in a ray of sunlight. I followed the strand up and saw it was still attached to the rear end of a spider that had all eight legs gripping a tiny branch. It was yelling, "Cut it loose, somebody! Cut it loose!"

Elaina stared at him for a moment, then burst out laughing. "You made that up."

"No, seriously, I saw a leaf floating like that. I just made up the spider."

"I can't wait to tell that one to daddy," said Elaina as she started walking down the trail.

"Do you think he'd be surprised that I know what spiders are thinking?"

"Not at all. They train us rescuers in that sort of stuff."

They zig-zagged through the forest and before long broke into a clearing. Elaina could see the Facility far in the distance, and wondered when she'd get to meet some of the other Mojave People. It had confused her when she and Arcon first arrived that the members of the Community didn't approach them. But Arcon explained they were simply giving the two of them some space, waiting for Arcon to give them a signal it was okay to approach them, but he'd chosen not to. But now it was time for him to introduce her to the Community of ArcPoint, and start the conversations he told her they were eager for.

As Arcon and Elaina got closer to the Facility, she noticed there were a few women staring at them. Pretty soon, she realized they were staring at her. It made Elaina nervous, so she asked quietly, "Why do you think those women are staring at me? Are they mad that I'm alone with you?"

"Oh no, not at all," said Arcon. "They're just letting you know they want to talk with you."

"Well, they can talk to me all they want."

"Did you let them know that?"

"I never told them they couldn't."

Arcon stopped and gave Elaina a quizzical look. "How do strangers on the outside start a conversation?"

She shrugged her shoulders. "We just start talking ... or if we're interrupting them we'll say, 'excuse me' first. Sometimes, when it's a stranger who works somewhere, like at a fast food place, we skip everything and order a, 'cheeseburger with fries' but I like to at least say 'hello' first. It's more polite." She chuckled to herself. "Is that what you mean?"

"Oh, I see the problem," said Arcon. "We do things differently here. Remember what I told you about being quiet? How it's difficult for us to be alone with our thoughts, especially around the Facility? Well, we have a signal we give each other when we want to talk. Do you see how those women are staring at you? Not just looking in your direction, but actually making eye contact?"

"Yes, and it's kind of unnerving."

"Where you come from, maybe it is. But it's our way of communicating a desire for fellowship. If you'd like to talk with them, then just make eye contact with one of them and nod like this." Arcon did a quick, almost imperceptible nod of his head. "When you do that, they'll understand that you're free to talk."

"Wait a minute," said Elaina. "Is that why you were staring at those people at the Shop Again store?"

"Well, yeah. They looked like they'd be fun to talk to. But nobody wanted to talk to me. I thought they were kind of rude."

"If you would've walked up and said hi, they would've talked with you."

"But what if I was interrupting some deep thoughts they were having?"

"Arcon, nobody in our world has deep thoughts," said Elaina, folding her arms across her chest.

"Really—?"

26

"Oh, I'm just exaggerating. This place is so special. Everything here holds so much value, and we ... on the outside we tend to take so many things for granted."

"Well, we sure can't do that. If we don't all stick to the same rules, things break down." He looked over at the group of girls. "Is there someone over there you'd like to talk to?"

"Any of them. All of them."

"Give it a try. Just focus on one girl, make eye contact with her, and nod. It doesn't need to be much of one, because they'll be looking for it."

"Who's that in the blue sorta jump suit?"

"Is she blonde? The one in the middle wearing dirty blue coveralls covered with colorful patches?"

"Yeah, her. She looks like she'd be fun to meet."

Arcon grinned. "That'd be Brina Ashford."

Elaina pulled a face. "The one the Community wanted you to marry?"

"She's the one." Arcon eyed the group.

"Do I have to nod at everybody I ever want to talk to?"

"Oh, no, not at all," he responded. "Only when you think you may be interrupting, like if they're alone and may be deep in thought. Or, like with us being together, we may not want company. Or when ... well, it's complicated." He put his hands on his hips. "If you don't know for sure, just stare ... like Brina's doing. She's staring at you. Give her a nod."

"She wants to talk with me?"

"Looks like it," said Arcon.

Elaina felt a little strange about it but said, "Oh, why not?" She looked directly at Brina, nodded her head, and right on cue Brina left the group and started in her direction.

"Go ahead," said Arcon. "I see someone who wants to talk with me. We'll get back together later. Then he smiled and said, "Just stare at me."

Elaina returned the smile. "Your world, your rules," she said and walked away to meet Brina.

As Roberto swallowed the last bite of the chocolate muffin, he looked over at a very somber Ranger Dan. "You seem deep in thought this afternoon."

"Sorry," said Dan. "I've just been running these last few weeks around in my head. It's been a strange time."

"You really think so?" asked Roberto sarcastically.

"I mean, to start with, you and I both violated a law that's been on the books for over a century. We didn't get in trouble for it; we essentially got promoted."

"But as we discovered, the one who gave the law moved us to break it," countered Roberto.

"Yeah, you're right."

Roberto saw the look on Dan's face and said, "But that's not what's really bothering you, is it?"

Dan was quiet for a moment. "Do you ever wonder why Arcon crossed the Rift where he did?"

"Well, Elaina and I determined it was the best place to manage it."

"But it wasn't," countered Dan. "If you would've told me about it, I could've given you permission to simply drive around the Rift at Twenty-Nine Palms. You could've picked him up when he exited the Forest."

"I wasn't prepared to violate the restrictions," said Roberto. "The way we did it, only Arcon violated the restrictions."

"No, he didn't. I checked the regulations. There was never a law that specifically said people from that area couldn't leave it. All these years, they've been the ones who had permission to walk anywhere on the planet. We were not allowed to go there."

"Wow, I never realized that. So, you mean that Bible verse people quote about that place has never been true?"

"So, you've heard that one too?" asked Dan. "The one in Hosea that says, *For this reason, I will fence her in with thorn bushes. I will block her path with a wall to make her lose her way.* I wish I had ten credits for every time someone said that verse to me. They were so convinced God locked those people away because they were evil. But I also gathered from Arcon they never knew they lived in a restricted area. They never wanted to exercise their freedom because they thought we were evil. It's a strange conundrum, isn't it?"

"Sure is. But I still think there's something you're not telling me."

Dan turned his chair to face Roberto, stretched out his legs, and leaned back in his chair. "Arcon and I have been called to Jerusalem."

"Did Jesus appear to you again?" asked Roberto excitedly.

"Oh, no, nothing like that," chuckled Dan. "This came down through official channels. They want to have a meeting to discuss the procedure for removing the restriction on the Mojave. Right now, I'm still the only one who can authorize anyone to enter it. I can't be doing that forever. To be honest, I'll be glad to finally have this monkey off my back."

"Do they plan to give the authority to someone else?"

"That's an unknown. But if they lift the restriction, the curious can check out the Mojave Forest for themselves instead of pestering me."

"What if the Mojave People don't want to be checked out?"

"That's why Arcon is coming with me. He'll be their ambassador, their voice, in the proceedings. If they decide they want the restrictions to stand, they may."

"Have you told Arcon about the trip yet?"

"No, I just learned about it myself. I'd appreciate it if you let me tell him."

"Absolutely!"

"Just be prepared—he may want to take Elaina with him. She seems to be his security blanket right now."

"Whoa, yeah, I understand what you're saying. This is all happening way too fast."

"If it's any comfort, I'll be their chaperone. If it's not, you can come along and do that job yourself."

"I may take you up on that," responded Roberto. "I've always wanted to visit Jerusalem, but never had an unselfish enough reason."

"Great. I'll request to bring you and Elaina. Besides, I think you're still officially Arcon's keeper."

"He doesn't have his paperwork yet?"

"They just arrived at the Ranger Station. It's not official until he officially receives them from the official person officially responsible for him."

"And that would be?"

"Confusing. It would either be you or me, so I'll give them to you, and then you can hand them to him, just to make it official. But I won't let you have them until you're approved for the trip. He doesn't need those papers right now, anyway."

THE PRODIGAL

CHAPTER FOUR

Arcon approached Madelyn with just a bit of trepidation. He'd known Jarden would welcome him back, but he still wasn't so sure about others in the Community, especially her. She'd been very close to his parents, and knew they both opposed his being a hunter. *Except for Jarden and himself, no one took their deaths harder than she did.*

When he'd ordered a large amount of hemp ropes for his swingway, she was the one who questioned Jarden about it. Then Arcon used those ropes to betray the Community by doing another thing Madelyn was opposed to, which was leaving it. *She's wearing her dye-shack smock, with splatters of every color ArcPoint had for clothes. Evidently the arrival of a helicopter had interrupted her work. I hope she's not as mad as she looks.*

As soon as she was close to him, he saw her hand reach out and grab his left ear. As her calloused hand twisted it, he dropped to one knee. Her gray hair belied the fact that she had a grip like a vise. He cried, "I admit it. I was wrong. Please forgive me, Maddy!"

She stopped twisting his ear but didn't let go. She pulled up on it until she'd gotten him back to a standing position. "You're forgiven. Now, give me a hug before I twist it again."

Arcon grabbed her and gave her a "Patty Abrams" hug, hard enough to lift her off her feet. "This is how they do it in the

31

outside world," he said, then set her feet on the ground. "Thanks for welcoming me back."

She laughed. "You didn't use to like the old ear twist. What has that evil world done to you?"

"I still don't," replied Arcon. "But I was harboring a little guilt, and that took it away. The forgiveness, I mean. Not the ear twist." Then he looked at her seriously and said, "The world isn't evil out there anymore."

"I heard that," she said, her voice trembling. "People are saying Jesus is ruling in Jerusalem. Is it true?"

Arcon nodded. "I haven't seen him yet, but he appeared to one of my friends out there a couple of weeks ago." Then Arcon looked around. Seeing no one within earshot, he said, "Can I share something that's just a you and me thing for a while? I'll tell everyone soon, but I need to tell someone now."

"If it's a good thing, I agree to your terms," she replied.

"I think it's very good," he said. "This friend of mine who saw Jesus—his name is Ranger Dan—was given dominion over the ArcPoint land. He's to make sure no one in the outside world violates our desires or enters our land without permission. And he told me Jesus wants me to let him know what our people want. I have to confess; I don't feel like I'd be the best person for the job." Arcon started getting choked up and couldn't continue.

"What is it, child?" Madelyn asked. "What's troubling you?"

Arcon fought to compose himself. "I didn't always show the people of the Community the respect they deserved. I'm not worthy to represent all of you."

"How dare you talk that way," she said jokingly as she grabbed his ear and twisted it again. "Don't you dare call someone unworthy that Jesus has deemed worthy."

Arcon looked at her and smiled. "Thanks, I needed that."

"Anytime you need something, child, you can trust me to let you have it." Then she looked past Arcon and said, "I think you need to talk to Jarden. He just came out of the Facility, and he's staring this way now."

Arcon turned and saw Jarden make eye contact with him. He nodded back at him and then said to Madelyn, "I guess I need to go." With outstretched arms, he said, "Give me one more hug, please."

"Easy now," she said. "I'm still trying to catch my breath after the last one."

Arcon hugged her with a quick, typical, ArcPoint hug. "It feels good to be back here, and I mean it. I'm going now."

As Arcon walked toward Jarden, he glanced over to see how Elaina was doing. There were now three girls she was talking to. They seemed to be enjoying the conversation, laughing and gesturing with their hands like lifelong friends. *Good. I think she likes my people as much as I like hers.* Then he stopped for a moment to consider what he was thinking. *My people? Her people?* He started walking again and thought, *those ideas need to go away. We're all God's people.*

"Hey, son, can I talk to you in private for a while?" yelled Jarden who was still quite far away. *Sounds like he wants a father-son type of conversation,* thought Arcon. He jogged toward the Facility but Jarden didn't wait for him to get close, instead he headed straight for the south man-door.

As Jarden held the door open for him, Arcon asked, "What's the problem?"

"We have a lot of people asking about the outside world and what's going on. I want to persuade the leaders to have a talk with you."

"Would that be a good talk or a bad talk?"

"Both, I would imagine," said Jarden. "The way you showed up here has some folks excited and some concerned."

"What do you mean?"

"Well, you know how the vote goes every year. Almost everyone likes it here, but some are open to change if it's good. Folks like the Separatists think we need to fight to stay independent." Then he chuckled and said, "Most of them are now thinking if push comes to shove, the helicopters win. Problem is, until you tell us what's going on out there, nobody knows for sure what to think."

"I have a lot to tell them, that's for sure."

"I suggest doing it in an organized manner. Let's start with the leaders and get their help to plan a meeting of the Community. My only comment is that we better be quick about it."

"Amen to that."

"Before we do, I'd like you to come up to my office."

"Sure, boss. I mean ... you know what I mean."

Arcon followed as they went up the long flight of stairs and into Jarden's office. "Have a seat," said Jarden, as he shuffled through some papers on his desk. "Does it feel like you're back home?"

Arcon took off his hunter's vest he'd been wearing since he dropped down from the helicopter, and placed it on a hook near the door. "I don't know if this is my home anymore, but it does feel good."

"I understand, son. More than you realize. But this will always be your home, no matter where you live."

Before he took his seat, Arcon gazed out the west window that looked toward the tiny houses. He could see Brina pointing to where she lived up on the hill, and showing Elaina the grouping of tiny homes. Elaina seemed to be enjoying talking with the girls. This was all happening a lot better than he envisioned. "Is this going to be another father-son type of discussion?"

"Absolutely, and then some," responded Jarden, as he opened the middle drawer of his desk. "I've got something to show you. Your grandmother Mary gave me a letter years ago. I was supposed to hand it down to you when the time was right. I believe that time is now."

"What? A letter for me?" Arcon knew that in the ArcPoint Community a letter was extremely important, and formal. Communications were usually delivered in person, since there was very little to write on or with. "What's it about?"

"I don't know. The envelope is sealed, and she didn't tell me."

Arcon stared in disbelief. "All this time you've had a letter from Grandma for me and you never told me about it?"

"It's not addressed to you—not exactly anyway," said Jarden. "And the letter wasn't from Mary. She just gave it to me. Someone else wrote it."

"What? I don't get it. Who?"

"Lee Franklin."

"Wait, let me get this straight," said Arcon. "Grandpa Lee wrote a letter, gave it to Grandma, who then gave it to you. And it's for me, even though Grandpa Lee died long before I was even born. What makes you think it's for me?"

"You fit the instructions."

"What instructions?"

"There was another letter that told your grandma Mary, and then me, how to handle the letter you should read. Those instructions were very minimal. They said this letter should stay in your family, until the one day someone leaves ArcPoint and travels to the outside world. And if he returns, hand him this." Jarden handed the letter to Arcon. "You should probably read this privately, but if it's not too sensitive, I'd sure like to know what it says."

Arcon stared at the envelope. "And you're sure Grandpa Lee wrote this?"

"All I can tell you is that your grandmother was certain he did. She should know. She was very close to him and Victoria." Jarden got up from his chair. "I'll leave you alone with it. I'm going back down to see how things are going. I'll tell Elaina you may be a while."

"Yeah … okay … thanks."

Arcon stared at the envelope for a minute, too unnerved by the whole situation to open it. The Community hadn't possessed sealable envelopes for well over a hundred years. It was made of paper that was only seen now in the Room of Remembrance or the technical libraries. The block letter address written on the front looked similar to the handwriting in his Grandpa Lee's journal. It was simply addressed to The Prodigal. Arcon's heart sank. He remembered Jarden calling him the prodigal son. *What could this all be about?*

He opened the envelope and then carefully pulled out and unfolded the old paper. The first line made his hand shake and almost caused him to drop the letter. It read:

Dear Arcon,

If that is your name, then you truly are the correct person to be reading this. You are the answer to my worries, concerns, and prayers. Let me explain.

For years I have agonized over whether I did the right thing by persuading so many people to join me here in the Mojave Desert. Desert. It isn't a barren wasteland anymore, but it certainly was when we got here. I'm not sure if God changed the climate just to help our little group survive or whether it was to help feed a lot of hungry mouths in the outside world. Maybe both.

I never expected us to be here this many years, but God has allowed me to know I will never see the outside world again, and I'm fine with that. We've had our struggles in this place, that's for sure. But I still shudder when I remember back to the way it was. Mankind should not have to witness the things we saw, let alone have them happen to us. Why were children always on the front line of sexual perversion, medical experimentation, and religious warfare? I tried to find a way to make a diffe ence. Then this opportunity appeared.

I plan to make sure we can hold out here until we know the outside world is right with God again. In order for that to happen, Jesus will need to return and establish God's order, and rule the world from Jerusalem. Maybe that's already happened, but we can't risk leaving to find out. That's where you come in.

If my instructions were carried out as I recommended, then you have already been to the outside world and made it back. If you're wondering about how I knew your name, it's because I chose it for you. I named you after my parents and asked God to give that name to you. Your name, Arcon, is his proof that he has guided you to do what you have done. His Holy Spirit helped your parents choose your name, just as He allowed me to choose it just a few hours ago. Please let them know this, since they probably don't realize it.

As Arcon read the last line, he started weeping uncontrollably. Memories of his parents, his life with them, and the tragic accident that took their lives all flooded back to him. He felt so guilty about his disobedience, rebellion, and rejection of the ArcPoint lifestyle. Now he realized he'd merely been battling the traditions of the Community as God developed in him the desire to leave.

Maybe it was my parents who were rebelling against what God was trying to do. Arcon rejected that thought and focused on what was in the letter. He composed himself, wiped his eyes so he could see, and started reading again.

My prayer for you, Arcon, is that God will lead you to people who can help you restore the ArcPoint Community to a world that is flourishing under the rule and dominion of Jesus. That, my child, is the Promised Land, the long-awaited Sabbath rest for mankind. What we have here is just a protected space in the wilderness.

Hopefully, your parents or others have told you what it's like to be born again, of the Spirit, as it says in John, Chapter 3. When you have that gift, you hear God's voice and become like-minded with others so blessed. We have that gift here in ArcPoint, and now you know if it is universal in the outside world. I pray it is, or wisdom may dictate that we stay isolated.

What peace there is in knowing the truth, to be separated from the world while yet a part of it. Our people, especially my wife Victoria and our grandson's wife, Mary, looked for a rapture event that would take us out of this lawless world. I am no longer convinced of that happening, but I won't say anything to Mary. It doesn't hurt to have hope. We got this place in the Mojave, and it truly is a peaceful place, and yet it's still a part of this planet God created. It appears God had something diffe ent planned for us, but that's okay.

I pray the God of creation will gift you with wisdom to carry out the task that now faces you and to choose those who can help you do it, whether from within the Community or in the outside world. I highly recommend one of those people be your wife. It is the ultimate blessing to share your life with someone who is close to the heart of God, as Vic was.

In His Service,

Lee Franklin

Arcon took care folding the letter and slid it back in the envelope. All his life, he'd felt he differed from others in the

Community. He didn't seem to fit in, didn't want to follow tradition, didn't even cherish the peace of this place. Now he understood he wasn't a different person; he just had a different purpose.

He remembered back to his childhood when he and the other boys would play the stick-and-tire game. They'd run through the woods with a motorcycle tire rolling at their side. They would occasionally have to nudge or hit the tire to keep it rolling straight and to push it over bumps. The rule was you couldn't touch it with your hand; you had to use the stick. In real life, he was the tire, and God held the stick. All his life, God was at his side, keeping him moving, and wouldn't let him fall. There was no greater evidence of that than when he'd nearly died trying to cross the Rift. God had Ranger Dan there at the right time, with the right skills and the needed strength.

God hadn't chosen him to lead the ArcPoint Community as so many had told him when he was young. God wanted to set them free from the barriers created by the decades of unwarranted fears. Like Joshua and Caleb, Arcon has seen the abundance that is available outside of these tangled vines. And even better was the fact that the things they feared no longer existed. His job was simply to open their eyes to the possibilities and allow God to help him do it. He was ready.

Arcon stood and walked to the window. Elaina wasn't where she'd been, so he went to his apartment to check the south courtyard. From there he could see her walking with the other girls toward the cloth shed. *She told me God had a plan. Wait till she finds out God gave it to Grandpa Lee first.* He darted out of his room and down the stairs. *Jarden just has to read this letter.*

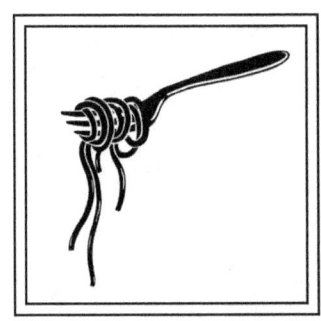

CHAPTER FIVE

Jarden spotted Petra Valerio, leader of the ArcPoint Community, standing alone in one corner of the large gathering room. Petra was more a man of wisdom than of action, which had worked well for guiding the Community since he'd taken over the role a few years ago. ArcPoint needed a wise counselor, not a political dictator. Petra was perfect for that. He had the innate ability to fit in anywhere, to learn quickly and to pitch in wherever help was needed. Then he'd step away to help somewhere else. *I bet with Arcon's return—and outsiders in our midst—he's probably worried someone will want him to help make sense of it all.* Jarden decided to join him, stopping by the kitchen on the way for a glass of apple juice. "Hey, Petra. How are you holding up?"

"This whole day has been a little overwhelming, don't you think? When I accepted this position, I assumed I'd just continue to organize our labor force—you know what I mean."

Jarden nodded. He knew exactly. Where Jarden distributed the products ArcPoint needed, Petra knew which workers could produce them. But dealing with outsiders was not something either one of them was familiar with. "It sure has been different," said Jarden, taking a sip of his juice. "I don't think I'll be able to sleep tonight. How about you?"

"Not likely," said Petra.

"I see you got news of family in the outside world. Exciting, isn't it?"

41

Petra examined the family envelope he'd received. "Look at this paper. In the Room of Remembrance, we read how paper was so common people used to crumple it to start fires. I've helped create paper. We can't make it this smooth, and we'd never waste it." He looked up at Jarden. "The outsiders are going to change everything."

"They sure are," replied Jarden. "But I think it'll be good, very good."

"I sure hope so." With pleading eyes, Petra said, "I'm going to need your help."

"I know you will, Petra, and I'm here for you. To be honest, God has prepared me for this day for quite some time. That's a long story we won't go into right now, but rest assured, this'll all work out okay. Just hang in there, buddy. Right now, I need you to talk to the leaders of the different groups. Arcon needs to have a discussion with us before he shares other news with the whole Community. Can you arrange a meeting for tomorrow, late morning?"

"Sure thing," said Petra. "Tell you what. I'll suspend all work details for the next couple of days. I'll have skeleton crews keeping essential operations going, like power, aquaponics, things like that." He thought for a moment and then said, "I guess we'll have to change the name."

"The name of what?"

"The meeting tomorrow night. We'll have to call it 'The State of the World' meeting. That's what Arcon should be sharing with us, right?"

"I haven't talked with him, but I'm sure he will. But let's not break up the union quite yet. We'll just have Arcon be the guest speaker. That'll be enough of a routine change."

"You know what, life was getting too routine, anyway," said Petra. " Who knows, I may even lose my job!" Then he smiled."At least I'm used to that." He looked beyond Jarden and said, "Talk about that routine breaker; here he comes now."

Jarden turned and saw Arcon coming down the stairs. "I think I need to talk to him. Will you let me know how it goes with setting up the meeting?"

"Sure thing, Jarden. I'll start doing that right now."

"Thanks, Petra."

When Arcon got closer, Jarden said, "Hey, son, was that letter as interesting as I think it was?"

"Look for yourself," said Arcon as he handed him the envelope. "I think it answers a lot of questions. As soon as you finish it, I'd like to talk to you about it. I'm going to go find Elaina. I saw her walking toward the cloth shed."

"Yeah. I know Brina wanted to show her how we make our clothing. I'll read this in a few minutes after I check on a few things for the kitchen."

"Great, boss, see you later."

As Arcon jogged toward the west man-door, Jarden looked down at the envelope and made a change of plans. He walked over to the stairway and sat on the stairs to read the letter. Numerous times through the years he'd pulled it out of his desk, and been tempted to open it. He'd come dangerously close when Arcon left the Community. After resisting the temptation for this many years, he wasn't going to put off reading it any longer. The first words gave him goose bumps.

Arcon walked into the cloth shed but found only a couple of people, a woman sitting at a loom and a man carrying a reed basket full of goat wool. He saw movement near another door and heard Madelyn yell, "If you're looking for your lady friend, she's out here in the dye shop."

"Thanks, Madelyn," Arcon yelled as he jogged to where she stood, wiping her hands on a towel. "Have you put her to work yet?"

"It won't be long," she quipped. "We've been teaching her a few things." As they approached the group of girls, Madelyn added, "She already knows more than you do."

"Somehow, that doesn't surprise me," he said as he laid his hand on Elaina's shoulder. "She learned how to swing through the trees pretty quick. Didn't you?"

"You didn't give me much choice, did you?" said Elaina as she punched him on the arm.

When he heard all the girls laugh, he asked her, "You didn't tell them what I did, did you?"

"Sure, I did. Why not? You'd already told Brina."

"If word gets out, we won't have any fun training new hunters how to swing."

Madelyn spoke up and said, "The secret is safe with us, right girls?" When she said that, all the girls gave her a thumbs up.

"I see you've taught them something too," said Arcon. "So, what have you learned?"

"Well, the Nigerian dwarf goats are good for milk, and the Angora's are good for wool. And when you crossbreed them, you get Nigora goats, which are good for both. Let's see, they get the yellow dye from turmeric—that surprised me—and the red comes from, uhh, wait a minute …"

"Madder," whispered Brina.

"Right, dyers madder."

"Rubia tinctorum," said Arcon. "That's the scientific name."

"Sure, smarty pants. And the different, kind of dirty blue color comes from the ArcPoint berries."

"It's what we call 'berry blue.' I'm sure you noticed a lot of people wear that color."

"If you don't need to look nice," said Madelyn, "you wear berry blue. Either that or goat skins." When she said that, they all looked at Arcon and laughed.

"I suppose I really should change out of my hunter's skins, huh?" he said. "Speaking of that, can someone find Elaina a place to stay while she's here? It's about time for evening meal, and she may want to, you know, freshen up. Madelyn? Brina? Somebody?"

"I already told her she could stay at our place," said Brina.

"Yeah, we got it covered," said Elaina. "Do you have a place to stay, Arcon?"

"Oh, no problem. Tawny said I can use my old apartment while I'm here." Then Arcon's tone became serious. "Can I steal her from you for a while?"

"Of course you can," said Brina.

"What is it?" asked Elaina. "You sound a little stressed."

Arcon walked her away from the others, then whispered, "I just need to tell you about this letter I just read. It's kind of intense—in a good way."

"A letter from who?"

"Grandpa Lee."

"Who did you say?" asked Madelyn, who'd walked up behind them.

Arcon snapped his head around. "What're you doing here?"

"I was just going to walk to the kitchen to get something to snack on. Thought I'd join you. What were you saying about Lee Franklin?"

"He said he got a letter from him," said Elaina.

"Oh, okay," said Madelyn. "Yeah, he inherited all of Lee's letters and things. Did something turn up you hadn't read yet, Arcon?"

"Uh, yeah. Jarden just gave it to me."

"Jarden must've found it when clearing out your apartment. No one thought you were coming back, so it was decided we were to turn it over to someone else. Tawny, I think."

"Yeah. Tawny's letting me use it again while I'm here."

"While you're here?" asked Madelyn. "You mean you're not staying?"

Arcon burrowed his gaze into her. "Maddy, remember the me-and-you thing? Could we keep all this between us until Elaina and I can figure a few things out? I don't want all of ArcPoint asking questions we don't have answers for yet."

"Okay, I understand," said Madelyn. "On one condition. If that letter is from Lee Franklin, I'd like to read it, unless it's too personal. I like reading whatever I can from any of the Founders."

"I agree to your terms," said Arcon. "I'm leaving now and taking Elaina with me."

As they walked away, he took Elaina's hand and asked, "You're going to have evening meal at the Ashford's?"

"Brina asked me to, and I told her that'd be great, but I needed to talk to you first. How about it? Will you join us?"

"Those of us living in the Facility usually eat there together. As much as I hate to be away from you, I think we should follow ArcPoint customs while we're here. I know it shouldn't apply to you, but single girls usually eat with their families. Will you be okay eating with Brina's family?"

"Sure, I understand. Besides, I like Brina. She's smart, pretty, energetic, all the things I'm not. I don't know why you didn't want to marry her."

Arcon looked at Elaina, trying to tell if she was joking or serious. Then he said, "She was certainly my first choice, but I didn't have time to build a companion swingway to get her out of here."

Elaina stopped walking, so Arcon did, too. He saw a stern look on her face and thought she might be mad, but he wasn't sure. Then she burst out laughing. "What's so funny?"

"I just tried to picture Brina swinging through the trees in a little Jane outfit."

Arcon stroked his goatee and said, "Come to think of it, I've never seen a girl in hunter's clothes. You know, I think she'd look really cute in that yellow vest."

Elaina punched his arm and said, "I know you're joking with me. She told me all about you two. You knew you weren't meant for each other. She knew you'd probably want to leave the Community someday."

Arcon was shocked. "Are you telling me that Brina knew about the letter?"

"What is it with this letter? No. She just said you were always fascinated with the outside world, wondering what was beyond the forest and about finding out someday. She knew you'd have to leave to do it. Plus, it was something strange that her grandpa told her."

"Grandpa Lars said something about me?"

"You seem surprised."

"I didn't think he liked me very much."

"Well, one day, he told Brina that if you ever left, to just let you go and not worry about it. He just said it out of the blue. They weren't even talking about you. But Brina told me that no boy in the Community intrigued her like you did. She was wrestling with her feelings for you when her grandpa said that. It helped settle her mind, even though it made little sense at the time. But she didn't say anything about a letter. Are you going to tell me about it?"

"Actually, I want to show you," he said as he started walking again. "We need to find Jarden. I hope he's still in the Facility. He has it."

"You gave it back to him?"

"Yeah, so he could read it."

"What? He never read it while he had it? Was it only addressed to you?"

"It wasn't addressed to me, exactly."

"Now I'm confused."

Arcon smiled and said, "Welcome to my world."

Jarden was in the kitchen when he looked through the serving window and saw Arcon and Elaina coming toward him. "I need to go," he said to one of the cooks. "I'll find someone to get you some more tomatoes and basil."

"Jarden, we found you," said Arcon. "Can I show Elaina the letter?"

Jarden stepped out of the kitchen. "Of course you can. Excuse me for a minute. Imelda, can you run out to hydro and get about a dozen tomatoes and a handful of basil for the kitchen? Thanks."

Imelda grabbed a basket from the kitchen and traipsed off. Elaina tapped Arcon on the shoulder and asked, "Hydro?"

"That's the hydroponics garden where we grow vegetables. Have you seen that yet?"

"No, I'd like to."

"After evening meal, I'll show it to you. Speaking of evening meal, what are we having tonight, Jarden? No, wait a minute. Let me guess. Tomatoes. Basil. I'll bet it's spaghetti. Am I close?"

"Hilarious, Arcon. Of course, it's spaghetti."

Elaina said, "It sounds like you have it a lot."

"If you eat here in the Facility like us hunters do, you have it about every other day. You'll be at the Ashford's, so you'll have something else. But us single guys living in the apartments love the spaghetti, and it's easy for the cooks to make a lot of it."

"Oh, okay. Well, now I don't know what to think. I made you spaghetti once, and you never asked for it again."

"That's … that's because I wanted to try new things," Arcon stammered. "And, well, I don't mean to offend you, but you don't use enough basil."

"Is that all?"

"Well, you don't use goat's meat. But I like the skinny noodles you use."

"Not to change the subject," said Jarden, "but here's the letter for you."

"Oh, good." Arcon turned to Elaina and said, "Come on, let's find a table away from everyone so you can read it."

Arcon felt guilty watching Elaina read the letter, but she'd told him it was okay. Her pretty brown eyes were the most expressive he'd seen since meeting her. When she finally looked up, he asked, "So, what do you think?"

"Wow. It's profound. It sort of reminds me of that day in Patty's container."

"I hadn't thought about that, but you're right. You can see God's hand in all that's been happening."

"And then some," remarked Elaina. "God was setting this up long before you were born. And if I'm reading this right, you may not have even been related to your Grandpa Lee. Wait a minute, that didn't sound right. What I mean is, the Arcon in this letter could've been someone other than a Franklin."

"What? What do you mean?"

"I think I'm right. It's not addressed to Arcon Franklin specifically. Whoever it was, would've been named Arcon by his parents, no matter who those parents were. Your family was just supposed to hold this letter for someone who left ArcPoint and came back. Here, read it yourself."

Arcon took the letter and read it again. "Whoa, you're right. I was thinking Grandma told my parents to name me Arcon because of this letter. But she never read it. When I got this, it was still sealed up in an envelope."

"I hope you're going to let Daddy read this. And Ranger Dan too."

"Yeah, I'll let them. I bet they'll be shocked."

"Maybe not as much as you think."

Arcon stared at the letter. "You may be right." He slowly lifted his head and looked at Elaina. "Should I show Madelyn? She already knows about it."

"Does she know what it says?"

"Nobody did, not even Jarden." Then he smiled and said, "Now *she* will be shocked."

"I'm sure she will, but I'd hold off telling her. You should probably discuss it with Jarden. I think the whole concept of reuniting with civilization should be presented carefully to your people, rather than leaked to one person at a time."

"Yeah, you're right." Jarden was staring at him from the other end of the Facility. "I have a feeling Jarden is thinking the same way you are." Arcon nodded to Jarden, who immediately started walking toward them.

As he approached, Jarden said, "I wanted you to know we're having a short meeting with a few of the leaders. We'll be discussing plans for you to speak at a gathering tomorrow. They'd like some information from you first."

"It's not a big meeting or a bad meeting, is it?"

"No. It's to discuss the big one. They want a little info so they can decide whether to go local or global with it."

"What does that mean?" asked Elaina.

"Either we let Arcon tell a few key people what's in the outside world and let the news trickle down to everyone else, or we gather the entire Community into the big meeting room."

"I think it would be best to have everyone here," said Elaina. "Don't you Arcon?"

"That's a decision we leave to the leaders," confessed Arcon.

Jarden's brow furrowed as he stared at Arcon. "I'd like to tell them about the letter, and I'd rather you weren't there when I do."

Arcon fell silent. He saw Elaina's eyes get big as she stared at him. There had been an excitement within him to share the letter with everyone, and he'd expected to be the one to do it. But as he thought about it, what Jarden had said made sense. The Community needed to hear Jarden's side of the story first. "I agree to your terms. Do I need to be there at all?"

"I'm glad you agree about the letter. It's nothing personal, but I think they should hear the words of your Grandpa Lee. If those words come from your lips, they'll only hear you. I think they should be given a quick explanation of what the outside world is like, from your perspective. But I could do that for you if you prefer."

"To be honest, your idea hurts, but it seems right. Besides, I'd like some time to think about what to tell everyone." Then he glanced at Elaina and said, "You'd have to stay out here for this meeting, and that'd make me even more uncomfortable."

Elaina scrunched her face and asked, "Why? Are women not allowed?"

That wasn't the response he'd expected. It shocked him at first, but then he remembered Elaina was strong-willed, independent, and capable. And she had quirky humor. "Actually, you have three strikes against you," said Arcon.

"What do you mean, *three strikes*?"

"In our leadership meetings, we don't allow women, or outsiders, or people with black wavy hair."

"He's joking with you, Elaina. But he could be correct about you being an outsider. It might keep some people from being completely free to speak their minds. Why don't you two wait out here while I talk to them, just in case they want Arcon to testify. Right now, I need to get in there. I tried to have them do it in the morning, but they were anxious. People are waiting for me."

"Actually Jarden, I'd like to take Elaina to see the view from Lookout Tree. We need to check in with her dad and we'll have good reception from up there. We'll come back when we're through."

"Don't stay too long, just in case the leaders have questions," said Jarden.

Arcon smiled. "May God give you good words so they *don't* have questions."

"Thanks, son. Gotta go."

CHAPTER SIX

The Franklin meeting room was packed with Community leaders, representatives from every work group in ArcPoint, and others who were simply curious. Jarden was especially glad to see Lars Ashford sitting in a place of honor near him. The room got quiet as Jarden stepped to the head of the enormous conference table. He looked at all the faces in the room and asked, "Is there anyone here whose life has been more disrupted than mine?" A rumble went through the room, then erupted into laughter when Petra slowly raised his hand.

Jarden rapped his knuckles on the table to silence them and asked, "How many here blame Arcon for that disruption?" Some threw their hands in the air, others raised them slowly, but the vote was nearly unanimous. "Well, I'd like to share something with you at this time, and it may change your opinion." He held the letter up for all to see. "It's from our great Founder, Mr. Lee Franklin." The room went silent, all eyes on Jarden.

"Lee wrote this letter about seventy years ago and sealed it in an envelope. He gave it to Mary Franklin—wife of his grandson Josiah—with instructions not to open it. It was addressed simply to The Prodigal. Years ago, Mary trusted me with it after her son Zoreb and his wife Sasha died in that terrible explosion. The instruction she gave me, that was given her by Lee, was that it should only be opened and read after someone left the

Community and returned—just as the prodigal son did in the Bible. Recently, Arcon did just that. On his return, I handed him the letter. He's asked me to read it to you. As I do, please remember that it was written before Arcon's parents were married. It starts out, Dear Arcon…"

At the mention of Arcon's name, gasps were heard around the table. As he continued, mouths dropped open, tears fell, and hands were raised. As he finished, Jarden said, "This writing appears to be a true word of prophecy because all things written have come to pass. None of it is self-fulfilled because none of it was known beforehand. God answered the prayer of our leader for a God-directed reunification of our Community with the outside world. There are already God-fearing people prepared to help us make the transition, and their mandate is for the ArcPoint Community to be in complete control of any changes that are to take place." Jarden saw a raised hand and asked, "Keenan, do you have a question?"

"When is all this going to happen?"

"That's really up to us, but as Head of Procurement, I recommend that we don't delay on coming up with a plan. We'll need to stay here in the forest for a while, but there are already people working on making our life easier here. One of them just happens to be a distant cousin of mine."

"And I've met him," said Keenan. "Victor Merrick. He's a good man."

"Thanks, Keenan. I agree. Anyway, tonight at the State of the Union meeting, Arcon will give us his understanding of the outside world. From what I've heard so far, Jesus made significant changes from the way things were." All around the table, people started talking, and the room exploded when Jarden said, "I think we can now get rid of the room of Ancient Evil."

When the noise subsided, Jarden asked, "Are there any questions?"

"I have an obvious one," said Bill Winters. "How will we obtain goods out there? Or a home? Do they all share things as we do here?"

"From what Arcon tells me, they do things very similar to how we do it. Just as we have our own dwellings, so do they. They do share things, but they also have an exchange system and personal accounts. That way, they can be rewarded for personal effort and also share their resources far and wide. When we enter that world, people will share their resources with us so we can get established without debt. Just as with us, greed has no foundation to build on." Jarden saw a raised hand. "What is your question, Lars?"

"What about the folks who don't want to leave here?"

"You shouldn't have to," said Jarden. "In fact, it'll be important that some people stay. It turns out our ArcPoint trees are a valuable resource that the outside world needs. Of course, things won't ever be the same as they were, but how much and how quickly things change is up to those who want to remain." A murmur of comments went around the table.

"Are you saying they want to cut down our trees?" asked Lars. "Can't have that."

"No, just the opposite. It seems your father was onto something with the oil that comes from the trees. We've taken that fuel for granted here, but good diesel-type bio-fuel is scarce out there. And that's not the biggest asset we have. A lot of their technology uses rare earths, which are in our trees, and better yet, probably in the runners. If it is, they'll want to chew up all the needle-brush to get it. Does anyone here have a problem with that?"

Derik got the group fired up by chanting, "Hack them back! Hack them back! Hack them back!"

"Amen to that, everyone," said Jarden. "All of this is preliminary until they can test a few things. Those tests would include some medical exams. It appears the trees also absorb a lot of heavy metals, some of which can cause infertility issues. Since we're already experiencing problems in that area, they want to run some tests as soon as possible. At this point, all of this is voluntary, and I hope, as the leaders in the Community, you'd encourage people to volunteer. Some of the hunters have already agreed to be tested since it's assumed they have the highest intake of ArcPoint fruit. Our medical people are reading through a report on testing performed on Arcon while he was out there. There is also a report on the rare earth harvesting for anyone interested."

Petra interrupted. "The people studying those reports are here, correct?" When a few people raised their hands, he asked, "Are you going to share your understanding of those reports at the meeting tonight?"

"As much as we can," said one of them. "Some of it is pretty technical, but it's some good stuff."

"Great. If you need help, let us know. We can connect you with the technical experts who wrote it. Jarden, back to you."

"Thanks, Petra. I'd mostly like to ask all of us leaders to encourage those under us to pursue wisdom and insight from our Lord regarding this coming change. We should let neither fear nor zeal cause us to act foolishly. I now give up the time to discussion by others."

As they stood on the platform at the top of Lookout Tree, Arcon pointed toward the hills. "Your dad is in that direction," he said. "And this is where Jarden was standing when I dropped down from the helicopter. He saw Raymo shoot at me, and Tawny tackle him."

"I'm sure glad Jarden disabled those bullets," said Elaina.

"So am I. But Raymo didn't know it was me. He'd created this whole scenario in his mind of me being captured and tricked into giving away our location. He spent far too much time in the Room of Ancient Evil, studying what the world used to be like. Quite a few people thought everything got worse after our people moved here."

"A lot of people thought this place was still like that," said Elaina. "Even I did for a while. Daddy definitely did. But God knew what He was doing."

"Amen to that." Arcon sat on a bench built around the trunk of the tree while Elaina looked down on the South courtyard. He turned on his earpiece and waited a minute for the control room to see the signal. "Do you think your dad is there?"

"He's supposed to be."

"Roberto here. Is this Arcon?"

"Yes, sir. Elaina is here with me for the 4 PM check-in."

"Good. Have her turn her earpiece on."

"Okay, sir." Arcon motioned to Elaina. "He wants you to turn your earpiece on."

"Hi, Big D. Girl here."

"Hey, girl. How are they treating you?"

"Great. I'm going to spend the night with Arcon's old girlfriend."

"His what?" asked Roberto, incredulous.

"Oh, you know. The girl he was going to marry if I said no." Arcon shook his head and Elaina laughed.

"Sorry, missed that," said Roberto. "Didn't know he had a backup."

"I didn't have a backup, sir," said Arcon, smiling at Elaina. "She wasn't a tree swinger."

"Hey, speaking of swinging, I saw you push my daughter out of that tree."

"You did?"

"Just remember, I've got eyes everywhere. Okay, down to business. How did the meeting go?"

"We didn't attend it, sir," said Arcon. "Jarden is still meeting with them."

"That's okay. You can give me a report after you talk to Jarden. I wanted to give you a heads up so you can prepare for your next mission."

Arcon stared at Elaina and asked, "What does that mean?"

Roberto answered, "You remember we gave Noreena permission to air the documentary about your people as soon as it was completed and approved? Well, last night, she aired a teaser. It was only a 30-second blurb about your escape from there, but it's already starting a commotion. There are folks petitioning the authorities for permission to enter your area."

Arcon pictured hundreds of strangers walking around ArcPoint. "Ranger Dan isn't going to let them, is he?"

"Oh no, there's no threat of that," said Roberto. "But it's driving a need for an official ruling on the restriction. Brace yourself, Arcon. You and Dan have been called to Jerusalem to discuss it with the authorities."

"We have? Jerusalem?"

"You sure have. Exciting stuff, isn't it?"

Elaina interrupted, saying, "Can I go too, Daddy?"

"Ranger Dan is getting approval for you and I both to go. It probably won't be for a few weeks, but you two will want to discuss it with the leaders of the ArcPoint Community. They'll need some time to think it through. They'll need to know they can continue with complete isolation if they desire, but Dan and I think it'd be best for a certain amount of openness. Too much, though, and ArcPoint will become a tourist attraction. Elaina girl, make sure Arcon understands what that means. He's probably never seen a zoo."

"Roger, Big D. We'll talk about it later."

"Good. As I said, there are no real worries because there are no roads in or out of ArcPoint. We can't shuttle very many people by helicopter, since we have no safe place to land, thanks to all the trees. Right now, this base camp is the closest we can get by driving."

"Would it help to have the Community clear some land for the helicopter?" asked Arcon.

"Yes, a lot. But mostly we want to get a long-term transportation plan started, and Dan would like to be able to schedule a date for a trip to Jerusalem."

"Understood. I'll talk to Jarden about it." Arcon saw movement in the south courtyard. "Mr. Roberto, sir, we need to go. I see some of the leaders coming out of the Facility. Did you need anything else?"

"No, Arcon. Find out from Jarden how the meeting went, and discuss privately with him what we just talked about. Then let me know. Roberto out."

"Arcon and Elaina out."

"Bye, Daddy. Love you."

As they entered the Facility, Elaina checked the faces of those still leaving the Franklin room. She leaned closer to Arcon. "It doesn't look like the meeting went as we hoped."

"Why do you say that?"

"Well, after hearing what that letter said, I thought they'd be swarming over here to talk to you."

"Were any of them staring this way?"

"They seemed to be avoiding eye contact."

"Okay, no problem then. Here comes Jarden. He wants to talk." Arcon waited until he was closer and asked, "How'd it go?"

"Boy, it was powerful," said Jarden. "A lot of them are already planning on how to work toward integration. They've got a lot of questions for you."

"I don't get it," said Elaina. "Why didn't someone ask him when they came out of the meeting?"

"I told them not to," said Jarden. "I said Arcon was going to explain a lot at the meeting tonight, so they should wait until after that to see if they get answers. I'll give you some hints on what they want to know."

"But did they say anything about the letter?" she asked.

"They accepted it as a God-inspired work," said Jarden. "I think if this whole affair had been a plan of Arcon's, or mine, or an outsider, they would've rejected it. But they could see that even your Grandpa Lee couldn't have made all these things happen. God is doing something, and they want to be a part of it. We'll have to work fast to keep up with them."

"That's perfect," said Arcon. "The authorities would like to get started on designing some way to get people in and out of here. They'd like to know what our desires are."

"I think we'll need to know what our options are," said Jarden.

Elaina said, "Can I make a suggestion?"

"Sure," answered Arcon and Jarden in unison.

"Ranger Dan is scheduled to come here tomorrow afternoon," she said. "Why don't you guys have another meeting, and he can tell everyone what options are possible?"

"I like it," said Jarden. "I'll talk with the heads of the different groups and see what they're thinking."

"And I'll talk to Mr. Roberto and have them work on different transportation options."

"People like to talk to me," said Elaina. "So, I'll try to find out discreetly what the regular people think about joining the 'outside world', as you call it."

"Are you going to find Brina and head over to her house?" asked Arcon.

"That's what I was thinking, unless you need me."

"No, that's fine. I need to change clothes anyway." Then he looked her in the eyes and grinned. "You'll need some extra charm for Lars. He's a real Separatist and doesn't like a lot of change."

She leaned closer to him, smiled, and batted her long eyelashes. "Will this work?"

"I think that'll work fine," piped in Jarden. "But I'd suggest you not try that with Tawny."

"Understood," she said, as they all laughed.

CHAPTER SEVEN

Arcon stood on the balcony outside of his apartment and watched people file into the main meeting room at the Facility. Each went to his usual location, most of them carrying a chair, as they had done every year for their entire life, and several times a year. He knew these people, some better than others, some barely at all, but that was his fault. At over a thousand strong, they'd completely pack this room, including this second-story perimeter walkway in front of the apartments.

He'd never been in front during this annual meeting. He was usually at this spot, occasionally in his apartment, and sometimes hiding in the forest, working on a secret swingway. But as private as he tried to be, everyone knew him because he was a Franklin. *Until this day, I'd never realized what Grandpa Lee must have gone through.* The time had come, so he walked to the north stairs and down to the makeshift stage, where Elaina waited.

"Took you long enough," said Elaina.

"Sorry. Just trying to shake off the nerves." He led her onto the stage and the chairs waiting for them.

"Welcome, everyone," shouted a large black man standing in front of the crowd. The boom of his deep voice made Elaina jump and Arcon smile. "Who is that?" she asked.

"That's Willem Bowman," said Arcon. "He's the only person with a voice loud enough to be heard over the crowd.

63

Everyone in the Community has their job, and calling a large meeting to order belongs to Willem. It's about all he does at a meeting, but he does it well."

"Find your seat, and we'll get started," Willem continued.

"In five minutes, the room will be silent," said Arcon. "Just watch. If it's not, you'll hear Willem again."

"I notice there aren't many black people in your community," whispered Elaina.

"Quite a few, I'd say—since it only started with two. One of them, Evan, worked for Norm Ashford when they started planting trees here. Then, just as ArcPoint was getting settled, a black woman came here with a white boyfriend."

"You mean every dark-complected person I see in the crowd is related to those two?"

"I didn't say that. We had a number of Hispanics who were very dark-skinned. In fact, Evan married one, and Willem is descended from them. Remember, I introduced you to Raymo? The other couple, Aniyah and Gerhard, were his great-great-grandparents."

"Is that why he's ..."

"Black-skinned and blue-eyed? Probably. But here at ArcPoint, we don't believe there are different races. We believe God only made one race that had a lot of mixed colors in its genes." The room quieted to a low rumble. "Sshhh—let's talk about it later."

Arcon could feel his heart beating faster as the time for him to speak got closer. He recalled the last time he'd had to speak in front of a crowd. This stage differed completely from the one he stood on at the family reunion. This one was nothing more than the large conference table from the Lee Franklin room. They pushed it up to the kitchen so he and the other speakers could sit on the serving line and face the crowd. Bench seats provided stairs to access it from the front. There was no sound system.

Sitting on the kitchen pass-through with him were Victor and Elaina, representing the outside world. Petra was there to start the meeting, and Jarden would get up and speak just after him. Next to him was Minda Polk, the Medic who got the infertility information, and at the end was Wendell Firsten, head of the Machine Shop, who examined the rare earth proposal.

Petra stood up and walked to a podium at the middle of the conference table stage and the room fell silent. "I'd like to start this meeting with a word to our Lord," he said as everyone raised one hand to the sky.

"Lord Jesus, we recently learned that you are once more on this earth with us, ruling in Jerusalem. But we also know your Spirit is in us, hearing our thoughts and spoken words. Please guide those thoughts and words this evening as we hear from your child, Arcon. Thank you for guiding him back to us. This meeting is now yours, Lord. Amen."

"AMEN!" shouted the crowd so loud the silverware shook in the kitchen, making Elaina jump again. She whispered to Arcon, "That was impressive."

"I'd like to turn the meeting over to Jarden for a few words," said Petra. "He knows a little more than I do." He started to walk off the table and then added, "About everything."

Everyone roared with laughter as he sat down, and Jarden took his place at the podium. Then they all started clapping for Jarden and didn't stop when he held up his hand. But when Willem stood up, they instantly went silent.

"Thanks, everyone," said Jarden. "By now, many of you have heard about the letter written by our founder, Lee Franklin. I'll read it now so all can hear its words. Then we'll post it in the Room of Remembrance so you can see it. Please don't touch it, because it's seventy years old. Now let me read it to you. Dear Arcon ..."

As Jarden read the letter, he had to raise his voice a few times because of the murmuring coming from the crowd. But it came from emotion, not talking. When he finished, he said, "Because of this letter, and the things Arcon is about to share with you, we believe the time has come to reunite with the outside world. To some of you, that may seem frightening; to others, it is overdue. But we, your leaders, believe now is the time that God is in control of it, so please listen carefully to Arcon's words."

Jarden continued. "On this day every year, we usually vote on whether we should send someone to the outside world, so we can know what the world is like. I think it's no coincidence that today—the one day each year that we vote on this subject— is when we have our answer. Arcon, please share with us your understanding at this time."

Arcon stood up, and there was a thunderous applause. He still couldn't get used to it, and just like at the reunion, he pointed toward the sky. He allowed the applause to continue just so he could shake off his nerves and compose himself. He laid his notes and a glass of water on the podium. Then he looked at Willem seated in the front row and nodded.

Willem stood, faced the crowd, and there was silence. He took his seat.

Arcon smiled and said, "In the outside world, there is nobody like Willem."

The crowd erupted in laughter, and when Willem stood, it immediately stopped and then started right back up again. Willem just shook his head, threw his hands in the air, and sat down.

Arcon cleared his throat, and the room went silent, so he said, "Let me tell you what I've seen, or actually, *not* seen. I have seen none of the horrors displayed in the room of Ancient Evil."

The crowd applauded and then stood, showing their relief and excitement. He let them have their moment. He knew most people hated that Ancient Evil room, but accepted the fact that they shouldn't forget. Now they could.

"I suppose you've all heard the other news," he yelled over the noise. As the room calmed down, he yelled, "Jesus is ruling in Jerusalem!" When he said that, Willem shot to his feet, raised his hands, and started singing a song of praise. The room exploded in song as Arcon dropped to his knees. He was still like that when Willem brought the song to an end.

As he stood, he swiped at his tears and returned to the podium. "I want to share a few things about His return." Arcon cleared his throat and steeled himself, finding it hard to continue. "You know how our Founders believed we'd be taken up to the sky to be with Jesus when he came? It didn't happen like that, but now we're in the midst of that thousand-year reign of Jesus that our Founders also looked forward to."

Arcon checked his notes. "I've put together a brief timeline of events. The first thing that happened was the falling away of many from God. They didn't realize they were, but they started turning to spiritual practices that weren't sanctioned by God but were actually doctrines of demons, such as meditation and divination. They even looked to rocks for healing, instead of God who is the source of healing.

"At the same time, the world turned lawless—stealing, killing, and destroying—while the government turned away. It was at this point our people moved here. While we were preoccupied with establishing a livelihood in this place, evil people were taking over important positions in both the government and the church. Respect for authority was lost, and they mocked and rejected those who advocated for lawful behavior. Many of those people moved away from the crime of the cities, as we did. How many is unknown.

"When the Rift opened up, it sealed our fate, and our Community accepted it. But it was only the first of many large earthquakes around the globe. These quakes damaged oil and gas well casings, causing major ecological disasters, as well as financial ruin for many nations. Major dams were damaged, causing floods and widespread power outages."

The murmuring of the crowd got loud, so Arcon took the opportunity to check his notes again. "Not long after that, Earth's magnetic field weakened. It had a devastating effect on the world, but worked to our benefit here at ArcPoint. The weakened field allowed a lot more solar radiation to enter our atmosphere. That caused the climate to change dramatically around the globe. It was a blessing for us, giving us rain and turning our desert into a lush forest. Other places that had been too dry or cold to produce crops eventually became farmland. The world, however, had grown dependent on computers for control of commerce and for military superiority. The increased radiation destroyed electronics, including the satellites that circled the earth. Wars erupted as countries blamed each other for causing it. But our Lord predicted it would happen. He said the stars would fall from the sky, and from our perspective, they did. Brina, you have a question?"

"Grandpa Lars would like to know what happened to America."

"Okay. You're probably all wondering what happened to America. I had a lot of questions about that myself. It's hard for any of *us* to imagine what it's like to suddenly lose a computer. None of us grew up with one. But people in developed nations like America used them for shopping, entertainment, finances, everything. Even people in poor countries were using them, and they were all connected to each other by something called the Internet. It all failed faster than experts could fix it. For a few weeks, Americans simply waited for the government to make things work again. But soon, there was panic and then rioting. As government services were overwhelmed, some other nations took advantage of the situation and attacked us. The same thing happened in Europe."

Arcon took a sip of his water. "With America preoccupied, other countries started turning on each other. When they turned on Israel, Jesus appeared. As with the Assyrians, many died on the battlefield before ever reaching Israel. Like it was for the Apostle Paul, Jesus' appearance caused many people to become believers. But like Ananias and Sapphira, the hearts of many others failed. Jesus purged the earth of the evil spirits that had influenced human behavior since Adam and Eve. People who'd given their lives over to those spirits lost those lives. And somehow, we here at ArcPoint were oblivious to it all."

Arcon saw Brina waving her hand. "Oh, sorry. To get back to your question, America was attacked, but only briefly. It took many years for the damaged infrastructure to be rebuilt, and a lot of the old stuff needed to be abandoned, such as the I-15 freeway. But to understand where America is *today*, you need to understand how Jesus changed the nature of government around the world. Every country was plagued with corruption, even America.

"When Jesus returned to earth, He raised to life individuals who had died during the tribulation era because of their devotion to Him. These people had resurrected bodies that couldn't die. They were incorruptible—I suppose that's obvious. How can you bribe someone to betray Jesus when they've already died for Him?"

The room erupted in conversation, and Arcon let it run its course. When it began to die down, he nodded to Willem, who stood and silenced them.

"All governments around the world are now under the authority of Jesus and those who rule with Him. They are divided into a few large land masses, and those areas are divided smaller, and so on. These are called Authorities and are governed by Judges, just as God did it with the tribes of Israel. Jesus operates from Jerusalem with his group of Judges, called

Central Authority. They're all part of the First Resurrected, as mentioned in Revelation, chapter twenty. In the beginning, Jesus exposed and removed corruption from existing governments. It was a process that took many years to accomplish, since he wanted us humans to learn to govern ourselves. There were many international disputes, as even God-fearing people needed to unlearn their selfish ways.

"In terms of geography, the United States is pretty much the same as it was, except Alaska is now part of Canada, and Hawaii is part of the Pacific Island Authority. Not every government that used to exist still does, but most do.

"What you'll like is that people out there now share things as we do here. They just have a lot more resources to work with, and a lot more people who need those resources."

Arcon saw Petra waving both his arms furiously. "Petra, do you have a question?"

Petra spoke loud enough for all to hear. "Yes! What about us? How does the ArcPoint Community fit into this new world?"

Arcon shrugged. "No one really knows."

A murmur went through the crowd and Arcon put his palms up to settle them down again. "I can say this. I've been reading through my Grandpa Lee's journal, and I found something that I think made our experience unique. Like everyone else in the world, our group panicked when communications went away. By that time, the government was already in chaos, and talk of war was everywhere. The whole Community was called together into this very room to discuss it. They decided to pray."

Arcon opened the journal where he'd placed a bookmark. "Grandpa Lee recorded that prayer, and I'd like to read it. It says:

Heavenly Father, your Word says we shouldn't worry about anything, but we should pray about everything. Right now, it appears we need to pray about everything in the world. We know we can't change the world, so we ask you to change us. From this day forward, we ask that you alone govern us. Give us your Holy Spirit to guide our thoughts toward each other, and allow us to live by your laws and not those that are constantly changing in the outside world. Until a future day comes, one that only you choose, keep us physically and spiritually separated unto yourself. Remove all evil and error from our midst, and create a barrier around us. We look to you, and only you, for our provision, our security, and peace. Please, Father, let there be only one spirit guiding us—your Holy Spirit. We desire to be under no other authority until Jesus is on the throne in Jerusalem. In His name, we ask this. Amen.

"I know many of you have a copy of my Grandpa Lee's journal and have probably read this prayer. I honestly read it for the first time only a few weeks ago. For that, I'm ashamed, but I have to admit that it probably had a more powerful impact on me when I did, due to its timing."

"For over a hundred years, Jesus has been ruling the world from Jerusalem. All that time, we never realized it. Why not? The simple fact was, it wouldn't have changed anything. Jesus had to establish his governance, or the world would've destroyed itself. Because of the influence of evil spirits, the rest of the planet was on a fast track to annihilation. But those spirits were removed from our people, as we requested. The authority of Jesus was established here, as we requested. Our people didn't need to be a part of God's new government. We were already committed to the governance of Jesus."

"Did any of you know that over a hundred years ago, we were put under quarantine by the outsiders? On all the maps, a line is drawn around our area that says 'Restricted.' Jesus himself told the world to leave us alone. But now, he's telling us to get prepared for that restriction to be lifted and to choose how we want that to happen. If we want this area to stay isolated, then it will be. If we want to open it up to a limited number of people, we can choose, ourselves, how to govern that. If we want to walk away from it all and blend back into the outside world, we can. But everyone would need to agree to that.

"I need to share with you what is already happening in regards to living under the authority of Jesus officially. For a few years now, one man has had authority over all of our land, as far as the world is concerned. Over the *land*, not the people. Only Jesus has had authority over us, and the only thing this man could do regarding the land was to keep people out of it. His name is Ranger Dan Wilson, and he's become a close friend of mine.

"Over a week ago, Jesus appeared to Ranger Dan in his home. Jesus told him that he was giving Dan dominion over both our land and the people." A murmur went through the crowd, and Arcon gestured for them to calm down. "Let me explain what that means. Ranger Dan is expected to care for us like a father, to nurture us and protect us. We'll remain under his care as long as we remain on this land. But we'll have complete freedom to come and go as we choose."

"Tomorrow we'd like to have another meeting here, same time, same place. I'll have Ranger Dan explain what's going on in the outside world regarding us. As I said, his primary goal is to find out what we need, and he'll work to obtain it for us. He'll also want to know how we want to proceed, and he'll lay out the possibilities for us. So, between now and then, talk to your leaders about what's going on and what you see as immediate needs in the Community. For instance, we're already working on getting a new generator in here."

Arcon didn't know what to say next, so he scanned the crowd, hoping for more questions. Then he thought of something.

"Speaking of the quarantine, when someone leaves this area, the authorities require a health test to be performed to ensure we don't have some disease that could spread to others outside our area. When they tested me, I told them about our infertility issue. They ran more tests and believe they've discovered something. I had Minda Polk look at what they found, and I'd like to have her tell you about it. Minda ..."

As Arcon watched Minda approach, he had to smile. She had a bounce to her step as she waved enthusiastically to the crowd. As the doctor to the women at ArcPoint, and the main midwife, she had to be excited with this report. *I can't wait to hear what she says.*

"Hi everyone," said Minda, as she took over Arcon's position. "You know I've been studying this problem for most of my adult life, so I was excited to get a different perspective on it. It appears to be caused by chemicals in our soil being sucked up by the ArcPoint trees. That's just a theory right now, but it looks pretty convincing. They need to draw blood from more people, so I'd like some volunteers, particularly women who are trying to have babies. For now, they recommend that we limit the intake of foods directly linked to the ArcPoint trees. I agree that would be wise, but it's not something to panic about. Speaking of the trees, here's Wendell Firsten."

With the same streaks of gray in their hair and similar square jaws, Minda and Wendell could have been siblings. But where she was diminutive and outgoing, he was tall and shy. She was over twenty years his senior, but it didn't show. Arcon knew of one other similarity ... their work ethic. They both worked hard to be the best at their jobs—for the sake of the ArcPoint people.

"Hi, folks," said Wendell. "As many of you know, our Founder, Norm Ashford, developed these trees as a commercial source of bio-fuel. It turns out they're actually good for that and more. The harmful chemicals in those trees are a valuable resource to the outside world.

"I was called on to look at a machine that may be able to gather those chemicals from the needle-brush without hurting the trees. It looks like it could work, so I'm recommending we test one of the machines. Back to you, Arcon …"

"Thanks, Wendell," said Arcon over the noise of the people. "There will be a lot more information for you soon, but I don't want to keep you folks any longer right now. I want you to have time to think about what's happening and talk about it amongst yourselves.

"Right after lunch tomorrow, our leaders will be meeting to discuss everything once more. So, between now and then, I want all of you to let them know what you think so they can represent you. Come evening we'll have Ranger Dan here to speak with us. The following morning the plan is to take some volunteers away in that noisy flying machine."

Murmurs rippled around the room at the mere mention of flying. Arcon gestured with both hands, reassuring him as he said, "Don't worry. They won't go far, and they won't be gone long. They will represent us, so Ranger Dan has someone to verify his report on our desires.

"That's all I have to say, so you're free to go. By the way, you are all officially allowed to leave ArcPoint now and see what the outside world is like. However, I don't recommend it. There's still a lot of needle-brush between here and there. Wait until we can do something about that."

There was a lot of laughter and applause for Arcon, but he could hear murmuring mixed in, and some were frowning like they weren't quite convinced. He sensed their uncertainty. *That's understandable. I hope Dan can ease some of those fears.*

CHAPTER EIGHT

All around the Facility people were talking, joking, hugging, and then picking up their chairs and leaving. This scene was unfamiliar to Arcon. In all the years he'd attended this annual meeting, he'd always been the first one out the door. He never liked the attention or the encouragement he got from others to take on the responsibilities of his forefathers. But today, he could've used some of their annoying advice and "can do" coaching.

"I think that went well," said Elaina, as she nudged him with her elbow.

"Yeah ... well ... I hope so," responded Arcon. "It's hard for me to tell."

"You don't sound very enthusiastic."

He turned to her. "It's funny how you get a certain picture in your head about something, and then things don't turn out as expected."

"Kind of like me?"

He smiled. "It's okay if things turn out better."

"Good answer, Mr. Ambassador."

"I guess that's the problem," he said. "Not a single person came up afterward to talk with me. I'm still not sure if I'm the right person to represent them. To most people, I'm probably still the one who turned his back on this place."

"Now, now, don't make me twist your ear," she said, shaking her finger.

"Madelyn told you about that, huh?"

"Yes, and I agree with her. It's up to your people to choose their representative, but if Jesus chose you, don't be surprised if they do, too. And if they do, don't be surprised if you can actually do the job."

He smiled and nodded. "I will plan to not be surprised."

"All right then. Now, don't you think we should contact Ranger Dan?"

"Yeah, you're right," he said, as he pulled his communication earpiece out of his pocket. "You got yours?"

"It's right here," she said, as she placed it in her ear and turned it on.

Arcon heard a voice say, "Base one, go ahead."

Arcon said, "Hi, BJ. Is Mr. Roberto there?"

"I'll connect you. Just one moment."

The radio was silent until he heard Roberto say, "Hey Arcon, buddy, how did the meeting go?"

"It went okay," said Arcon. "It seemed like everyone understood. We'll see what happens next. Is Ranger Dan there, too?"

"He's in his office." Roberto's voice grew quieter. "BJ, could you page Dan? Tell him his kids need his attention. Thanks."

"Hi, Daddy!"

"Hey, girl. Are you staying out of trouble there?"

"No comment."

"Uh-oh. That doesn't sound good. Hey, Ranger Dan's here. Just a second."

"Hey, miss Jane," said Dan. "Did Tarzan do okay with his speech?"

"Hi, Ranger Dan. I think he did great. He's not so sure, though. He didn't get the response he was expecting."

"Well, that happens. As long as they didn't tar and feather him, it's probably good."

Arcon asked, "What does that mean?"

"Sorry, son. It's a Wild West term. Well, older than that, actually. I'll tell you later. I've got some ideas for tomorrow. Would you like to hear them?"

"Shoot," said Elaina, then whispered to Arcon, "That's a Wild West term. too"

"Okay. I'm bringing a media package so we can show folks what's out here," said Dan.

"Do you mean like a disc player and a computer and a roll-up screen?" asked Arcon.

"Something like that," said Dan. "I'm also going to bring an overland vehicle to haul myself to your Facility. There's no way I'm going to shimmy down a rope."

"Awww, I was so looking forward to seeing that," said Elaina.

"So was your dad. Tells me something is amiss in the Gonzales family. Anyway, I'm also bringing a small generator, fuel for it, and some parts we've gathered up for Luther. This'll take a few trips, so I'd like to take something back with us while we're at it."

"What were you thinking?" asked Arcon.

"To get started on the rare earth study, if you could gather up several of those sticker vines, some of the ArcPoint fruit, and maybe a piece of goat meat, that'd be great. And a sample of the refined ArcPoint oil would be good to study, if you don't mind."

"I'll talk to Jarden about getting that together."

"Thanks, Arcon. We'd talked about a few people volunteering to come visit us. I was planning to do that after the big meeting—flying them to the Ranger Station and housing them in cabins near Calico. Have any more come forward yet?"

"Only a few," said Arcon. "I think they're still sort of overwhelmed."

"Understood. It's not critical. But if they do, it'd be nice to take a few of them during one of the earlier trips rather than waiting until later."

Elaina said, "I'll see if I can talk Brina into going, and maybe Madelyn."

"That'd be perfect," said Dan. "Dr. Stone would like to run tests on them, so you can prepare them for that as well. That's all from me."

"Us too," said Arcon. "Tarzan and Jane out."

They both removed their earpieces, and Elaina said, "I thought you didn't like being called Tarzan."

"It is kind of demeaning," said Arcon. "I'm a much better swinger than him."

With a straight face, she responded, "Maybe. But you've probably never wrestled an alligator."

"I've never rappelled down a cliff, either. When do I get to try that?"

"Rappelling or wrestling an alligator?"

He turned to her, put his hands on her shoulders, and stared into her eyes. "Whichever one you're willing to teach me."

"Tell you what," she said, smiling, "I'll think it over and let you know. But right now, I need to find Brina. She wanted me with her when she fixed dinner."

"To be honest, I need a nap. I think I'll take one before they fix us dinner. Just so you know, around here, it gets dark right after we eat, and most people go to bed not long after. And we get up as soon as it starts to get light. We may not see each other until tomorrow. Is that okay with you?"

"It'll have to be. We need to live in this place as you normally would. I can adapt. Besides, I've got a job to do."

"What's that?"

"To find out what the Ashford family thinks about us outsiders."

"What kind of meat is this?" asked Elaina as she poked another piece of it with her fork. "It's really tasty."

"That's rabbit meat," answered Brina. "Haven't you ever had any before?"

"Never have. Could this be one that Arcon caught?"

"Oh, no, he's been gone for weeks," answered Brina's mom, Sybil. "This is fresh. We cooked it this afternoon when Sander brought it to us."

Elaina flushed with embarrassment. "I'm sorry. I forget you may not have ways to preserve meat."

Sybil smiled at her. "We have several ways. We can dry it into jerky, salt it down, or use cookers to can it. We used to freeze it, but our freezer hasn't worked since before Brina was born. Does the outside world have other ways?"

"Well, a few maybe. But we mostly do the same thing. I guess you're more resourceful than I thought."

Brina laughed. "Don't be embarrassed. We heard through Madelyn that Arcon said you outsiders thought we lived in caves and cooked around a campfire."

"I never said that," said Elaina defensively. "But we sure wondered when he showed up wearing animal skins."

"He does like to make an entrance, doesn't he?" Brina said, laughing. "He told me he always wanted to fly, and the next time we see him, he drops out of the sky."

"I'll bet that was a shock. What did you think was happening?"

Brina looked at her grandfather. "When we first heard sounds coming from the sky, we didn't know what it was. We were here in the house, so it took a while for me and Grandpa to get out the binoculars and see where the noise was coming from. When we saw that big flying thing in the sky, I heard Grandpa say—"

"God help us," interrupted Lars.

"But I wasn't scared for long because I could see it was Arcon dropping down from it. Ever since he left we've been concerned he might *cause* an invasion of outsiders, but I knew he'd never lead one here himself."

"So, you're not afraid of us outsiders?"

"Oh no, I've never been. How about you, Grandpa?"

"I'm not afraid of anything," grumbled Lars. "Pass me the butter."

Brina's dad, Thomas, complied. "Most people in ArcPoint would rather have things stay the way they are—"

"And most of us know we won't be able to do that forever," added Brina.

"None of you have ever given a thought to leaving here?" asked Elaina.

"I wouldn't say that," said Brina. "I'd love to know what's on the other side of these trees. We have books that show us how beautiful it used to be."

"Used to be?"

"You know, before the evil time, when everything was being destroyed. None of us really knows how much of that beauty is still out there."

"Would you like to see?"

"Do you have some books that show what it's like now?"

"Better than that. How'd you like to see it from a helicopter?"

"Oh, you're kidding me. What do you mean?"

"Ranger Dan is coming here tomorrow in a helicopter, and he wants me to find a few people who'd like to fly back to his headquarters. Would you like to go?" The excitement showing on Brina's face suddenly turned to fright. "What is it?" asked Elaina.

"Will I have to go up on a rope?"

Elaina remembered Arcon saying she wasn't comfortable with heights. "Don't worry about it; it's no big deal. We'll just tie a rope around your waist and hoist you into the helicopter. You don't even have to hang on." She saw all of their eyes get big as saucers, so she added, "We can even fly you all the way there just hanging by the rope. Trust me. I do it all the time."

"I ... I don't think ..."

"Relax Brina, I'm just kidding. Ranger Dan will have a safe way to get you into the helicopter. I know *he* won't ride a rope up to one."

"Well, okay, maybe. I'll think about it. But you'll have to go with me."

"I could do that."

"Mom, Dad, would it be okay with you? How about you, Grandpa?"

"How long would she be gone?" asked Lars, his gray eyes searing Elaina.

Elaina swallowed. "I don't know, but I hope it would at least be overnight. There's a bunch of things I'd like to show her. To watch the sun break over the Mojave Forest is spectacular this time of year. I mean, the ArcPoint Forest."

Lars loaded his fork, jabbing vegetables. "Nope. Sorry, dimples. I don't want you to go."

"Grandpa! Why not?"

"You're too young. Let someone older go."

"I'm older than Elaina by five years!"

"It's too dangerous. We don't know anything about those things. You should let someone else go."

"It's not dangerous, is it, Elaina?"

"Not at all. If it was, I wouldn't get on it myself."

Lars put down his fork, slowly raised his head, and looked each one of them in the eye, one at a time. He got to Elaina last. "Is there a reason she needs to go?"

Elaina thought for a moment and said, "Sir, Arcon told us about the infertility problem here at ArcPoint. Our medical people think they've figured out a solution, but they need to test some of the women here to be sure. They'd like to have a mix of older and younger women, if possible, as well as a few males. No, it doesn't have to be Brina. But I don't know any of you very well, and I don't know who else to ask."

Lars stared intensely at Elaina, then said, "Will she be with you the entire time?"

Elaina exhaled and, with a serious tone of respect, said, "She will never leave my sight, sir, and I will bring her back myself."

"Then it's up to her parents. I won't stop her."

"Mom? Dad?"

"Brina, honey, we'll discuss it and pray about it," said Sybil. "Right now, let's finish our dinner and talk about something else, okay?"

"Yes, ma'am," said Brina.

Elaina nodded, but she wasn't entirely confident Brina would be allowed to go. Then she felt a tap on her leg. She glanced down, and where no one else could see, Brina gave her a thumbs up sign.

CHAPTER NINE

The Community gazed in the early morning sun, watching a cargo basket being lowered from the helicopter. Standing closest to the landing zone, Arcon could see it contained an open ATV with a smiling Ranger Dan sitting at the wheel.

As the cargo basket settled on the ground, Dan beckoned him to unlatch the gate. He then stepped aside, and Dan drove the vehicle out and away from the basket. As soon as it was clear, Arcon latched the gate, and the basket went back up to the helicopter. Then he climbed into the passenger seat of the ATV, and they headed toward the rest of the crowd. Arcon pointed out Jarden and Ranger Dan drove right up next to him.

"You must be the famous Ranger Dan Wilson," said Jarden as he watched him slowly climb out from the driver's seat.

Dan looked at him and said, "That's right. And you must be the infamous Jarden Merrick, cousin of Victor and friend of a young man named Arcon."

"That's what I'm told," said Jarden. "Would you like a tour of the place?"

"Not quite yet," said Dan. "I want you to see some goodies we brought you."

"Goodies?"

"Oh, yeah," Dan said as he looked back toward the helicopter. It was just leaving when he stated, "As soon as that thing returns, let's get it unloaded. We can throw some of it in this ATV. Tarzan, excuse me, Arcon, get over here and give me a Patty hug. Where's Jane?"

Arcon smiled as he saw the wide-eyed look on Jarden's face. There was nobody even remotely like Ranger Dan at ArcPoint. He walked over, wrapped his arms around Dan, and lifted him off his feet, almost.

Dan laughed and said, "Good effort, son."

"Can Patty do it?" he asked.

"Since she was twelve years old." Then he looked around and said, "Where's Elaina?"

Arcon looked toward the Facility and saw her walking toward them. "Here she comes. She's bringing the people who want to take a helicopter ride."

"That's great. How many did she get?"

"Only six, and she'll ride back with them."

"Mostly women?"

"Two hunters, the rest women."

"That'll work great. Will you be okay without her?"

"Why wouldn't I be?" said Arcon, as he smacked Dan on the shoulder. "I have you." As Elaina walked up with the others, he added, "Besides, she spends all her time with these girls, anyway."

"You bet I do," said Elaina. "Give me a hug, big guy."

Ranger Dan wrapped one arm around her and lifted her off her feet. Then he held out his other arm to the others and said, "I can do two at once."

"Oh, no," said Madelyn. "I'm still trying to catch my breath from Arcon."

As he set Elaina on her feet, he looked behind him. "I hear the chopper coming."

They watched as the helicopter maneuvered into position and then lowered down the cargo basket. When it hit the ground,

Dan jumped in the ATV and yelled, "Jarden, hop in. The rest of you men, follow me."

With Dan barking orders, they soon had the heavy items loaded in the ATV, and what didn't fit was in their arms. Over the roar of the helicopter, he told Arcon to lead the men back to the Facility with the goods and asked Jarden to stay. As they left, he motioned to Elaina to bring the passengers up to the cargo basket.

Dan chose the young men to go up in the basket first. As they passed, he recognized one of them. "Do I know you?"

Jarden answered for him, saying, "This is Tawny. He's the one that tackled the shooter."

"Yes, that's why he looks familiar. Well, thanks for your help, Tawny."

"And this is Chad, the one who helped him."

"Hi Chad, welcome aboard. Here, you two, take this harness and strap it around your waist and go sit in the basket. Elaina, will you pick one of the girls and help her get hooked up? Then you can go with them."

"Sure. Brina ... you want to go first?"

"You know I do," said Brina.

After all three were strapped into the basket, the others moved a safe distance away and watched it climb into the sky. Then Dan leaned in close to Jarden and gestured toward the ATV. "Hop in. I want to show you something."

The crowd followed as Ranger Dan drove the ATV to the nearest tree. He stopped, grabbed a box from the pile on the back seat, and opened it up. "Here's what you folks need," he said as he held up a strange-looking saw. Then he turned to Jarden and asked, "Do you need that branch for anything?"

Jarden looked at the branch Dan referred to and said, "I don't know. Firewood?"

"Perfect," said Dan. He reached up, laid the blade on the branch, and pulled the trigger. In a few seconds, the branch was on the ground. "It's a cordless reciprocating saw. Should make clearing the property a bit easier. Here, take a look."

Jarden looked it over and carefully pulled the trigger. He'd seen one in the Room of Remembrance, but it was much heavier and didn't work. "Where does it get its power?"

"Little things called super-capacitors. We call them caps. All small electrical things use the same ones, so we always have a few spares with us. Some use more, some less. We can talk about that later. Hop in, and I'll give you a ride to wherever it is we're going."

"I owe you a tour. Let's start at the generator shack. Head toward that building."

The tour of ArcPoint went quick in the ATV. Jarden was embarrassed about how little there was to show him, but Dan seemed impressed with it all. "I suppose after more than a hundred years there should be more to it," said Jarden.

Dan stopped the ATV near the Facility and looked seriously at Jarden. "Do you want to know what I was thinking? I was concerned that after this amount of time, you may have all died off. With this land being under my authority, I was afraid they'd send me in here and I'd discover your bones. I'm not kidding. You have no idea how excited I am to meet you people."

"Arcon tells us you now have dominion over this place."

Dan laughed. "Isn't that a turn of events? Don't take this wrong, but when I took over that position it was considered a demotion."

"How's that?"

"I used to be in charge of an area ten times this size, that included this land. So, ninety percent of the land was taken away, but now I'm in charge of the people too."

"That's too bad."

"Are you kidding," said Dan. "I love it. Or at least, I *will* love it once it all settles down." He got serious again. "Jarden, you're a big part of what I need to make this job change work. Arcon tells me how you're the one that makes this place function. You know all these people; the jobs they perform, the needs they have. My sole purpose in life now is to make sure every one of the Mojave People thrives, wherever and whatever they decide to do. I'd like you to help me do that."

"I'd certainly want to help these people do well. I mean, I've just been trying to help them survive. But how exactly do you need my help?"

"Is there a place we can talk? I've been working on a plan."

When the helicopter lifted off, Elaina had the pilot fly low and slow over the Facility so they all could look down on it. Brina could see her grandpa and parents watching from their house on the hill. At Tawny's request, they located the Sunset trainer and then the Outpost. They tried to figure out the route Arcon took as he traveled through the forest.

As they approached the Rift, Elaina showed them where they first saw Arcon burning the grass. "We're the first people to ever fly over this area in over a hundred years," she said.

"Is that why we've never seen sky vehicles?" asked Chad.

"Uh-huh. This area has been restricted. No one has been allowed to cross the Rift, not even in a helicopter." As she said that, she had the pilot fly low over the Rift and follow it north. When they first got over the canyon, she saw Brina lean over so she could see better out of the window. "I thought you were afraid of heights."

"So did I," answered Brina. "But I think it's more a matter of trust."

"What do you mean?"

"I don't trust myself when I climb a tree or a ladder. But I trust the helicopter, as long as I can hang onto something."

"Oh, I see what you mean." said Elaina, then to everyone, "If you watch to your right, you might be able to see the nest Arcon built in the trees."

Tawny quickly moved to that side of the helicopter. "Let me try to spot it." The pilot slowed down, and Tawny yelled, "There it is, there it is, in that open spot."

"Arcon cut away the branches so we'd be able to see him," said Elaina.

"How could you?" asked Tawny. "Where was it you were looking from?"

Elaina pointed out the left side of the helicopter. "My dad and I were way up on that hill over there. In fact, that's where you'll be staying tonight." Then she said to the pilot, "Now turn so they can see where the freeway broke in half." When they were in position, she said, "If you look down here, you can see where Arcon crossed the Rift. He tied a super-rope from the barricades on that side to a vehicle over there where those people are standing."

"Whoa," said Tawny. "Chad, can you believe Arcon did something like that?"

Chad looked and said, "I wouldn't."

"We need to move on," said the pilot.

"Roger that," said Elaina. "As I said, this area is restricted, so we don't want to make too much of a commotion yet. But since we had special permission, I couldn't resist taking another look at it."

Ranger Dan admired the rustic wooden chair in Jarden's office. "This is beautiful wood. Is it from your acacia trees?"

Jarden nodded. "Most everything is from these trees. Can I get you some tea?"

"Acacia?"

"No," Jarden chuckled. "Mint. But we do use acacia tea for medicinal purposes."

Dan sat carefully in the chair, making sure it would hold his weight. "It's solid. Did you make it?"

"Sure did."

"And the desk?"

"Naaa, someone made that years ago."

As Jarden brewed the tea, Dan looked around the room. He saw a colorful rug on the floor made of woven material. A bookcase, a chest of drawers, a couple more chairs, all made of the same wood. He marveled at the craftsmanship, and how these people didn't seem to lack many creature comforts. "Have you ever heard of a kibbutz?" Dan asked Jarden.

"Can't say that I have."

"It's a Hebrew term for a group of people who share things communally."

"Similar to what we've done here at ArcPoint?"

"Precisely. Like you folks, they banded together as a way to survive the Jewish persecutions of the 20th century. Most kibbutz compounds started as farms, but farming in Israel was intense work, and dividing up that work equally was difficult. As with many communes, they struggled to maintain the unselfishness required in order to succeed."

"I don't remember it being said that selfishness was a problem here. It was more the remoteness of the site. And the weather. This was a desert, you know. But God provided us with a lot of resources at the beginning."

"It's really amazing how you've made it work all these years. Imagine you've had some creative solutions for problems."

"That's for sure." Jarden set the tea on the desk in front of Dan, then sat down himself.

"Let me tell you what I'm thinking," said Dan. "One interesting thing that took place in Israel just before Jesus returned was, many outsiders volunteered to work at a kibbutz just to experience Israeli culture. They wanted to spend time in the Holy Land and bless Israel, as the Bible recommended. I was wondering if you'd consider doing something similar to a kibbutz here at ArcPoint?"

"What do you mean exactly?" asked Jarden.

Dan leaned back in his chair. "For many years, people have petitioned me to be allowed to come into this place and look around. Rumors, good and bad, about the Mojave People were rampant, and people were curious. Now that word has gotten out that there are still people—good people—living here, I'm getting even more requests. I think I've come up with a way we can help each other."

"I'm listening," said Jarden.

"There hasn't been an official discussion about what your people want to do in the future, but some of the feedback I'm getting from my spies is that there are a number of people living here that really like this place and would prefer to stay."

"You have *spies* among us?" asked Jarden, incredulous.

Dan laughed and said, "Yeah, you know … Arcon, Elaina, Victor."

Jarden tipped his head. "Okay, I understand. Yeah, I'd say there are those who are understandably still uneasy about being thrust into the outside world."

"Well, have no fear, Ranger Dan is here. Nobody has to leave if they don't want to. In fact, I hope some will want to stay. Here's what I'm thinking. You folks have a resource here with the trees. You may need extra labor to develop it, but you also have a resource just by being who you are."

"Who we are?" asked Jarden, furrowing his brow. "We're no different than other humans on the planet."

"Of course not," said Dan. "But the way you live certainly is. Back in the 20th century, there were native tribes who were an oddity to the outside world. People would visit them to gawk at how primitive their lifestyle was. Trust me; you don't want that here. With a kibbutz, visitors volunteer to work in exchange for being able to *experience* the lifestyle. You can share with them how God brought you through it all."

Jarden thought about that. "I'm not sure how we'd work it all out, but I don't think we'd mind allowing a few folks to live among us and work alongside us."

Dan looked intently at Jarden. "We? Us? Sounds like you're one of those who'd prefer to stay."

"I'd certainly like to see what the outside world is like, and meet more of my family. But this is what I know, and I think it's my home."

"That's completely understandable," said Dan. "And really, you can make of this place whatever you desire. What I'm tasked with is preparing to go some direction with it all. If you don't mind, how about if you and I brainstorm on a plan? Then you can share it with everyone this evening. We can always make adjustments, but I need to start figuring out the logistics for getting folks in and out of this place."

"I can take some time today," offered Jarden. "Let me make sure the cooks have everything they need for lunch, and we can work on it right after."

"Works for me," said Dan. "I'll find Arcon and then see you at lunchtime."

CHAPTER TEN

Elaina had fully expected to hear statements of astonishment during the helicopter ride, but the comments made afterwards during the walk to the Ranger Station surprised her.

She heard observations like, "You can see such a long way without being in a tree," and, "Not much grows on the ground here," and, "How do you make the land so smooth?" and, "Look how uniform the logs are on this building!" Elaina couldn't wait to show them a viewscreen and hear their response after they accessed the worldwide info-net.

After introducing the first three passengers to Ranger Becca, Elaina left on the helicopter to get the others. On the way back to ArcPoint, they piloted down to the Rift and followed the I-15 freeway up to the interchange that had once been the access to the ArcPoint area. Then they flew down where the old road to ArcPoint should have been. As they flew over it, she took surveillance pictures for Ranger Dan so they could start designing a new road. After they landed, three more people were waiting for the flight.

The first two to get there were Nola and Steph, two girls she'd met at the dye house. "Hi, girls," said Elaina. "Hop into the basket and have a seat."

Elaina thrust out her hand to the last traveler. "I'm so glad you decided to come, Maddy. Don't worry; it's safe. We didn't drop Brina. Just take a seat next to Nola."

As Madelyn approached the basket, Elaina helped secure the other two. Madelyn's hands were shaking. "I don't know if I can do this," she said.

"Please try," begged Elaina. "It's too late for me to find someone else to go in your place, and the doctor needs to take as many blood samples as she can get. If it helps any, Brina calmed down as soon as she sat inside."

Refusing to step into the basket, Madelyn said, "It won't hurt to have one less, will it?"

"Trust me," said Elaina, as she put her hand on Madelyn's shoulder. "Don't make me twist your ear."

Madelyn's top lip stretched into a nervous smile. "I agree to your terms, reluctantly."

Elaina smiled back. "Good enough for me." In a few minutes, they were strapped in and being hoisted up to the helicopter. She tried to point out the overhead view of the Facility as they took off, but Madelyn just moved closer to the middle of the helicopter and closed her eyes. But by the time they reached the Ranger Station helipad, Madelyn was ready to keep going.

Elaina said to her, "When we get back to the forest, I'll get Arcon to teach you how to swing."

"I don't trust either of you *that* much," joked Madelyn.

Ranger Dan had given Elaina the driver code for his vehicle, so she gathered up her six guests from inside the station and let Becca know she was taking it. "Men, if you don't mind, I'll have you sit in the cargo area. The girls can sit up front on the seats. Don't worry; we don't have far to go. Oh, here, let me show you how the door opens."

The first place she took them was to their cabins. As she walked into the corner unit, she said, "Remember I told you we were looking at Arcon? This is where we watched him from. If you look right down there, you can just barely make out the opening in the trees."

94

They all looked, and Chad said, "You must have had some powerful nocs."

"Some what?" said Elaina. Then she remembered, "Oh, yeah, binoculars. No, we had a telescope. I'll show you the pictures later." She stepped outside and said, "Chad and Tawny, your cabin is right there." Then she motioned the other direction. "Nola and Steph, you can stay in that one, and I'll stay with Madelyn and Brina in this one since it has two bedrooms and a full kitchen. Go ahead and check out your rooms and get settled in, and we'll meet back here in a half-hour."

They all gave her a strange look, and she remembered, "That's right, no watches. I'll come knock on your doors."

"Do you think the kibbutz model is the one we should pursue?" Dan asked Jarden, Arcon, and Petra.

"I'd say so," said Petra. "It would certainly limit the number of people entering the ArcPoint area."

"It would also minimize the amount of road we'd have to construct," added Dan. "We would only come down the I-15 from the north, where there's already a security gate. For now, we could leave the I-15 pretty rugged, maybe just move in a pre-built one-lane bridge over the earth crack south of Baker. The earthquake damage could really add some ambiance to the experience."

Jarden added, "I liked Arcon's idea of having the visitors abandon their vehicles on the freeway, like some of our people had to. Make them park next to the rusted-out carcasses. That way, we'd only need a trail in here from the highway."

"If it's an ATV trail, I like it," said Dan. "But it's about eight kilometers, so they won't want to walk that far. I'll have the engineers work on giving us a timeline for making it happen. Until we have a way to travel in and out of here, you folks will remain pretty isolated, but that's okay. There's no need to rush things."

"I agree," said Petra. "I'll make sure we're on track for the meeting tonight with the leaders. I may even say a few things myself."

Jarden and Arcon gave each other a knowing smile.

Elaina was glad when Noreena Chan finally left the cabins. She stayed longer than she'd said she would, but it wasn't her fault. The ArcPoint people were just as inquisitive as she was. For a people who coveted quiet time, they certainly hadn't showed it. Neither did they mind the time they'd spent with Dr. Stone, who was excited to get blood samples from some women. She also thought it fortunate to get two more hunters to test, since they had the diet highest in ArcPoint fruit. She'd hoped for someone who was trying to get pregnant, but the only two such women in ArcPoint had husbands who refused to let them fly away in a noisy machine. "Are you all tired of meeting people yet?" Elaina asked them.

"We've only met two so far," responded Chad. "Not counting Ranger Becca."

"Well, I have to apologize that you're still in sort of a quarantine here," she said. "But I do have permission for you to meet four of my friends. They've been praying for Arcon for years and for all the Mojave people since we found out about you being there."

"Why have they been doing that?" asked Madelyn.

"Because they're my friends, and they knew my mission to

help Arcon was important to me. You should all be impressed, and not just because they prayed for so long. They actually kept it all secret."

"I'd sure like to meet them," said Tawny.

Elaina laughed. "I'm sure you would."

"Why do you say that?"

"They're all girls."

The Franklin meeting room was packed, but the ArcPoint crowd was quiet as Petra explained to them about the Israeli way of life known as a kibbutz. They murmured a little as he pointed out the similarities with their own way of living. "Before I have Ranger Wilson talk to us about the outside world, I'd like to have Jarden share a few things with you. Jarden, take it away."

The crowd applauded loudly, but Jarden thought it was more for Petra than himself.

"Thanks Petra, hello everyone. Okay, so Petra talked about the communal nature of a kibbutz, but I'd like to talk about its educational nature. People ... outsiders ... used to visit Israel for the express purpose of working at a kibbutz. It was a way for them to immerse themselves in Israeli culture. Ranger Wilson told us there are many outsiders who'd like to experience life at ArcPoint. So, he suggests we put them to work so they can."

Jarden scanned around the room and pointed at various people as he said, "Can you imagine them shearing goats? Or these folks dying wool and spinning it into yarn? Pedaling the pump for the aquaponics? What about sawing logs for a new home, or making soap?" He cringed and finished with, "How about hacking needle-brush?"

The crowd roared their approval with that particular suggestion, so he added, "I agree. If we can get them to beat back this needle-brush, this place could be heaven again."

Once they'd quieted down again, Jarden said, "Seriously, I know many of you have told me you'd like to stay here, and I think this is a way we could do it. Without help with the work, though, it'd be hard on those that remain. I told Ranger Wilson we'll consider a kibbutz type of plan for our future, but we need a lot more information. Is anyone opposed to at least *studying* it?"

Jarden's recommendation brought on plenty of noise from conversations and joking around, but no one raised their hand in opposition. "Then we'll proceed with that in mind. We can always go a different direction if we want. Right now, I'll have Ranger Dan Wilson tell us how the outside world will try to help us. Ranger Dan …"

The people started to applaud, but their applause drifted away as soon as Dan stood up and they saw how big and tall he was. Jarden said, "Don't worry, he won't hurt you." Then added, "Unless he hugs you."

Dan waited as the noise died down "I want to thank you all for being here, and I mean that literally. You've probably heard that I've been in charge of this land for over four years, mostly trying to keep people away from here. I was afraid you people all died off a long time ago. To find out this is still a thriving community is a tremendous blessing. I can see God has been good to you. Let's thank him."

Then he lifted one hand to the sky and started reciting the slightly altered words to an ancient hymn: "O Lord, my God, when I in awesome wonder, consider all these people you have saved. I see their peace, their praises rise like thunder, your love throughout the Community displayed."

Jarden nodded to Willem, who stood and led everyone in the chorus: "Then sings my soul, my Savior God, to thee. How great thou art, how great thou art. Then sings my soul, my Savior God, to thee. How great thou art, how great thou art."

"Thanks, Willem," said Dan. Then he turned to the crowd and said, "Isn't God good?"

"AMEN!" came a shout from the crowd.

Dan stepped back like he'd been struck. "Whoa, if I'd been on a horse, he'd have bucked me off for sure." The crowd went notably more quiet and he suddenly remembered—none of them had ever seen a horse.

"Never mind. I'd like to tell all of you what's been going on behind your backs. We have a group in the outside world called Helpers Anonymous. When people have more credits than they need, they donate them to this group, and the Helpers track down people in need. So, if any of you are in need of something, let your leaders know. Until we get a road into here, we'll have to bring in supplies with that noisy flying machine. But we can't keep dropping a basket down on a cable. We'd like you folks to clear a landing pad for us. I'll give the dimensions and such to Jarden and Petra. It doesn't need to be fancy. Just a level place where the blades won't hit the trees."

"I think a number of you have met Jarden's cousin, Victor." Victor stood and waved, and Dan continued. "He tells me the parts are in for your backup generator, so pretty soon, you'll have all the power you need. We're getting you pumps for the hydroponics, so the pedal-pumpers will soon be out of a job." Sounds of a commotion came from the back of the room. "There they are now!"

Ranger Dan continued talking about how the outside world was trying to help them but he noticed they were more receptive, mellower than he'd expected. He wasn't quite sure if they wanted help or not. He decided he shouldn't try to push his own ideas. There was plenty of time to get their input. *It's probably better to work through Jarden. They all seem to love him.*

Lars watched as Brina tapped Jarden on the shoulder. He wanted more time with the man who claimed to be in charge of ArcPoint land. *I'm not sure if we've asked him the right questions yet.*

He let them talk a while. Then Jarden's eyes met his and he pointed to Ranger Dan, Arcon, and himself as if giving him a silent invitation to join their party. Lars nodded. Jarden gave his own temple a tap—his sign for Petra, the head of the Community. Lars nodded again and cast his own vote by pointing toward Jarden's office upstairs. Jarden gave a nod.

Lars was at the foot of the stairs when Brina caught up with him. She took his hand and said, "Now, you're going to be nice to him, aren't you?"

Lars huffed. "As nice as I always am."

She grabbed the other handrail. "You should try to do better than that."

"Don't expect me to be as nice as you."

"Wouldn't think of it." They grinned at one another and then worked their way up the stairs. In Jarden's office they sat in the two spare seats to the right of his desk. Arcon came through the door next, with Dan close behind.

"Lars," said Arcon, "I don't think you've met this big fellow yet. Ranger Dan, this is the patriarch of the ArcPoint Community, Lars Ashford."

"I've certainly wanted to meet you, Lars," said Dan, thrusting out his hand.

"Sounds like you want to take my job," said Lars, scowling.

Dan shook his head. "From what I've been told, that would be impossible."

Lars winked at Brina, who smiled back at him. "Good," he said, turning back to shake Dan's hand. "I see we understand each other."

"That will take some time." Dan took a seat in the chair Jarden had set up for him next to Lars. "And you can have all the time you need. I hear you have questions for me."

"Sure do." Lars waited until Petra and Jarden were seated. "I want to know what it's like out there. And I don't mean the workaday world. I'm sure that's all changed. I want to know what's going on with people's hearts—what they're like on the inside. Are they good or evil?"

Dan leaned over and looked Lars in the eyes. "We're good."

Lars held Dan's stare. "Completely?"

Dan leaned back in his chair. "From our perspective, we are, but not always from someone else's. But we settle differences pretty fast. Jarden tells me you folks are the same way. You work out any disputes right away, and if you can't, you get someone to help you."

"That's right."

Jarden leaned forward and put his forearms on the desk. "Does the entire world operate that way?"

"For the most part," said Dan. "Since all authority flows down from Jesus—and His Spirit assists us in judging matters—there's very little jurisdictional difference. But we're all free to make our own decisions as well, so it's not perfect. I imagine it's the same here."

Jarden laughed. "Yeah, we all work together, but there's that occasional person who insists on doing things contrary to the desires of the Community."

"You mean like him?" asked Dan, pointing his thumb at Arcon.

"Or Raymo shooting at the helicopter," added Jarden. "I have another question. What about goods and services? Arcon told me about a train that can ship food all over the world. Do people share resources long distances like that? How does that work?"

"Food is important," said Dan. "It's shared locally as much as possible, but certain things—like coffee, bananas, spices—they'll go wherever in the world they're needed."

"Does everyone share freely, or do they get paid, or what?"

"Every worker is worth his wages. No matter what work you do, you get compensated for it. But no longer do people get paid to do nothing. That's one more function performed by the judges—to determine what's fair. But we're taught not to think more highly of ourselves than we ought to."

Lars interrupted. "How did it all happen? Was there a huge war, or what?"

"That'd be hard to explain," said Dan. "Part of my training as an Authority involves understanding what happened during the times of tribulation. But that doesn't involve which people or nations caused the conflicts. We're told that people ignored God, so He stepped out of the way. For centuries He'd limited the influence that evil spirits could exert on mankind. He still guarded those who asked for His protection, but those numbers were too small to keep nations from enacting laws in favor of sinful behavior. The ones who'd steal, kill, and destroy were ignored, while those who loved life, liberty, and justice were persecuted. So it wasn't a declared war, per se, but more like worldwide chaos."

"Then Jesus returned," said Arcon, "and established His government."

"Not exactly," corrected Dan. "When things got bad, humans created a universal government. For years, people had been developing a world-wide system of control, with artificial intelligence, digital currency, and something called 'the internet of things.' With everything controlled by one government—and ultimately one person—they hoped peace could be attained through control. But with Satan controlling that one person, it turned into mutually assured destruction."

"It sounds like Lee and my father were wise to move here to the Mojave," said Lars.

"They sure were. Even after Jesus returned, it took years to get the planet cleaned up from the damage inflicted on it. But the governing part was simplified by the apparatus already in place. There just needed to be people at the highest levels that money or power couldn't corrupt."

"That'd be Central Authority, right?" asked Arcon.

"That's right. They're part of what we refer to as the first resurrected—those who gave their lives for Jesus during that tribulation time."

"You're talking about chapter twenty in the book of Revelation," said Lars. "Am I right?"

"Absolutely right," said Dan.

"I knew it," said Lars as he shook his fist. He looked at Brina. "Isn't that what I told you? That righteous people would govern this world?"

She nodded. "You were right."

"And all those notions about people disappearing and leaving their clothes behind? That never happened, right?"

"It really couldn't," said Dan. "Those ideas relied on verses in chapter four of first Thessalonians and chapter fifteen of first Corinthians, which require a resurrection to take place. That didn't happen until Jesus returned, which was after the tribulation years. Those particular verses refer to the final resurrection on Judgment Day, at the end of this time period we're in."

Lars nodded. "Thank you, Ranger Dan. That answers my question. I will let you govern our land."

"Naah, I'll let you folks govern it. I'll just make sure us outsiders respect it."

CHAPTER ELEVEN

Victor wiped his brow and neck as he finished installing the last water pump in the hydroponics greenhouse. It wasn't arduous work, but the room was hot and humid. When he finished this project, he'd suggest installing an automatic temperature controller. When that was done, he'd try to think of some other reason to spend time working with Brina.

When Jarden had asked if he could help in the hydroponics greenhouse, Victor had pointed out that he was a mechanic, not a gardener. But one of the hydro workers had just come back from the outside world and had all sorts of ideas on how to change things. It would require pumps and valves and lights and aerators, and, well, Victor was needed there more than he was in ArcPoint's mechanic shop. That fact stung his ego, but it was true. All they ever needed in the shop were materials and parts, and he supplied those. When Brina heard from the hydro worker about these pumps, Victor felt obligated to make it happen for her. He showed her an irrigation design program on his computer and helped her design one for the hydroponics greenhouse. He enjoyed working with her. A lot.

Hydroponics was a completely different world. It was quiet and bright, and the air smelled fresh and clean. Very few people worked there, except when they needed to pump irrigation water to the feed tanks. Various people stopped in to harvest fresh herbs and vegetables. Victor always preferred to work alone, and right now the shop would be swarming with people repairing machinery. In this place, there were only two key people to contend with, Thomas and Sybil Ashford. And occasionally, their daughter Brina, who was the most mechanically savvy gardener he'd ever met.

"It's a work of art," said Brina.

Stepping back to admire his work, he remarked, "Oh, I wouldn't say that. But it doesn't look half bad if I do say so myself. The important thing is that it works."

"If it doesn't, I'll hold you responsible," she replied with a smile.

"If it doesn't, I can fix it."

"I'm sure you can. You remind me of another person I know."

"Jarden? If that's the case, I'll take it as a compliment."

"Well, yeah, you sort of look like a young Jarden. But I was thinking of Arcon. When he was younger, he was always taking broken things apart and trying to fix them. Were you that way?"

"Yeah, I've always been fascinated with how things work," said Victor.

"Okay now, don't tell me," said Brina. "Let me guess. Sometimes you get so into working on something you lose track of time. And sometimes, when you're trying to figure something out, you don't like to be distracted. Am I right?"

"Am I that transparent?"

"No, you're just like Arcon. Once in a while, he'd tell me to leave him alone. But I learned not to take it personally."

"You seem pretty mechanically minded yourself. Did you learn that from being around him?"

"You're going to laugh. We used to have contests to see who was fastest at completely disassembling something and putting it back together without parts left over. I was faster than he was with a toaster."

"Really?" asked Victor.

"I'm not kidding," said Brina. "But he's the one who got into making things work. He especially got into electronic stuff. Of course, now we know why."

"Oh … yeah … he told me about the radio and stuff. And about Elaina and all that."

"Well, she seems to be perfect for him. We kind of drifted apart once he became a hunter. I just never had a desire to climb up a tree."

"I totally agree. I'd rather smack my knuckles or get shocked with electricity than fall out of a tree."

"I still like doing mechanical things, but now I'd rather get my hands in the dirt than in the grease."

They both looked back at the sound of footsteps. Victor saw Brina's father, Thomas Ashford, rounding the corner of the hydroponic tanks. "Are we about ready to start the pumps?" asked Thomas.

"I'm just going to do a quick leak test," said Victor. "Then I'll have one of you start it up while I check the operation."

"Great," said Thomas. He turned to Brina and said, "Your mom just left to go make dinner, so you should probably go help her. I'll stay here and help Victor."

"Sure, Daddy." Brina took off her gloves and moved toward the door, then stopped to ask, "Victor, would you care to join us for dinner?"

"If it's not a problem, I'd like that very much."

"No problem at all. Arcon and Elaina will be there too, so the more, the merrier."

"Great. Thanks."

"Here they are," said Brina as her dad and Victor walked into the house.

"Hi everyone," said Thomas. "Sorry we're late. Victor had to make sure everything worked perfectly before we left. Hey, I see we have another guest. Hi Jarden."

"I ran into him on the way home," said Brina. "I had to twist his ear, but I finally persuaded him to join us."

As Thomas washed his hands in the kitchen sink, he said, "I hear all of your newfound friends are leaving you tomorrow morning."

"That's the plan, but I don't think it'll be for long," said Jarden. "Victor, here, has a few more parts to install, and I know Elaina wants to bring her dad here, eventually. What about you, Arcon? Don't you still feel more at home here than out there?"

"Well, maybe," said Arcon. "It's good to be back, but I'm not going to fight Tawny for my old apartment. I saw how he tackled Raymo."

They all laughed, and Elaina said, "You may not have to fight him. I had a tough time bringing him back. He seems to have taken an interest in one of my girlfriends."

"Which one?" asked Arcon.

"Malika."

"Did you warn him she doesn't swing through trees?"

"Neither did I when you first met me."

"That's true. They'll work it out."

Elaina punched him in the arm. "Are you going to become a matchmaker now? Has Ranger Dan been teaching you things I don't know about?"

Arcon looked over at Victor and smiled "Hey, Victor. You better marry somebody like Brina, here. You'll never find anyone better."

Brina's face turned red. Victor stared at his plate.

Elaina smacked Arcon again and said, "Now you've embarrassed them."

"I'm sorry, you two. I was just kidding. That never worked on us, did it, Brina? Owww. What was that for?"

"Now you embarrassed me," said Elaina.

Sybil set the last bowl of food on the table. "Okay, kids, enough of that. It's time to eat. Thomas, would you like to thank our Lord?"

"Sure. Dear Lord, once more, we sit before a table full of food, and we see how you've provided for not only us but the friends who share it with us. Thank you again for it all." He waved his hand slowly over everything on the table and said, "All of this …"

Everyone but Victor responded, "From Him!"

After they finished their meal, Arcon said to Victor, "Come here. You've got to try this." He led him to a strange-looking object in the living room. "It's called a macramé sling-chair. Go ahead, sit down. It's really comfortable."

Victor carefully negotiated his backside into the chair. "Wow, you're right. It is. Who made it?"

"Lars made it originally with branches from the ArcPoint trees. He used canvas from an old tent, but it wore out. Then Brina took a macramé class from Madelyn and made a new sling for it. Pretty impressive, huh? I think she was only twelve years old when she made it."

"How long ago was that?" asked Victor, hoping to discover Brina's age.

"Oh, about fourteen years."

She's my age. Victor smiled. He settled back in the chair and crossed his ankles. "It's really held up well."

"And it fits you perfect. I thought it would. I'm too tall for it. The top branch hits me in the shoulder blades. But if you see Jarden coming, you'd better get out of it."

Just then, the man himself stepped through the door. "Hey, what're you doing in my chair?" barked Jarden.

"Sorry, sir." Victor pushed his way out, but the chair buckled and dumped him on the floor.

Jarden and Arcon started laughing, and the noise brought the others in from the dining room. "Arcon!" yelled Brina. "You didn't pull the sling-chair trick on Victor, did you?"

"Don't feel too bad, Victor," said Elaina, "Brina pulled that on me too."

Victor got to his feet. "Is that why the macramé is in such good shape? Because nobody sits in it?"

"Oh, you can sit in it," said Jarden. "You just can't get out."

"Don't believe him," said Brina. "You just have to know the trick. I sort of made the macramé lop-sided."

"Wait," said Victor. He carefully sat down in the sling chair again. He rocked a little back and forth, then side to side. He sat still for a moment, then threw his weight onto his left foot and stood right up. "No problem."

As they all applauded, Lars said, "I think he just set a record."

"Arcon never has figured it out," added Brina.

They settled into the living room, sitting in what looked to Victor like rustic patio furniture. It appeared to be made entirely of tree branches, with cushions of the same material most of the men in the machine shop wore. Brina sat in the sling chair, while Elaina sat on the floor in front of Arcon.

Jarden asked, "Are the pumps all working now in hydro?"

"They're all running," said Thomas. "Now we'll see how well Brina's design works."

"Victor chose a different pump than what I saw on the computer thing," said Brina. "He said a low-head pump would work better in our application. It'll move more water with less energy."

"And you only did half of hydro?"

"That's correct," said Victor. "We left the other half original for the visitors to see how you used to do it."

"And, of course, we'll make the visitors do all the hand-cranking to pump the water," added Thomas. "Especially in the middle of the night. By the way, Dad had a great idea. Tell them, Dad."

"You know that old tractor by the Griffin house?" said Lars. "You should get it running again—if they've still got parts for the old lady."

"I like that idea," said Jarden. "Hey, Victor, how'd you like to restore an old tractor?"

"I've never done it before, but I'd love to try. How old?"

"Older than me," said Lars.

"And hasn't run since I was a young man," added Jarden.

"Sounds like an interesting challenge. Uhh, wait a minute. After the sling chair, how about if I let you know ... after I see it?"

"That only sounds fair, son. If you want, we can go look at it now."

"Sure. Why wait?"

Jarden and Victor said their goodbyes and left the Ashford home. Arcon stepped outside too and said, "Can I talk to you alone for a minute, Jarden? It won't take long."

"Sure. Victor, how about if I meet you at half-way bench?"

"Fine with me. See you in a few."

They watched as Victor walked down the trail. "Nothing serious, I hope," said Jarden.

"Oh no, not at all." Arcon glanced back at the house. "I'm just trying to think things through, you know, with Elaina and everything. I mean, we still have to do the courtship thing for a while. But to do things right, after that, I need to have a home for us to move into."

"You know you have—"

Arcon held up his hand. "I don't want to move into the Franklin tiny home. I know that's the tradition, but I've always wanted to build my own. Something like this place—on a hill with a view. I'd just like to get your wisdom on the idea. Not right now, just think about it."

Jarden put his hand on Arcon's shoulder. "Son, if you want to build yourself a house, I'm sure the Community will help you do it. We'll talk about it later. I need to get back to Victor."

They didn't see Elaina eves-dropping in the doorway.

When Victor spotted Jarden coming down the trail, he got up from the bench to greet him. "I gotta say, I'm excited to fix up this tractor. Tell me more about it."

Jarden sat down on the bench. "Belonged to Harlon Griffin. He was an important help to the Community, even though we considered him an outsider at first."

"Why is that?"

"Well, after the Rift happened, we became cut off from outside resources. Harlon owned a farm that ended up on the ArcPoint side of that earth crack. He was friends of another outsider who worked for Lee Franklin on the Facility."

"Sorry, Jarden, but I've gotta ask. What do you folks mean when you say outsider?"

Jarden chuckled. "Don't worry. It's not a derogatory term. When people first moved here, they knew they had to be committed—to each other and to God. At one point, they almost split up. So, they had a meeting where they made a verbal—what would you call it, a contract maybe—with each other and with God. Those outside that meeting were eventually called outsiders. Harlon was like that. He was just a local farmer."

"And he became important to the Community?"

"He sure did, and so did his tractor. We used that tractor and a trailer to haul a lot of the building material that make up our buildings. We disassembled his farm and brought it here. Then he got permission to take materials from other abandoned farms."

"How far away were those farms?"

"Oh, it'd take about two hours to get there with the tractor. Then we'd work all day, maybe a couple more, and come back here the next morning. Took half a day with a full load." Jarden stood up from the bench. "Now, look out there, on that other hill. That's the house he built with materials from his old one."

"Why that far away?"

"It was actually closer for him. We went that direction to get to his farm, so that spot was on the way. The tractor is just on the other side of the trees below the house." Jarden began walking down the trail.

"How far is it from there to the machine shop?"

"Oh, I don't know. Half a mile, maybe. Why?"

"If I'm gonna work on it, I'll want it close to the tools I'll need. But I'll figure out what those are once I see it."

When they reached the storage shed, Jarden said, "I haven't looked at her for a while. Looks like the roof has sprung a leak since I was here last. The old girl's starting to live up to her name."

"The tractor has a name?"

"Yup. She's called dirty Gertie, the 730."

"That's, uhh, unique. How'd she get that name?"

"Well, the story goes, Harlon completely restored her to be like new in 2009, when she was fifty years old. He went back to using her, plowing fields, hauling hay. One day, he took her to a tractor show without cleaning her up first. When other farmers saw how filthy she was, they started calling her dirty Gertie, the 730. You see ... she's a 1959 John Deere 730 Diesel."

"Were they making fun of the tractor or Harlon?"

"Neither. Everybody liked Harlon. And from what I've heard, dirty Gertie used to beat all the competition in the antique tractor pull."

Victor looked the tractor over, opened its hood, turned the steering wheel, and inspected the axles. When he was done he used a rag to wipe the grease from his hands and said firmly, "I'll do it. But I'm gonna warn you. When I get finished, she'll need a new nickname.

CHAPTER TWELVE

Roberto glanced around at all the workers who'd helped get Arcon back to ArcPoint. *This abandoned fi ehall has worked well as a base camp, but now it's time to close this chapter of its life.* He cleared his throat and yelled, "Could you all take your seats and please quiet down?" Then he smiled at everyone. "I know you're all excited and waiting for Ranger Dan. He'll be here shortly; his previous meeting went a little long."

"Are you going to give us the good news?" yelled BJ.

"Officially, no," said Roberto. "That's Dan's job. But I'd like to say these have been a hectic couple of weeks, and you should all be proud of what we've accomplished. None of us knew what to expect when we entered the Mojave Forest. Would the Mojave People scatter like rabbits or defend their home like coyotes? What we discovered was God in control, and the time was right. Oh good, here's Ranger Dan now."

Dan sauntered in and sat on an empty barstool. "Hi everybody. Sorry, I'm late. I don't know what Roberto told you, but if it wasn't good, don't believe it. I don't think we could've asked for a better outcome. The ArcPoint Community has accepted the modified kibbutz plan, and as we speak, they're preparing the place for visitors. The primitive helipad is finished, and they're also marking a pathway from their facility out towards the intersection. On our end, crews are just starting to rebuild one side of the I-15 from the security gate at the highway 164 interchange. It'll take a while to get the road easily navigable again. I guess what I'm trying to say is, you'll have a rough road ahead of you."

"Are you saying we can leave?" asked BJ. "Officially?"

"Yes, the film crew can officially go home. One helicopter and pilot will remain, but the other one and all the flight support can leave. We'll essentially drop to a skeleton crew for a while, then maybe this poor town of Baker will become a ghost town again. Yes, Victor?"

"Will anyone be working with the ArcPoint people?"

"You, if you want the job. Otherwise, I believe we have them on their feet again for a while. They have the tools and supplies they need to make necessary changes to accommodate kibbutzniks. It doesn't make sense to move forward until the road is in. But we've overcome the biggest obstacle to that. I just talked to Redi-Span, and they have a 25-meter bridge section for us, which is a full ten meters longer than the earth crack is wide. But we need to improve the rest of the road first, especially through Mountain Pass."

Noreena Chan asked, "Where's your office going to be?"

"For a while, nowhere," said Dan. "The Rangers are handling my old duties just fine, and ArcPoint can take care of themselves. I'm taking a few weeks off."

"Going any place in particular?" she asked.

"Home. I've been away from my wife's cooking for too long. And, no offense, but you people are just not as enjoyable to be around." He chuckled, but could tell by Noreena's countenance that she wasn't satisfied with the answer.

"And?" she asked.

"Off the record?" he countered.

"Of course."

"Arcon and I need to take a trip to Jerusalem," said Dan.

"We'll be taking Elaina and Roberto with us, but no reporters," he said, narrowing his eyes at her. "But you already knew all that, didn't you?"

"Hey, I'm a reporter."

"And Arcon's got a big mouth," said Dan.

"Well, this time, it was me," said Roberto. "I didn't know you wanted to keep it hush-hush. Sorry."

"At this point, I don't think it matters. But Noreena, I'd prefer if you reported on it after we get back. And, yeah, I'll sit for an interview."

"I agree to your terms," she said as they all laughed.

Elaina was glad to be back home. She could make coffee the way she liked it, could eat what she wanted for breakfast, and have a little more privacy when the urge struck. But most of all, she was happy to get back in her recliner. She even enjoyed the embarrassing worn spots where her hands always rested. Right now, they felt good.

Even with a one-day head start, she and Arcon probably only beat her dad home by a couple of hours. It was a long drive around the Restricted Area, and she was exhausted. She could imagine her dad walking in the door, unpacking, and tossing his dirty laundry in the basket before she could get hers in there. He might try to do some of it himself, but he'd probably collapse on the bed for a nap. Then it would be too close to dinner to start a load, and nobody would want to do it after dinner. Tomorrow her dad would check in at the Search and Rescue office, and she'd be stuck washing clothes.

Arcon didn't know how to use a washing machine, and he was surely making his own pile of dirty clothes. *If I was smart, I'd get out of this recliner and start a load of my own.* In three days, they were getting on a tube train for Jerusalem and would need everything clean. She thought more about it, then kicked back in the recliner and went to sleep.

Arcon lay on his bed, staring at the ceiling. He'd slept on the ride home, and now he was wide awake. He couldn't get his mind off of his grandma. She wanted so much to go to Jerusalem, especially if Jesus was there. If only he'd tried to escape the forest before she died, he might have been able to take her with him. But he knew better. God was in control of all that had taken place, and he had to accept that it was the best way to have happened. Besides, at over a hundred years old, a long trip would've been difficult for her.

He got up and walked over to his luggage sitting on the desk. He opened up a small box, and, one by one, pulled rocks out of it and placed them around his room in the basement. They were all beautiful rocks he'd collected around the ArcPoint Forest. He'd painstakingly polished a window on one side of each stone to reveal the colors. He'd done some research on the computer and found out they were sagenites and plume agates. In the outside world, he could have polished them in fifteen minutes. But with ArcPoint resources, they'd taken him days, and sometimes weeks, to polish by hand.

He'd given each one to his grandma as a gift at one time or another. Thankfully, Jarden had saved them for him, or they'd have been distributed throughout the Community. He would've felt guilty to ask for them back since he knew the people would've kept them to remember his grandma. She always displayed them prominently in her room.

When he had them all laid out, he looked at each one carefully. He thought about their color, their beauty, their size, and how much his grandma had liked each one. Then he chose one and set it aside—her favorite. It was one Jarden had given him that he'd found on Far Ridge. He knew what he had to do. *Grandma can't go with me to Jerusalem, but this rock of hers will.* And he would remember her.

Victor felt fortunate as he stared at the picture on his monitor. It appeared to be an exact match of the tractor at ArcPoint. He still marveled at how old it was. He double-checked the photo and saw it was correct. It was a John Deere 730 Diesel and had been manufactured in 1959. It was over a century old when they were still using it, and now another century had passed. Now that he knew what he was dealing with, the question was where he would restore it.

The machine shop was too cluttered with projects to provide enough space. It was too dirty of an environment to paint in. But to be efficient, he'd need ready access to the shop. He scanned a plot plan of the Facility site and chose a level spot between the shop and the hydroponics greenhouse to build another utility building. Then he'd make sure it had a window facing the path that Brina walked every day.

He'd have to get approval from the Welcoming Committee; the one formed to prepare ArcPoint to receive outside guests. That shouldn't be a problem, since the tractor was an important part of the welcoming process. Plus, he already had a relationship with two people on the committee: Jarden and Thomas Ashford, Brina's dad.

If he built the structure out of materials that matched the Facility, it wouldn't be distracting. He could build it so it could be disassembled and materials used to repair the existing Facility. Or he could build it to be used for some other purpose once the tractor was finished. Maybe Brina could use it for something.

There was no denying it. He couldn't get Brina off his mind. He'd always noticed attractive girls, but most of them seemed focused on maintaining that image. Brina focused on caring for her grandfather, her plants, and helping others. She wore pretty clothes she made herself, or work clothes she adorned with colorful patches. She never wore makeup and didn't need to. The big surprise was that she enjoyed working with him and wanted to learn rather than just assist. He'd certainly met no one like her.

Now he was glad he'd made friends with Arcon. Since he and Brina had been close, Victor now knew a lot more about her than he normally would have. But there was one thing Arcon had said to him that he still didn't fully understand. At the Facility, after eating at the Ashford's, from out of nowhere he'd said, "If you do want to marry her, I'm going to be one of your life guarantors." *What had he meant by that?*

Elaina jerked upright and dropped the footrest on the recliner. Arcon was coming up the basement stairs. As he walked into the living room, she said, "I thought you were going to take a nap."

"Couldn't sleep. Too much on my mind."

She wondered if it had to do with building a home. "How did it feel, going back to all your friends?"

He plopped down on the sofa. "It was good; getting to see Jarden again and the hunters. What did you think of Tawny? People say he's like a goofy version of me."

"Well, he's tall and thin like you. I still think you're my first choice." She winked at him. "Besides, I think he and Malika are kinda fond of each other."

"It's probably just bunny love," said Arcon.

"So, I didn't mean to eavesdrop, but I heard you say something to Jarden about building your own home. Do you plan to talk to me about it?"

Arcon hung his head. "I suppose. I mean, right now, I don't know what I'm gonna do."

Elaina saw the troubled look on his face. "You sound a bit lost. Why don't you tell me what you're thinking? Then we can be lost together."

He smiled. "I take it you don't know where you're going, either."

Elaina got up from her recliner, walked over to the sofa, and sat down next to him. "I know where I should be," she said as she snuggled up against him. "I just left my most comfortable place, my recliner, and found my new place of comfort—next to you. Tell me what you're thinking."

Arcon put his arm around her and kissed the top of her head as she melted into his chest. "You'll think this is funny," he said. "I was thinking about when we met Patty. Remember when we climbed that hill and looked out over Twenty-Nine Palms?"

"Of course. Beautiful view."

"Well, that was the first time I saw the area surrounding ArcPoint. Remember the hike we went on and all the places I said I wanted to see? I still do. I'm not ready to settle down in the forest again. But I still consider ArcPoint my home, and your home is in Apple Valley. I want somewhere to be *our* home, and I don't want it to be either of those."

"I can certainly agree with you on that. Why were you talking to Jarden about it?"

Arcon laughed. "That's just because I talk to Jarden about everything. Always have. Well, except about the transmitter."

"And leaving ArcPoint."

"True. Anyway, I didn't mean to leave you out of the conversation. I was just trying to get the ArcPoint perspective on the idea from Jarden. It's kind of a tradition that us Franklin men move into Grandpa Lee's tiny house when we get married. Then the Community helps us build a log home. I told Jarden I didn't want to do any of that. But I still don't know what it is I *want* to do. We'll have to figure that out together."

"I agree to your terms," said Elaina. "But I think we need to talk to Daddy, too."

"Of course. And Ranger Dan will probably be a big factor as well."

Elaina chuckled. "He's definitely that." She looked at Arcon, and they both burst out laughing.

"But you know who'll be the biggest factor?" asked Arcon, then answered his own question. "The Authorities in Jerusalem. I think we should wait to see what they say before we make too many plans."

Elaina looked into Arcon's bright blue eyes and said, "I agree to those terms as well."

CHAPTER THIRTEEN

The Junction Restaurant was busy for a Thursday evening. Jenny, the waitress, did her best to locate the quietest booth in the place, as Dan had requested. When they'd had some time to look over their menus she returned and with her usual cheerful tone asked, "Are you ready to order?"

Meredith set down her menu. "I'll have the fish and chips, with side salad and ranch dressing."

"How about you, mister Ranger, sir?" asked Jenny.

"I'm still a bit undecided," answered Dan. "Would you recommend the filay mignown or the lobster?"

Jenny just smiled before explaining, "The filet mignon is very fresh today, but the lobster will cost you double what it did last time."

Dan's broad shoulders shook as he tried to keep from laughing out loud. A snicker slipped out. Meredith gave him "the look" from across the booth so he reined himself in just enough to say, "I sure do wish I could've seen Arcon's face when you brought him that lobster. His girl told me he thought it was a big *scorpion*." He raised his hand for Mery's benefit and brought his urge to laugh under control. "Thanks for helping me out with that Jenny—and be sure to thank Marla for me as well."

"You're welcome," said Jenny. "Did you know he was going to propose to her?"

"I don't think *he* knew," said Dan. "He was one clueless kid. But did you hear why?"

"Yes—that he was one of the Mojave People? It shocked me when Marla told me that. I would never have known by looking at him."

Meredith leaned forward and asked, "How *would* you ever?"

Jenny's expression turned quizzical. She looked up at the ceiling like it might have the answer, then seemed to come up with the answer for herself. "I guess I just don't know!"

Ranger Dan laughed and said, "Oh don't worry, you'd have known when he first showed up. He had long hair, a scruffy beard, and he was wearing goat hides and rabbit fur sleeves for climbing through the trees. Definitely a wild man."

"Now, Dan," scolded Meredith.

"Are you teasing me, Ranger Dan?" asked Jenny.

"Only a little. The Mojave People are no different from us, but that's honestly the way he was rigged out when we first saw him. I went in there—to where he's from—and met with the Mojave People. They dress and act much like we do. The difference is they have to make everything themselves. And they do a good job at it."

"Well, that's really something, isn't it?" Jenny eyed her notepad and said sweetly, "I'd better get myself back to work. Have you figured out what you'd like to eat?"

Dan ordered the salmon and Jenny said, as she collected their menus from them, "I'd like to hear more about the Mojave People someday."

"Check the *San Bernardino Portal* for news and a documentary about them," said Dan. "You'll get to see my smiling face in it as well."

"I'll do that. It'd be worth it to see you *smile* for once," said Jenny as she walked away.

"Yeah," said Meredith, "why are you grumpy all the time?"

Dan spread his napkin over his lap. "I've been away from your cooking for too long."

"And that's why, for your first day home in a week, you take me out to dinner?" asked Meredith.

"I just felt ... romantic," said Dan.

"That works better at home," she said with a wink.

"Well, once we get home, I'm not going to leave again for two whole days." He smiled lovingly at her but then his tone turned somber. He looked at the dessert menu in front of him. "I wish you were coming with me."

"Me too," she said, "but there'll be another time. Come on, let's hear about your plans. Are you excited?"

"You have no—wait, you know me too well. Yes, of course I am. Getting to see Jerusalem is huge. But being invited there by Central Authority? That's monumental."

"Do you think Arcon knows what to expect? I'm sure he's never even seen a tube train, much less ridden in one."

"He's excited to ride the train, but he's a hard one to read regarding Jerusalem. He's been kind of moody. Maybe he's feeling guilty because he wasn't as focused on the return of Jesus as the rest of his Community was. But they had this idea that all of them would see him at the same time. I don't know. Hopefully, he'll find out something about the circumstances involving his people."

After an uneasy time of silence, Meredith asked, "What else did you want to tell me?"

Dan chuckled. "I take it I'm easier to read than Arcon."

"For me, you are." She reached across the table and squeezed his hand. "Whatever it is you need to say, spit it out."

"Okay, here's the thing. I didn't mind getting stripped of my Ranger duties in order to concentrate on the Mojave People. It's going to be a tough transition, and you know I'm more than happy to help. But it'd be a lot easier if they'd replace the I-15 bridge. So far, they've been flying me back and forth in the helicopter, but that won't last much longer. Elaina told me it's an eight-hour drive from Baker to Apple Valley." Dan sighed and sat back in the booth. "Sixteen hours round trip! I can't do that every day."

"So, what are you saying? Are you wanting to move to the Mojave?"

"What I need to know," said Dan, pointing his fork at her and then back at himself, "is what *we* want to do. Care to hear the best idea I've come up with so far?"

"Sure. Go ahead."

"It looks like the ArcPoint People are going to want to do the kibbutz thing, and if it works, it may be a long-term solution. So, let's say that happens. I've made a few contacts and found out that if they do rebuild the I-15 bridge, it could take over ten years to complete. So, let's say that doesn't happen. They'll probably only rebuild the I-15 from Mountain Pass to Baker as a two-lane road. Baker will be used as a gateway to the Mojave area, complete with a Ranger Station. Do you understand it so far?"

"What about the I-40? Will they build a bridge there? It's nowhere near as bad as the I-15."

"They're pretty certain they'll start on that as soon as the Restriction is lifted. But that will only shave an hour and a half off the drive. When it's all done—which will take years—the best I can hope for is a six hour commute."

"How about the tube train?"

"That'd be faster," said Dan. "We could go from our place to Vegas in a couple hours. But it'd be a couple hours more driving to Baker. That's still four hours total one-way, and we'd need another vehicle. Naah, I don't think that'd work, either."

"Sounds like we'd have to find a place to live that's a little closer to Baker."

"That'd make the most sense as far as my governance of the Mojave. But we still have a life in this area. I've got Patty at the Survival Camp. I'd still like to do the Dude Ranch tours once in a while. Our kids are in San Bernardino."

As Jenny set the salad in front of her, Meredith added, "Don't forget the Junction Restaurant. We'd hate to leave it behind."

Dan smiled at Jenny. "That sinks it. We're not moving that far away. Maybe we could persuade Marla to open a restaurant in Baker."

"Speaking of Patty and BBL Survival," said Meredith, "could she make a second home for us there?"

"Would *you* want to live there? It's cold!"

"Guess you're right. Do you think Central Authority would allow us two homes?"

"You know, you just gave me an idea," said Dan. "Patty has been doing a pretty good job renting out space in the containers. She's got fix-it people she trusts. What if we could talk her into opening a motel in Baker? She could fix part of it up for us."

"If it were me, I'd say no, but it'd be up to her."

"Hmmm." Dan rested his chin on his hand and stared out the window. He looked up at Jenny when she brought his dinner and gave her a big smile, then said to her, "You still need to watch the documentary."

"I will," she said, smiling back. As she walked away, she added, "And you still need to leave me a tip."

When he went back to staring out the window, Meredith asked, "What are you thinking?"

"I don't see any other way than to have two homes. I'm going to talk to Central Authority. Can't hurt to ask."

"Or to pray."

"True enough. Throughout all that's happened, God seems to be working out a plan. Dealing with our living situation may just be another part of it."

"Daddy, you're home!"

"Hey, girl, you beat me. You must've driven straight through."

"We only stopped once at Vidal Junction for lunch," she said as she hugged him.

"How long did it take you?"

"Arcon and I got here before three, so almost exactly eight hours. But you know how broken up the I-15 is. I think it's worse coming this direction. Going toward Baker, driving over the earth cracks is like dropping off of curbs. This direction, it's like running into them."

"Where's Arcon?"

"After all that time riding in the car, he needed some exercise. He's jogging around the neighborhood."

"I'm glad they flew me out. I wouldn't want to drive it."

"Will you need to go back?"

"Just once more to clean out my desk and check operations. Then I'm done."

"You don't think they'll need you?"

"No. Road construction isn't my thing. Taking you guys in there was like a rescue mission. That's what I'll probably go back to. How about you?"

Elaina didn't know what to say. She didn't know if she'd be going back to work with her dad at San Bernardino Search and Rescue. For years, she focused her life on one goal, Arcon. Now they were together, but where her life went from here, she just didn't know.

"Girl?" said Roberto. "What are you thinking?"

"I don't know."

"It looks to me like we need to talk about it."

"Probably won't help. Arcon and I figure we'll have to wait until after the Jerusalem trip. Until then, I don't know what the future holds. I may not come back to the SBS&R."

"I've wondered about that. I was thinking about you on the way home. Our lives exploded a few weeks ago, and the dust is just now settling. But like I said, everything about it was like some crazy search and rescue mission. I know it was a bigger deal for you. If I put myself in your shoes, I'd be completely lost. I'm afraid I'm no help in this situation."

"That's okay, Daddy, I think it's something I need to work out with Arcon. But right now, he's in worse shape than me. For some reason, this trip to Jerusalem has him on edge. I don't think it's in a bad way, but it's something personal that so far, he hasn't wanted to share."

"Maybe you shouldn't even try to make plans before the trip. Who knows what might take place in Jerusalem? Why don't we put it all in God's hands and see what happens?"

"I like that idea," said Elaina. She put her hands on her hips and clicked her tongue before saying, "And *you* didn't think you'd be any help."

"Well, if I was, I'm glad I was. Speaking of help, do you need any to make dinner?"

"Naahh, I was going to default to mac and cheese and tuna peas, if that's okay."

"Sounds good to me," said Roberto.

"Good," said Elaina, "Then why don't you take a quick snooze, I'll call you when it's ready."

CHAPTER FOURTEEN

Arcon stared at the roll-up screen Elaina had spread out on the dining room table. She'd connected it to her comm-pad and opened up a map of the worldwide transportation network, showing highways and tube trains, air flights and water routes, with passenger and cargo designations. "These are all the ways we shuffle stuff around the earth," she said.

"This reminds me of how Don Denton handled procurement at ArcPoint," said Arcon. "He had a big piece of paper with lines all over it connecting things we had with where we needed it. Jarden does it all in his head."

"I bet he couldn't do this in his head," chided Elaina. "Would you like to see how we're going to be shuffled?"

"You mean our trip to Jerusalem? Sure."

"Okay. Well, first, Ranger Dan will take Connector 15 from Barstow to the Victorville Station."

"What is Connector 15?"

"Okay, let me back up." Elaina tapped the surface of her comm-pad on a link that said *Tube Train* and then another that said *Passenger Pods*. The roll-up screen lit up with pictures of various pod configurations. "We have two different kinds of tube trains. Remember how I told you the tube trains send pods down a tube with a combination of magnetism and a blast of air?"

"Right. I get that. Magnetism floats the pod and gets it moving and air helps propel it."

"Right. There are two different sizes of tube trains, and each has its own size pods. The small tube we call a connector, and the large one is the main. Pods for the connector only hold two people, while the main pods hold twelve."

"That's not very many. Don't they have bigger ones? I read about passenger trains that carried a lot of people."

"Right, and there are still a few around. But they are extremely heavy, consume a lot of fuel, and are difficult to travel on *when* you want to and go *where* you want to go. And they're slow, with a top speed of about two hundred kilometers per hour. Because of that, most above ground trains are used for moving freight."

"What about airplanes?"

"They move faster than the connector pods but slower than the mains. But they're even less convenient than trains. There are very few airports, and you have to schedule a flight far in advance. As far as danger, they have an outstanding safety record, but they require a lot of maintenance to keep from failing. Failure in one of them can be catastrophic. In a hundred years, no one has died traveling by tube train. No other form of transportation can claim that. Plus, the pods are contained in a tube, so they can't hit a car at an intersection or fall out of the sky onto a house."

"Wow. So how fast will we travel?"

"The connectors can travel up to five hundred kilometers per hour, and the Mains can go over a thousand. Fifteen minutes after Dan gets into the pod in Barstow, he'll be at the Victorville Station. Five minutes after he walks into a station, he can be in a pod—anytime he wants, day or night. The connector trains are all about convenience."

Arcon scanned through the pictures of the pods and saw how two passengers would sit in the small one facing each other. He tried to imagine someone as large as Ranger Dan in one and remembered being folded up in the back of Elaina's little three-wheeler. Then he saw the cut-away of the tube train traveling underground. "Isn't it kind of scary traveling like that?"

"No more than getting a tooth pulled," Elaina joked. "I'm just kidding, but it's kind of like that. The fear is mostly in your head. It's over quick and you eventually get used to it. But there are some who just won't unless they absolutely must."

"Like swinging through trees."

"Probably so. There are weight restrictions, so someone as big as Ranger Dan will travel alone. But they'll move some cargo with him to balance the load. Anyway, we'll meet him in Victorville and then get on one of the mains. Here's what one of those pods looks like."

Arcon looked at the cutaway view. "I see they hold twelve people."

"Right. Three seats facing three more seats, and two sections back-to-back like that, with a bulkhead in-between."

"Hmmm." Arcon looked at the different cross-sections. "How tall is it?"

"The pod is two meters in diameter, so, let's see, in feet, that would be … Let's put it this way. You and Dan will hit your head. The connector pods are worse. They're only a meter and a half."

"Why do they make them so small?"

"The obvious reason is so the tubes and the tunnel digging machines are smaller. They literally drive those machines through the ground, digging the tunnel and building the tube at the same time. It's a fascinating process. But if they had to make the tunnels as big as for the old railroads, they'd have to move ten times as much rock and dirt. They were considering connector pods as small as one meter, but tests showed people hated it. So they engineered them larger."

"Makes sense. How do you know all this stuff?"

"When I was a child, Dad and I visited a tunneling site and we took a tour."

"I'd like to do that someday," said Arcon.

"They're not digging very many tunnels anymore. But who knows? Maybe they'll want to build a tube train past ArcPoint. Now, there's one more big difference between connectors and mains, and that's coupling."

"What's that?"

"The connector pods always go through the tubes one at a time. But the main pods can travel connected to one another. Wanna know why they do that?"

"Of course."

"Okay, well, it's more stable with a larger mass moving. The mains have a lot smoother ride, which is important for long trips. It also allows the whole thing to go faster without the air in-between the pods. Plus, it's complicated to maintain the proper air volume and pressure between the pods. Every coupling removes that complication. I think the most they connect together are twelve, but usually, it's only six or eight."

Arcon looked at the picture of the main pods. "How are they connected? Is it like docking at a space station?"

Elaina stared at him. "I have no idea what you're talking about."

"Really? I read about things like that in the Room of Remembrance. There's an international space station orbiting the earth, isn't there?"

"Orbiting earth?"

"Uhh, yeah. Never mind, I'll look it up later. Anyway, how do they connect?"

"There's a magnetic coupler at the front and back of each pod that holds them together. They try to only connect pods that are going to the same terminal. But let's say somebody wants to go to a terminal that's closer than people in the other pods. They'd put that person in the back pod. When they get close to the first terminal, they de-energize the coupler, and that pod would drop off and go to that terminal. Get it?"

Arcon blinked. "I think so."

"Okay, let's do something else first. We need to get to Jerusalem. This is where you get to make your first decision."

"What do you mean?"

"We're going to let you choose how we travel to Israel and back. Here's a hint. It has to be by tube train. You get to choose if we go to the left or to the right."

"I don't get it."

"Let me show you." Elaina paged back on her comm-pad until she got to the rail map of North America. "To travel fast, you have to use the Mains as much as you can. They travel mostly clockwise around the country. Let me show you. Pick east or west. It doesn't matter which."

"Okay. East."

"To go east to, let's say, New York, we'd go north to Oregon, then follow this route through Montana, Minnesota, under the lakes, and then to New York. However, to go to Israel, we need to go through Europe, and there's only one way to get there: through Greenland. Okay, so now you're scooting across America. Choose east or north."

"Okay. How about north?"

"In that case, we'd split off here in Minnesota and go north of the Great Lakes, then to Greenland, Iceland, over to this island here, down to France, and then we have to make another decision—left, or right?"

"What if I would have said east?"

"Then we'd have gone under the Great Lakes, over to the east coast, up to Greenland, and blah, blah, blah, to France. Left, or right?"

"Uhh, left ... no ... right."

"Okay, going right will take us down to Spain, cross over into Morocco, then all the way across here to Egypt and then up to Israel."

"What if I chose left?"

"That would take us through all of these mountains and then into Israel from the north. I've heard you really need to dress warm to go that way, but most people do."

Arcon looked closely at the map and the lines that showed the tube train routes. Then he looked closer and said, "Does that say *Sahara Farmlands?*"

"It sure does. A lot of the food for this whole side of the map comes from there."

"And the desert will bloom," he mumbled.

"It sure has," she remarked. "One of the benefits of having a Creator who controls the rains. Just like the Mojave used to be a desert."

Arcon looked at her and smiled. "We thought God changed the weather just for us."

"Maybe He did. You guys sorta needed it. So, is that the route you'd like to take to get to Israel? Through the Sahara?"

"I think so. How would we get back?"

"Again, you have a choice. North or south? Both go east but in different ways. Just so you know, the rest of us will want to take the north route."

"Why?"

"Because here is Israel," said Elaina, pointing to a spot on the map. "And clear over here is where we cross into America across the Bering Strait. This south route is about ten thousand kilometers, so it hits all of these countries like India and China. The north route goes through all this farmland and is less than four thousand kilometers. That's about a full day's travel difference. This one in the south has to slow down a lot for cities. The train can go full speed for most of this northern route."

"But wouldn't there be a lot more people going the south way because of the cities?"

"Yeah, but that would mean more pods. Those of us who just want to get back to America won't want to go to those cities."

"I'd like to see them."

"So would I, some day. But now is not the time."

"Then we'll take the northern route."

"Wise decision, mister world traveler."

Arcon stared at the red lines crisscrossing the map. "You say all these tube trains only go one direction?"

"Right. That's because of how the air propulsion is set up. You'll have to ask Daddy about that. I was too young to understand it."

"Then … how do you get from, say, Minnesota to Oregon?"

"Okay, here's Minneapolis. You'd go to Chicago, then take this line to California, then north to Oregon."

"Wouldn't that take a lot more time?"

"At an average of eight hundred kilometers per hour? No. At the most, maybe an extra hour. Well worth not having to dig another three thousand miles of tunnels."

"Hmmm. Makes sense. What about Minneapolis to Fargo?"

"In most cases, you take a connector to go a shorter distance like that."

"Why do the routes go where they do?"

"They used a lot of the old railroad tracks. The land was already owned, and the ground was prepared. All they had to do was rebuild it so there weren't any road crossings. They started in the areas where the earthquakes had damaged the rails. That was mostly here in the West. The part that you see missing is the one where the Rift happened. A lot of the old track is still there in the Restricted Area, but they can't use it."

"There used to be railroad tracks that went right through ArcPoint."

"I thought I could see where they used to be. They went right past the Facility, right?"

"Right. Jarden helped tear them up when he was young. They mostly used the wood and gravel for foundations of houses, and the metal shop got the rails. Do you think they might put a tube train through ArcPoint?"

"I think that'll be up to your people. But I doubt it'd happen soon, even if you wanted it. Especially not a Main. There are other places that need it more. But they may build a connector. That'd be nice, wouldn't it? It'd be a lot faster to get from here to there."

"And what about the stuff they talked about getting from the ArcPoint trees? Can they use the tube trains for that?"

"Oh yeah. They have special pods just designed for cargo. And if it's liquid, they install pipelines alongside the Connector tubes. Did you know that when you drink water from our kitchen sink, it originally fell as rain in Nova Scotia?"

"Really?" Arcon scanned the map, searching around southern California.

Elaina reached over and tapped the map. "Look over here." When he looked where she pointed in Canada, she said, "Gotcha! You had no clue where Nova Scotia was, did you?"

Arcon didn't respond, but just stared at the map. "Can we go to Nova Scotia? I hear the water is fresher there."

"You can go anywhere the tube trains go," said Elaina. "Hey, I have an idea. When we go to Jerusalem, why don't you ask the Authorities for a connector tube to ArcPoint?"

"I can do that?"

"Can't hurt to ask. Jesus told Dan to get your input for what ArcPoint needs. Tell him they need a connector tube. Then you can go to Nova Scotia whenever you want."

"But I'll have to talk to the Authorities?"

"Ranger Dan will be with you, and knowing him, he'll probably do all the talking. But you'll see what that's like in a few days when we talk with Central Authority. There's no one higher than that."

"I thought Jesus was the ultimate authority."

"He is. Central Authority comprises all the people who work directly for Him. This is going to be so exciting. Many of them are from the first resurrection, the ones that died for Him during the tribulation days. They are directly connected with His Holy Spirit, so all of their decisions are according to His will. They are incorruptible, as He is."

Arcon stood there in stunned silence for a moment. Then he said, "Grandpa Lee was right. In his writings, he said the countries could never govern themselves until all the corruption was removed from their leadership. He said he didn't know how that could happen."

"Only Jesus could make that happen, and He did. But we still have our own free will, and our personal desires aren't always in line with the will of other people. That's why we have the Authorities. They settle our disputes, and Central Authority settles international disputes."

"So why are we going to see *them?* We don't have an international dispute."

"I don't know, but I'm excited to find out."

CHAPTER FIFTEEN

Arcon grabbed the armrests as a shudder moved through the pod. He looked at Elaina, sitting across from him with her arms folded and a smug look on her face. She smiled, folded her hands behind her head, and closed her eyes. As the pod shimmied, he put his hands in his lap and tried to be calm. *They're moving the pod into position.* Then another jolt jerked his hands back to the armrest. *Now the pod is in the acceleration lane.*

"Accelerating," said Elaina calmly. "Make sure you're buckled down."

Arcon tugged on his seat belt strap just as the pod sped up and tried to pull him out of his seat. "Woo-hoo," he yelled as he pushed hard on the armrests.

"Just relax," said Elaina, her voice warbling with the shaking of the pod. "The straps will hold."

The force of the acceleration increased and then almost as quickly began to ease. Within a few seconds, he was sitting comfortably in his seat again. He saw Elaina still had her hands cupped behind her smiling head. "I guess you were right," he said.

"About what?"

"About facing forward. Being pressed into the seat would be better than being pulled out of it."

"I gave you the option."

"But you didn't try very hard to convince me."

"Of course not. It's always fun to watch someone's first ride in a connector pod, especially when they're in that seat. It feels like you're going to do a face plant."

"Face plant?"

"Yeah, you know. When you fall face first. Like you did on the treadmill."

"Oh, right. Weren't you afraid you'd have to catch me?"

"That's why I told you to buckle up. I don't mind you being in my arms, but not at three hundred kilometers per hour."

"Are we going that fast now?"

"Pretty close."

"Sure doesn't seem like it."

"Like I told you, with no outside reference, you don't know how fast you're moving. You could just as easily think you're shaking in one spot."

Arcon leaned back in his seat and stretched his feet out on either side of her legs. Mimicking Elaina, he put his hands behind his head. With his eyes closed, he tried to imagine the pod sitting on top of a machine that was shaking it. He could feel a slight breeze and knew he was getting fresh air. In his mind, he pictured the pod moving underground at what he calculated was about three hundred miles an hour. Suddenly, their pod smacked into a stopped pod and he jerked himself awake with a snort.

"You fell asleep fast," said Elaina. "The rocking motion will do that."

"I'm just glad I was dreaming. I thought we ran smack dab into another pod."

"I told you that's impossible. Remember, we did the calculations. They send out the pods a minute or more apart. At five hundred kilometers per hour, there's over five kilometers of air between each pod. If one stopped in front of us, which is also nearly impossible, the air would compress, and we would

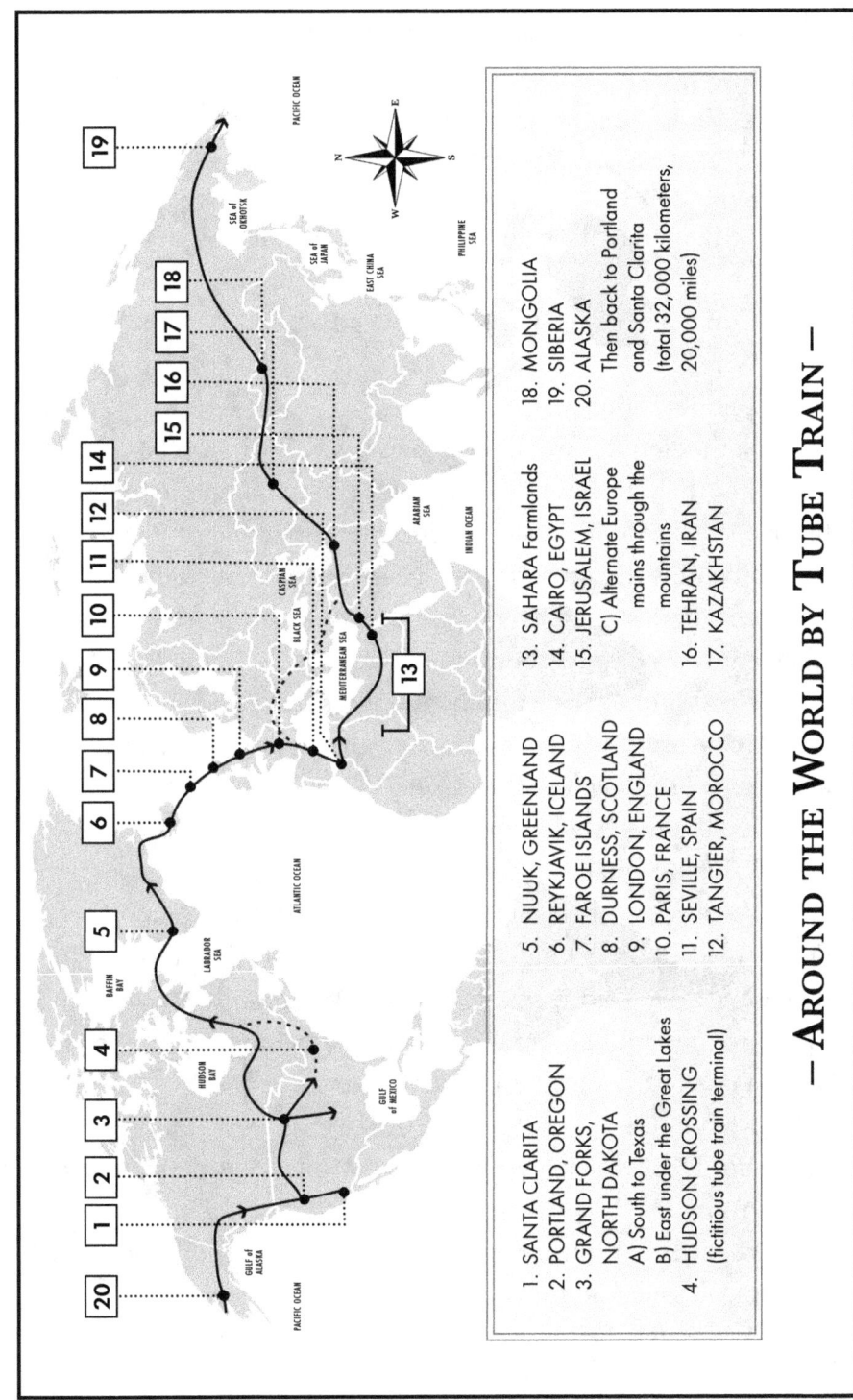

— AROUND THE WORLD BY TUBE TRAIN —

1. SANTA CLARITA
2. PORTLAND, OREGON
3. GRAND FORKS, NORTH DAKOTA
   A) South to Texas
   B) East under the Great Lakes
4. HUDSON CROSSING (fictitious tube train terminal)
5. NUUK, GREENLAND
6. REYKJAVIK, ICELAND
7. FAROE ISLANDS
8. DURNESS, SCOTLAND
9. LONDON, ENGLAND
10. PARIS, FRANCE
11. SEVILLE, SPAIN
12. TANGIER, MOROCCO
13. SAHARA Farmlands
14. CAIRO, EGYPT
15. JERUSALEM, ISRAEL
    C) Alternate Europe mains through the mountains
16. TEHRAN, IRAN
17. KAZAKHSTAN
18. MONGOLIA
19. SIBERIA
20. ALASKA
    Then back to Portland and Santa Clarita (total 32,000 kilometers, 20,000 miles)

decelerate, not crash. And the compressed air would push the other pod along, so no one can get stuck in a tube."

"Yeah, I know. I saw the demonstration, and it made sense at the time. It's just hard to get my brain to accept the truth while I'm sitting in this seat."

She laughed. "Eventually, the truth will set you free."

"I hope you're right."

"Cup your hands behind your head again."

"Why?"

"Deceleration."

He thought for a moment, then threw his hands behind his head. Just then, he felt a weight on his chest and had to pull with his arms to keep his head upright. He remembered her telling him something about raising the headrest, but he hadn't done it. The pressure lessened as the pod slowed down more gradually. Elaina appeared to be counting something.

"Hard shift to the left in five seconds," she said.

Arcon braced himself, then felt the pod lurch to the right and shake. "I thought you said left."

"Excuse me. My left, your right."

"What *was* that?"

"We were pushed out of the main tube. We're now in the decel tube, approaching the station and moving toward the unloading area. Daddy should be there waiting with our luggage. When we get out of the pod, you should be able to see the one behind us slowing down on a different track."

"Next to us?"

"No. It's less dangerous if we can unload away from each other. You'll see."

When their pod stopped, he saw the hatch pop open next to them. Elaina stood up while he was still figuring out how to unhook his safety belt. After she crawled out of the pod, he stood up and joined her on the platform.

She grabbed his hand and said, "I see Daddy in the waiting area. Let's go." She walked a few steps and then stopped. "Wait, here comes the next pod."

He noticed there were twelve spaces where the pods were parked. As the next pod pulled to a stop three spaces away, the pod they were in closed up and disappeared under the elevated waiting area. "Where did our pod go?"

"It went under the terminal to the screening area. If it were carrying cargo, it would get unloaded. Then it gets safety checked, shoots out to the other side of the terminal, and gets loaded up again to go somewhere else. Hey, look. The pod that just came in only has one person like Daddy's did. See how they brought him a roller bin? The man will unload his luggage and roll it to the waiting area. They like as many people as possible to travel like we did with just what we can carry. It gets the pods through the terminal faster. That's why we dumped everything on Daddy. I let them know we weren't carrying anything, so they didn't need to provide a bin for us."

As they left the platform, Roberto greeted them. "Hi Daddy," she said as she hugged him. "Is Ranger Dan here yet?"

"No. He planned to ping me when he gets to Bernie, and then he'll be about fifteen minutes. I haven't heard anything yet, so why don't you two check out the view? I'll ping you when he's about five minutes out."

"Sure, Big D. See you later."

As they walked away, Arcon asked, "What did he just tell you about Ranger Dan?"

"What? Oh. Ranger Dan went a different way than we did. If he'd gone to Victorville, he would've needed to change pods. Instead, he went to San Bernardino—Bernie—which was a little farther. But he could stay in the pod while they just switched it to a different tube. Then it's a fifteen-minute travel from there to here."

"Ping?"

"Send a message on the shoulder phone, which makes a ping sound near our ear."

"Oh. Okay. What's there to see? We're underground, aren't we?"

"Oh, no, the Santa Clarita terminal is above ground. We can go up to the observation deck, where you can see the beautiful view of the Los Angeles Basin. I think you told us most of the ArcPoint people came from that area. I'll warn you; it's huge. If you saw pictures of it in your Room of Remembrance, well, it's not like that anymore. You'll see."

After climbing two flights of stairs, they entered a large seating area with windows on three sides. There were hills in the distance, and in front of them was an odd-looking metal structure. It was straight on one side and arced on the other. They walked closer, and Arcon could see that it climbed high into the sky. "What is that?"

"That was an amusement ride at one time. There used to be a building over here, and people would get into a car and shoot straight across the ground and then up to the top of that tower. They called it *Lex Luthor*."

"You mean like in a Superman comic book?"

"You've seen a Superman comic book? Was it a real antique paper one?"

"Yeah. One of the Founders had a collection of old comic books that children weren't allowed to look at without an adult with them."

"Why? Did they think they were evil or something?"

"No. He didn't want the children to damage them."

"Well, you got one on me. I've never seen a paper one. Just the digital version."

He looked up at the towering mass of rusting metal again. "Why did they call it Lex Luthor? It looks nothing like him."

"I guess at the time they were really into superheroes. This place was full of a lot of rides named after them. But the park was severely damaged in the earthquakes and was closed. This one never fell, so they left it as a monument. They built the tube train terminal on the abandoned ground of the park. Now let's go over to the other side."

As they approached the south side of the room, they could see the valley stretching far into the distance. "I'm sorry it's not as impressive as when you're standing on the edge of it. But you can still see how big it is. Ranger Dan will be coming right up through the middle of it. But underground, of course."

"I'm amazed," said Arcon. "From the helicopter, it looked like the land went on forever. But here, it looks like buildings go on forever." Arcon scanned the valley and sighed. "So many people." The valley floor was hidden behind the hill they were on. "How will Ranger Dan's pod make it up this hill?"

Elaina scrunched her face and said, "I thought you knew physics."

"Oh yeah, right. Speed and inertia. If he's traveling at five hundred kilometers per hour and with his weight—but the hill *will* slow him down."

"It will, but he needs to slow down anyway as he comes into the station. By the way, I just got the ping that he's five minutes from here. Let's go over and see the distribution warehouse before we meet him. We'll have to hurry."

They jogged down a wide corridor, meeting and passing a handful of people on the way. At the end was another viewing platform overlooking a large area covered with machinery. Arcon saw people moving around the equipment and pods from the tube train scattered everywhere. "What's all this?"

"We call this the cargo dance floor," said Elaina. "When the cargo pods come into the station, some of the packages may need to be shuffled to different pods to go somewhere else. They automate as much as they can, but some of the stuff just has to be manhandled. When a pod has been repacked, it's sent to the insert timer."

"Insert timer? Is that some sort of scheduler?"

"Right. Every pod has a different priority need. Emergency pods carrying critical stuff have the highest priority, so they get shot down the tube first. Produce pods are next, to keep the food fresh. People pods have high priority, but they travel at different speeds than the cargo pods, so their timing is different—usually moving during the day. Low priority things ship at night. Anyway, all of that is carefully controlled and timed to insert the pods into the tubes at just the right moment."

Arcon watched a pod come out of a tube, land on a platform, and instantly get picked up by a machine. "Jarden would love this."

"I bet he would," said Elaina, "since this is basically what his job is. We better get moving. Ranger Dan should be here any minute."

CHAPTER SIXTEEN

Victor stood with Jarden and Petra, each with their arms crossed, admiring the recently poured cement slab of the new utility building.

"Well, what do you think?" asked Victor.

"Looks great," said Petra. "It's so brown—not gray like the ancient concrete in the Facility."

Jarden walked over and touched his fingers to the slab's surface. "Smooth. It's setting up well. I'm impressed. I couldn't understand how a few bags of dust could turn our dirt into concrete, but it did. When can we walk on it?"

"Couple of days," said Victor. He pointed to where pipes jutted out from under the slab. "That's where the power will go to the machine shop, and these two are the new water lines for the radiant heat. Then there are two more conduits out the other side of the building for powering the hydroponics area."

Petra gestured at the bolts protruding from the concrete near the edge. "And those are to hold the building down, right?"

"Exactly, anchor bolts for wind and such."

"Just a second," said Jarden. He stepped away and released a shrill choppy whistle through his teeth. Soon after, Brina's mom, Sybil Ashford, emerged from the hydroponic greenhouse. Jarden waved to get her attention, held his hand out about hip high, and then motioned in their direction. Sybil nodded and went back into the greenhouse.

"What was that?" asked Victor, perplexed.

"I just told Sybil to send Brina over here."

"You said all that with a whistle?" asked Victor.

Petra laughed. "Jarden has a whistle for everything."

"Saves me a lot of walking." He leveled his palm, repeating the motion. "This hip high motion told Sybil I wanted the little one, which she knows means Brina. I want her to come see this slab. I told her I'd keep her informed on your progress."

"Really?" asked Victor.

Jarden smiled. "Sure, Hydro will be her baby someday, so her parents are letting her take care of all the modernizing— which involves power from this building. She's excited at least half of their work will now be automated."

"Is Brina's family planning to stay here at ArcPoint?" he asked casually.

"You'll have to ask them—but from what I've heard, Tom and Sybil plan to do some traveling while Brina watches over things here. Brina may want to get out for a while and explore. I don't think Lars is going anywhere."

"I doubt any of them plan to relocate," said Petra.

"I agree," said Jarden. "As long as Lars is alive, they won't leave him. He may be slowing down, but we're all convinced it'll take him a good long while before he comes to a stop. Hey, here comes Brina now."

As Brina walked up to them, her eyes were scanning the slab of soil-cement. "Is the floor done?" she asked.

"All done," said Jarden. "Victor says you can walk on it."

"Really?" asked Brina, as she stepped toward it.

"In a couple of days," added Jarden, just as Victor reached to stop her.

Brina frowned at Jarden and fisted her hips. "Hey! Are you trying to get me in trouble?"

"I try all the time," he said, "but it never seems to work."

Brina narrowed her eyes at him, then smiled brightly at

Victor. "Well, I think you've done a great job. There's no way I'm going to make a mess of it."

"Would you like to?" asked Victor.

"What?" asked Brina.

Victor laughed. "There's a tradition of signing your name in the wet cement. Would you like to do that? I think it's still soft enough to be able to scratch it in with a nail."

"Shouldn't *you* sign it?"

"I already have, back where the machinery will be. Wanna see?" Victor led Brina, Jarden, and Petra around the slab and to where he'd signed the cement. "Right there. Victor 2165. The date tells everyone—including any future grandkids—when it was finished. Would you like to sign your name, Brina?"

"What? Why me?"

"Well, Jarden says this place will be part of your jurisdiction someday. Why don't you sign near where the hydroponics power conduits are?"

"Can't I just sign it right here?"

"Uhh, sure, that'd be fine." Victor reached into his tool pouch and pulled out a nail. "Here, use this." Brina used the nail to scratch a B lightly under his name.

"You can do better than that," said Jarden. "Put your shoulder into it."

"Yeah," said Victor, "we should've done this sooner. Just push hard. You can't hurt it."

Brina scratched, going over her name and date repeatedly until she was satisfied. "Jarden, do you want to do yours?"

"No, no, let Petra. He's the big boss around here."

"Not me," said Petra. "Looks fine the way it is. How long till it's finished?"

Victor paused and looked to the trees, appearing to make a mental calculation and then said confidently, "I've got help lined up and all the building materials are here. We plan to start framing it up tomorrow."

"What?" asked Brina, sounding perplexed. "I thought you said we couldn't walk on it yet."

"Well, we'll start with the outside walls so we can mostly stay off it. But we'll also protect the surface with plastic and carefully cover it with the plywood that'll get used on the roof later. That'll protect the cement where we need to walk. Trust me. I've got it all figured out."

"He's smarter than he looks, huh, Brina?" chided Jarden.

Brina quickly snapped back with, "Kind of like you, only he's better looking,"

Jarden sad-eyed a look at Victor. "Do you see how she picks on an old man?"

"I'm glad I'm not old," said Victor.

"Now they're ganging up on me, Petra. I should probably quit while I'm ahead."

Petra laughed. "Quit, you should ... ahead, you're not."

"So, Victor, you were telling us about these tubes sticking out?" Jarden pointed at the slab as he walked toward it, then stopped. "Down there should be the other ends sticking up?"

"That's right. The new generator, switchgear, pumps, and other equipment will be where we are now. The other end will be where I work on the tractor. When that's done, it'll probably become a repair shop for other machines you don't have yet. Or maybe a wood shop."

"When will the generator be up and running?"

"That's going to take a while, obviously. As soon as the shed is weatherproofed, we'll bring in the generator, the switchgear, and the other materials. I'll work with your people to get everything figured out and moved into place. Then we'll bring in our electrical expert to help put it together."

"So, you finally found someone?" asked Jarden.

"Yeah, that wasn't easy. I had a lot of volunteers until I told them they'd be working with twenty apprentices, none of which had been to school or worked on anything less than a hundred and thirty years old. But you want to know who finally helped me find someone? Noreena Chan."

"Who's that?"

"Oh, right. You've never met her," said Victor. "She's the one producing the story about the Mojave People. Uhh, I mean ArcPoint. She worked with Dolores Reid to track down relatives of you people. You've heard of Dolores Reid? She's descended from the Franklins. Anyway, Noreena's who told me about my being related to the Mojave People. Oh, sorry. ArcPoint."

"Don't worry about it. We don't mind being called the Mojave People. So how did this Noreena Chan find you an electrician?"

"He's related to Clive Barrows."

"Really? Our Clive Barrows?"

"Yep, same one. I saw his name on the Electrical Library and sent it to her. It was a long shot, but it paid off."

"I think he'll be surprised at the reception he'll get here," said Petra. "Clive is quite a legend among the ArcPoint people. When we moved here, he grabbed hundreds of old electrical books, not realizing how badly we'd need them over the years. He'd been a teacher for the electrician's union and an old-school tinkerer. Probably more important than Norm Ashford." He glanced at Brina and added, "To the electricians."

"I think this job is a little outside his comfort zone," said Victor. "But he has unlimited support on the outside. Besides, this is for your people to learn, so they shouldn't mind him learning along with them. I bet they can't wait to shut down the old generator."

"Me, too," said Jarden. "Every time it quits, Brina here throws a hissy fit."

"Jarden!" snapped Brina. "I've never had a hissy fit in my entire life!"

"You did just now."

She shook her finger at him. "I'm saving the next rotten tomato for your salad."

"Now, now, children," said Petra. "Don't let this war of words escalate into a food fight. You remember what happened last time?"

"What happened?" asked Victor.

"Brina put a hot pepper in his spaghetti."

"Oh," said Victor sympathetically. He put his hand on Jarden's shoulder. "I'll get that generator working as fast as I can."

"Thanks, son."

"And I'll have a big kiss waiting when it's done," said Brina. When she got stares from everyone, she added, "For the generator."

Victor could feel his face flushing, and he hoped no one noticed. What she said was probably just the sarcastic humor she was so good at. But he hoped, just maybe, she was trying to send him a signal.

Arcon reached across and gripped Roberto's wrist. He pulled hard as Roberto stood to his feet in the middle of their pod area. Settling back in his seat, he reached behind Elaina and pushed on her back until she was standing. After both of them had gotten out of the pod, He stood up, bent forward, and stretched, his hand sliding across the open pod door. Then he grabbed Ranger Dan's hand and pulled him to his feet, almost banging his head on the center hinge of the gull-wing door.

"Watch your head," yelled Elaina.

"What do you think?" Roberto asked him. "How did that

compare to the connector pod ride?"

"Completely different," answered Arcon. "Starting and stopping was smoother. It wasn't as bumpy or noisy. And it didn't seem so—what did you call it—close to phobic?"

"Close enough," laughed Ranger Dan. "It's claustrophobic, and it means you don't like to be in tight spaces. How did you like the viewscreen?"

"That was fun. I especially like the Highlights one where you can see the best scenery on the way. The one that showed what it would actually be like to move that fast kind of made me dizzy after a while."

"Yeah, that Real View screen makes some people sick," said Elaina, as she moved the roller bin toward the cargo door on the pod. "I saw you looking at the Map view a lot."

"Yeah. It was fun to see how fast we were moving toward Portland. The fastest I saw it go was a thousand sixty."

"When we get past the mountains of Montana, we should hit eleven hundred most of the time," said Roberto, as he and Arcon loaded their luggage into the bin. "Wait till we go across Canada. I hear some stretches are good for over twelve hundred."

"Heads up, people," said Dan. "We're scheduled to leave at noon, so that gives us about forty-five minutes to grab lunch. Roberto, you and Arcon get that bin into a locker. Elaina and I'll order us some lunch and meet you in the PDT lounge."

"See you there," said Roberto. "Arcon, grab that roller bin and follow me over to that wall. I'll show you how to store one of these so we don't have to drag it all over the terminal."

CHAPTER SEVENTEEN

Victor stared at his sandwich and said a silent prayer. He wasn't just thanking God for the food. He was also thankful for all these new friends from the machine shop he was eating lunch with. Mostly, though, he asked God to bless this food to nourish him because he still couldn't get comfortable with it. He enjoyed the flavor, and he was getting used to the texture. But a rabbit meat sandwich was a strange concept. So was bread made from the beans of the ArcPoint trees. He was glad the scientists certified it free from heavy metals.

The conversation at the other end of the table caught his attention. Someone was talking about Brina, so he had to eavesdrop.

"So, who do you think will get Brina's hand?" asked one of them.

"I still think it's going to be Raymo," responded another. "He's persistent."

"But she's never really liked him. And I don't think old man Lars likes him at all."

"I don't know. She's been talking with Raymo more, and they seem to get along. Things have really changed since Arcon showed up with another girl."

Victor could feel a heaviness building inside him. He'd noticed Raymo walking her to the hydroponics greenhouse once in a while. He assumed Raymo had some sort of job that involved meeting with her on occasion. Now he wasn't sure.

"Have any of you you noticed how Brina has changed?" one of them asked.

"Yeah, she's really come out of her shell. I mean, she's always had a sort of weird sense of humor, but she rarely used it. It's hilarious when her and Jarden get into it. What's funny is to watch old man Lars. He shakes his head like they're being utterly ridiculous, and then you see a slight grin sneak across his face."

"I think the grumpy old man routine is just a front. Brina probably got her humor from him. Hey, Victor. I notice Brina picks on you a lot, too. You don't seem to mind."

"Aaah, I've just got one of those faces everyone likes to joke about. I'm used to it."

They all laughed, and it made Victor feel welcome in this group. They were good, hard-working people, and they could talk technical. Not once did they make him feel like an outsider.

"Did you notice who else has changed?" asked someone. "Arcon. He used to be kind of depressing to be around. Now he jokes around as much as Brina."

"I think the common denominator is that outsider girl of Arcon's," said someone else. "It seems like everyone who hangs around her gets infected with sarcastic humor. I don't know how Arcon found her, but it sure seems to have worked out well."

"I've spent some time with Elaina," said Victor. "Her humor is pretty dry, but I agree. I think Arcon is learning a lot from her. Ranger Dan is the big jokester, though. You have to keep on your toes around him."

An older man sipping soup asked, "That's the big guy that spoke to all of us, right?"

"That's him," said Victor. "You'll be glad to have him on your side."

"Is it true he's our new supreme leader?"

"He'd laugh if you called him that," Victor answered. "He considers himself more of a protector. His job is to make sure you folks have everything you want or need here. Otherwise, he's happy to just watch the borders and make sure no one sneaks in this place."

The older man added, "Well, I think I can speak for all of us here that we're thankful for what you outsiders have done for us. Everyone will tell you we're happy here, but things are starting to get difficult. We spend all of our time fixing things that are wearing out."

"In the outside world, there are those of us who do that for a living," said Victor.

"Yeah, but it's a choice. Here it's a necessity. I can't tell you how many of us are itching to help you with that tractor. Until you guys showed up, none of us had seen a moving vehicle."

"The tractor isn't going to move very fast," joked Victor.

"If the tractor starts moving at all, we'll all start weeping," said the man.

They all laughed, but Victor could sense some nervousness. Then he remembered something. "That reminds me, what happened to the ATV that was delivered here? I haven't seen it for a couple of days."

The laughing stopped, and one of them confessed, "It's sitting outside the Parker home. We were using it to deliver firewood yesterday, and it quit running. It may be out of fuel, so we were going to ask if we could put ArcPoint oil in it."

"Oh, sure you can. It's considered a multi-fuel vehicle. I'll show you how to change the programming for bio-diesel, but it'll change itself once it senses a different fuel. After dinner tonight, let's go down there and get it running. There's a trick to priming it after you've run it out of fuel."

"Dietrich, you're not gonna start crying, are you?" said the older man.

They all laughed again, but Victor could tell the statement was partially true. Coming from a world that was constantly buzzing with activity, he'd found peace in the relaxed, simple life of the ArcPoint people. But they'd had enough relaxation. They needed stimulation. *Maybe they'd like a scooter that will work on rough ground.* He'd try to get permission to sneak one in. Maybe a few.

He wanted to know more about Brina and Raymo, but the subject had turned to machinery again, as it usually did with this group. Under normal circumstances, his mind would lock in on a conversation like that. And it did for a moment when they asked him about new tools and techniques. But his mind just wouldn't stay there. It kept drifting back to Brina, and the way she talked straight at him with that pretty smile of hers. He'd never met a girl who was more important to him than a tool kit.

Tomorrow he'd be able to throw himself into the utility building again. He knew she'd stop by every so often to check his progress. He'd be glad to see her, but with so many other people working around him, he'd have to struggle to act nonchalant.

Dietrich said, "Hey Victor, we're heading back to the shop. Wanna join us?"

"No, I think I'll take advantage of the downtime while I wait for the concrete to set up. Starting tomorrow, I'll be busy for like a month."

"Just remember, you promised we could help."

"I expect you to," replied Victor. "It's your tractor." As the guys walked away, he turned to look behind him. Above the stairs he could see a light on in Jarden's office. It wouldn't be easy, but he'd have to pay his cousin a visit.

Jarden heard a knock on the doorjamb of his office. Without looking up from the papers on his desk he said, "Come on in, the door's open."

"Hi, Jarden," came a now familiar young man's voice. "Can I have a moment of your time?"

Jarden looked up at Victor and said, "As long as you give it back someday. What's on your mind, cousin?"

"Well, I've been talking to some of the guys at the shop and, well ... I had something I wanted to talk to you about."

"Have they been picking on you?"

"Oh, no, nothing like that," Victor said as he sat in the chair near the desk. "I like those guys."

"Well, good, because picking on you is *my* job. What is it you need?"

Victor stared at the front edge of the desk, then said, "I've had something on my mind lately."

Uh-oh, something's up. Jarden softened his tone and said, "Go ahead, what is it?"

"Well ... I'd like to introduce the guys to some cool technology." Victor hesitated, chewed on his lip, then blurted out with ever-increasing enthusiasm, "It's just that, in the outside world, we have all *sorts* of personal transportation devices. We have these things where you stand on this platform, and in the middle is a wheel, and there's a motor that runs the wheel and batteries that power the motor, and you stand on the platform, see, and you can move around from place to place. You can ride it over rough ground, and it's a *lot* of fun."

"Okay, okay," said Jarden, feeling like he'd just been spun around the room on some imaginary goods. "So these things are what you want to bring in with the next shipment?"

"Yeah, I'd like to bring in a couple, but I don't know if it'd be keeping with the customary ArcPoint culture or not."

"Oh, I wouldn't worry about that," said Jarden, laughing to himself. "Why not? Until we're completely set up to do the kibbutz thing, we can do what we want. Just tell your contact what you need, and we'll get it coming."

"Uhh, great. I'll let them know. Thanks."

Jarden studied his cousin's demeanor. He was staring down; not looking him in the eyes. *Something is still troubling him, something he needs to talk about but may not want to.* Jarden leaned forward, resting on his forearms. His tone was matter-of-fact. "Whatever it is, son, just tell me."

"I wanted to talk with you about somebody."

Jarden wondered who it could be, other than the guys in the shop, Arcon, or himself. Victor didn't hang out with anyone else. *Except for one person.* He took a gamble and asked, "Is it Brina?"

Victor's eyes went wide as he looked up at Jarden. "Oh no, is it that obvious?"

"Is *what* that obvious? That you've noticed her? Everyone does. In this place, there are ten males for every female, so there's no eligible girl who goes unnoticed. But I'm not a very good mind reader. You'll need to tell me what's going on in your heart."

There was an uneasy silence until Victor ventured to ask, "Why hasn't someone grabbed her up before now?"

"That's her concern, not mine. But the problem goes way back to when her and Arcon were youngsters. The Community matched them up as life partners long before they were old enough to consider such things. They were best of friends as children, but the constant pressure forced them apart. Now we know how Arcon dealt with that problem, but I don't think Brina ever has. She knows she can have the pick of any boy in this place. But she takes more comfort in her family and her plants."

"I think I understand," said Victor. "Life is less complicated when I'm fixing things. I prefer to work alone, and I get lost in the oil and smoke." Victor went silent for a moment and then added, "At least I used to."

Jarden watched him struggle and had an idea about what was bothering him. "Let me see if I understand what you're going through. As I said, it's ten to one odds against a boy connecting with a girl here. When I was young, it was four to one. Several times, I was attracted to a certain girl, but I was too slow. Someone else always stepped in. But you want to know something? I now have a closer relationship with every one of those girls than I did back then. They're all my friends, and I can talk freely with any of them."

"Have you been satisfied with that?" asked Victor.

"Satisfied? Yes, with staying single. But I don't believe that's how God meant it to be. In my case, I eventually learned to enjoy the freedom of talking with anybody. But that's me. I think it's normal for a young man to be completely flummoxed by a pretty girl."

"Hmmm. Flummoxed. I'll have to look that one up."

"You do that. Meanwhile, let me give you some advice based on what I know about Brina. First of all, there's no one here in ArcPoint she's interested in."

"Not even Raymo?"

"*Especially* Raymo."

"Why do you say that?"

"He's too much like Arcon."

"I don't follow that at all. They don't seem anything alike."

"Just like Arcon, Raymo's mind is somewhere else. He wants Brina to fill the desires of his heart, and I don't think he really considers her needs and desires. When Arcon found Elaina, he found someone with desires so close to his own, they fulfill each other. Only God could have made such a perfect match. Brina knows every boy in ArcPoint, and none of them fit what she's looking for. And believe me, she's being wise in that, not selfish."

"How could I ever be the type of person she's looking for?" asked Victor.

"If you try, you won't succeed. To be honest, I think you've been doing well already. I can tell she enjoys working with you, and I know that's one of her main criteria. She talks with Raymo because he approaches her, and she's too kind-hearted to tell him to go away. But he distracts her from her work, and I know it annoys her. You, on the other hand, help her with her work, and then you let her go about it. That's perfect."

"Do you think she'd enjoy working with me on the tractor?"

"Oh, absolutely. As long as you didn't steal her from her other chores. You'd be surprised at how helpful she can be. Her and Arcon used to tinker on things all the time."

"I guess I just can't picture her with a black grease smudge on her pretty face."

Jarden laughed. "I've seen her with worse than that. Remember, she works with fertilizer."

Victor chuckled as the thought sunk in; then he got quiet again. "So, you think someone like me could have a chance with her? I mean, seriously?"

Jarden gave him a stern look. "I think someone like me could have a chance with her, minus about forty years. I don't know if anyone has pointed it out, but that'd be you. There would be no competition for her hand here. But that's an important point. This is her home, and I believe it always will be. Are you prepared to make that kind of sacrifice for her? To uproot yourself from the outside world?"

"I've already been thinking about doing that," answered Victor. "I like it here."

"Then let's start there. Why don't you take the apartment you've been staying in and make it your own? You'll be working on the tractor for a while, so you might as well get comfortable. We'll keep this conversation between us, and as far as Brina is concerned, just treat her like one of the guys. And don't worry about Raymo. He won't get it until you give her parents the Request for the Daughter's Hand."

"The *what?*"

"I'll explain that to you later."

CHAPTER EIGHTEEN

All four of the Jerusalem-bound travelers had their eyes glued to the Map view on the monitor. They were approaching the Grand Forks, Minnesota tube train terminal at over a thousand kilometers per hour. "This will get interesting," said Elaina to Arcon. I think there are seven or eight pods coupled together right now. They'll all decouple, one at a time."

"Why is that? asked Arcon.

"It helps the pods slow down as we come into the terminal. It's easier to stop a single pod, than it is a big mass of them together."

"Can't some of them keep going?"

"Nope," said Elaina. "This is a full-stop terminal."

"Everyone will get off the train at this stop," said Ranger Dan. "It's a major intersection on the tube train map. From this terminal, people can continue east below the Great Lakes, go north to Canada, or south to Texas. The pods, on the other hand, will all go through a major inspection before moving on."

"Will there be people joining us?" asked Arcon.

"Not on our side of the pod. I petitioned for privacy on our entire route, and that got approved. Maybe on the other side of the bulkhead, but it could just be cargo. They ship a lot on this route. After here, it's non-stop for the next three hours."

"Non-stop?" asked Elaina. "I hope we can stay here longer than fifteen minutes."

Dan laughed and said, "What's the matter, getting hungry? I know I am. Once our pod stops at the terminal, we'll have at least an hour break. But we have to unload our stuff, so that eats up some of our time. I'll check the stats and see if we can stay here for a while." If there are other passengers, it's courteous to be on time getting back.

"How long did you say the next stretch will take?" asked a drowsy Roberto.

"It's around three thousand kilometers, so it'll take about three hours. So do whatever you need to before we leave. I know I'm pushing the schedule, but I'd like to get to Hudson Crossing before we crash for the night. We'll get there about nine o'clock at night, local time, so grab something to munch on. I have rooms reserved for us there near the terminal."

Arcon leaned over and whispered to Elaina, "What does it mean to crash for the night?"

"He means going to bed," she answered, then smirked. "Did you think he meant falling out of a tree?"

"Been there, done that," said Arcon, as he settled back into his seat.

Arcon checked the map view once more, this time to find out what the local time was. They'd been traveling across Canada for two hours, and he calculated he'd spent over seven hours in these tube train pods. He looked over and saw Elaina was still asleep, leaning against the side of the pod. He tried once more to go to sleep, but he still couldn't get used to the shaking and noise.

Dan and Roberto were sleeping, too. Dan was so still you'd wonder if he was alive, but Roberto was curled up and restless, as if he was cold. Arcon could hear talking, but it came from the other side of the bulkhead. He tried putting on the noise-canceling headphones like the others were wearing. It calmed him down until the pod shook with no sound associated with it, which made him too nervous to sleep.

"Have you fallen asleep at all?" he heard Elaina ask.

"I've nodded off a few times, but not for very long."

"Don't worry about it. We can get plenty of sleep tonight."

"I'm not keeping you awake, am I?"

Elaina chuckled. "No, I was asleep anyway."

"What?" asked Arcon, sounding confused.

"You two are keeping *me* awake," said Roberto.

"Sorry, Daddy."

"That's okay. I couldn't get comfortable, anyway. How much farther do we have to go?"

Arcon glanced at the monitor. "About eight hundred kilometers."

"Good. In another hour, we'll be off this thing. I'm ready for a break."

Elaina looked across at Dan lying on his back, legs stretched out under her seat, and his head tipped back. He was lightly snoring through a partly open mouth. "Do you think Ranger Dan will wake up before we get there?" she asked.

"Unlikely," said Ranger Dan softly.

Elaina blinked in surprise. "I guess he's already awake."

"What makes you think so?" asked Dan, eyes closed.

"Do you normally talk in your sleep?" asked Elaina.

Dan raised his head to look at her. "How would I know? Do you normally talk to people while they sleep?"

"No. I usually talk abnormally just to mess with them."

Ranger Dan pushed himself upright and smiled at her. "Your normal is abnormal."

Roberto started laughing. "I think he got you with that one. So how about we talk about something else? Arcon, what do you think of the trip so far?"

"It's not as exciting as I thought it'd be." He changed the monitor screen to Real View and watched the wheat fields rolling by. "It's exciting to see all this food being produced, but I still can't wait to actually touch it."

"Tomorrow, son," said Dan. "I scheduled a two-hour layover in Greenland. That's on your list of things to see, right?"

"Actually, it's on Lars Ashford's list of places he'd like to go," said Arcon. "He knows he'll never get to do it, so I'm supposed to visit these places if I can and report back to him. I told him he could see these things now on a viewscreen, but he didn't care about that. He said anybody could make pictures. He wanted an eyewitness."

Elaina put her hand on Arcon's arm. "Why don't you read those prophecies to us? I'd like to hear them again, and I don't think the others have ever heard the whole thing."

"Lars didn't say they were prophecies, just predictions." Arcon turned the viewer off and dug papers out of the satchel Lars Ashford had given him. "These are the climate predictions of his father, Dr. Norman Ashford. Want me to read the scientific parts?"

"Is it long?" asked Roberto.

Arcon held up a handful of paper. "Dr. Norm went into a lot of detail about the science behind his predictions. That's why Lars said they weren't prophecies."

"But they all came true," added Elaina.

"I think they all did, so they were sort of prophetic."

"Can you summarize the scientific part?" asked Dan.

"I'll try," said Arcon, as he scanned the papers in his hand. "First, I'd like to say that I learned a lot about Dr. Norm as I read these papers. It seems his life's passion was to feed the world's population. His obsession was creating plants that were drought and salt tolerant and disease resistant. Genetic modification wasn't his thing, but he was okay with it if it worked. He said he hated fake science—that the world was in big trouble if everyone learned science from celebrities, politicians, and journalists. He called them phony, corrupt gossips."

"So, what science did he like?" asked Roberto.

"He loved raw data," said Arcon. "Lars showed me lots of boxes filled with paper that were covered with numbers and charts. Dr. Norm didn't agree with the politics of his day that said carbon dioxide was destroying the planet. He said plants need the extra CO_2 and hungry people need plants. Of course, he was fine with the world switching to bio-fuels. But he thought destroying the fossil fuel industry was foolish until there was a viable alternative, such as the ArcPoint trees. Then he and my Grandpa Lee had a discussion about DNA and building the Facility."

Dan leaned forward in his seat and cocked his head. "How do those fit together?"

"They both require planning," injected Elaina. When they all looked at her, she added, "I read about it in Lee Franklin's journal."

"Yeah. He wrote that DNA is the blueprint for building a *living* thing. I guess back then some people thought life just happened somehow—that we didn't have a Creator."

"That's hard to imagine," said Roberto. "Something that complex happening without intelligence even existing. Are you saying that's what Dr. Norm Ashland believed?"

"That's what Lars told me. But when Dr. Norm started believing in a creator, his outlook on the future changed."

"And how was that?" asked Roberto.

"He realized God was in control. When he read in the Bible how God changed the rains and the movement of the moon, he stopped worrying about sunspot cycles and volcanic eruptions altering weather patterns. Then the ArcPoint thing happened and his focus changed to feeding us rather than the whole earth. He did everything he could to help ArcPoint survive and asked God for help with what he couldn't do."

"So, what were his predictions?" asked Dan.

"There were six of them. Let me read them to you. Number one: *The Bible says the deserts will bloom, and our Mojave did. I predict the Sahara, the Atacama, and many other deserts around the world will become productive farmland, as Israel already has.*"

"That one certainly came true," said Roberto.

"That's why I wanted to take the tube train through there, to see the farms. Okay, number two says: *I predict the earth will get warmer. This will allow tundra to thaw and be available for farmland, as happened in Greenland during the medieval warm period. Many people fear the warming of the earth, but if God is in control, it will be good.*"

"Is that why you wanted to go to Greenland?" asked Roberto.

"Lars asked me to pick him a handful of grain from the hills of Greenland and bring it back to him. I hope it's growing this time of year."

"He may have to settle for grocery store grain that was grown in Greenland."

"I'll take what I can get, for Lars, that is. Here's number three: *The Bible says there will be horrific earthquakes. At ArcPoint, we experienced that fi sthand. I think he's talking about the Rift here. I predict tectonic movement will affect the whole earth for a time, and then it will be over after Jesus is on the throne in Jerusalem. The earth will then be at peace from this form of destruction.*"

"I've checked the earthquake statistics," said Elaina. "Ever since Jesus returned, there have been almost no earthquakes larger than a magnitude four. None of them have caused any destruction, and very few have even been felt. I'd say that one came true."

"You know what it's like?" asked Dan. "It's like the earth still has to make its adjustments, but with God's help, it doesn't do it destructively."

"Okay, here's prediction number four: *Considering the previous points, I predict carbon dioxide levels will increase in our atmosphere, but primarily from natural occurrence, not anthropogenic. Based on the carbon cycle, this will increase vegetation and thus food production, eliminating world hunger. Then the increased plant production will stabilize the CO2 concentration at an optimum level.*"

"I checked the statistics on this one, too," said Elaina. "At the beginning of the 21st century, there were nearly a billion malnourished people in the world. Half of that was from political or religious turmoil, meaning they may have been able to grow enough food, but conflict kept them from it."

"Corruption was bad," said Roberto. "Countries could send tons of food to help, but getting it to those in need required trucks, drivers, and fuel—often at overblown prices. Then bribes were required at checkpoints."

"But now there are no corrupt governments," said Elaina. "Any food that's grown can be freely shared, and these tube trains are better at spreading it around."

"So again, his prediction was right," said Arcon. "It goes along with prediction number five, which says: *Most hopefully, I predict wisdom and unselfish ess will allow the world to share resources efficien y, so all people prosper. That is the only outcome that makes sense to me, with Jesus ruling in Jerusalem and the Holy Spirit guiding our thoughts and actions.*"

"Amen to that," said Dan.

"The last one, number six, is kind of personal. It says: *Last, I'm not sure how it will happen, but I predict our ArcPoint trees will have a positive impact on mankind.* That was always our intention. It looks like that one is just now starting to happen."

"You want to know what I think?" asked Ranger Dan. "When all the test results of the ArcPoint trees come in—and we have a plan in place to develop their use—I think we need to have a meeting of all the ArcPoint people. We'll make Lars the guest of honor, and we'll read these predictions to everyone. Then we can honor Dr. Norman Ashford by declaring the prophecies completely fulfilled."

CHAPTER NINETEEN

Ranger Dan led the others into a small meeting room at the Hudson Hotel. "Grab a seat, everyone. Elaina, set up your laptop and get connected to Ops in Baker. I'll do the same."

"What's going on?" asked Roberto.

"I don't know," said Dan. "Sam Boardman sent me a message; said he wanted me to contact him at the operations center tonight if possible."

Arcon whispered to Elaina. "Who is Sam Boardman?"

"He's the one in charge of transportation in and out of ArcPoint," she whispered back. The screen on her laptop blinked and displayed pictures of charts and images. "Ranger Dan, I'm connected in. I don't see Mr. Boardman in the cue. Now I see you just connected."

"I'll ping him to let him know we're ready. It's six thirty there, so he's probably not in his office."

As they waited for Sam to connect, Roberto asked, "You don't think there's been a problem, do you?"

"I sure hope not," said Dan. "They were supposed to be setting the bridge span in place today, and that's no easy feat. I hope it didn't fall into the earth crack."

"Oh, don't even say such a thing," said Elaina.

"I certainly don't think that happened," said Dan. "Redispan has an excellent record. The last I heard, they'd come up with some idea they thought would save us some time, but they didn't say what that was. Oh, look, Sam just connected."

They watched as Sam made himself the host, and his face appeared on their screens. "Hi Ranger Dan," they heard him say through both laptops.

"I'll turn my sound off," Elaina whispered.

"Hey, Roberto. Sorry to interrupt your trip. I see Elaina on the other screen. Is that Arcon next to her?"

"Yes, it is," said Dan. "Hey Sambo, I'd like you to meet Arcon Franklin, the kid who got you a new job. Arcon, this is Sam Boardman. He's working on getting a road of sorts built into ArcPoint. He's also in charge of the helicopter flights until we don't need them. Sambo, what's going on over there?"

"To start with, it regards the helicopter flights. We probably won't be flying them much anymore."

"What do you mean? We're supposed to fly electrical gear in for Victor in a couple of days. I'd hate to have his project delayed."

"Well, that's the other thing. We're flying Victor out of there tomorrow morning."

"What? How come?"

"It seems he didn't like his accommodations. He's heading back home."

Dan threw up his hands. "He's coming back though, right?"

They saw Sam shake his head. "He didn't say, but he didn't act like it."

"That doesn't sound like Victor," said Arcon.

"I agree," said Dan. "Any idea what happened?"

"All I know is, him and Jarden got into a conversation, and then he suddenly wanted us to fly him out of there. That's all I know."

Dan slumped in his chair. "This is not good. He's going to be hard to replace. I'll have to track him down and have a talk with him."

"Just a second," said Sam.

They all sat there staring at their laptops. Arcon's mouth hung open, and a tear rolled past Elaina's quivering chin. They could see that Sam was moving his cursor around. Suddenly, Victor's face appeared on the screen and he said, "Gotcha!"

"Victor!" yelled Elaina.

The view became a split-screen with Sam's face up on top next to Victor's. "Sorry, you guys," said Sam. "It was Victor's idea, not mine."

Dan asked, "Victor, what's going on?"

"Hey, well ... nothing Sam told you was a lie," said Victor. I am leaving, but it's not like it sounds."

"So, what's the deal?" asked Dan.

"I've decided to move to ArcPoint," announced Victor. The meeting devolved with everyone talking at once and congratulating him. "I'm leaving for home tomorrow to gather up some things to make my apartment a little more comfortable."

"Victor, that's great," exclaimed Arcon.

Roberto added, "You certainly had us worried."

Dan held up his hand, getting back to business. "Sambo, what's the deal with the helicopters?"

"That's the main thing I need to talk to you about," said Sambo. "Redi-span got the bridge in place today. But they also gave us two mini bridges, one at each end of the span. They're little ramps that attach to the span so trucks can drive on and off the bridge. Good news Dan, the bridge will be available for use tomorrow about noon."

"Are you saying we won't need helicopters? We can drive across?"

Sambo nodded. "The ramps are just a little over three meters wide, so it'll be a squeeze. But they can handle all the weight we can throw at them. We can bring in bulldozers, dump trucks, whatever we need to get the road done. So, I'm proposing we focus our efforts and back off on helicopter flights. It should only delay the electrical gear a week or so. What do you think?"

"That sounds great," said Dan. "As far as any work on the I-15, just do it. I'd still like ArcPoint people to work on the road into their Facility, but now we can get them better equipment to work with. Victor, when will you return to ArcPoint?"

"Well, if I had my own off-road vehicle, I could be back in two days," said Victor. "But I'll need to track one down, and I don't know how long that'll take."

"Tell you what—you've met Jonathan Greywolf, haven't you? The guy with the braids?"

"The old miner?" asked Victor.

"Right," said Dan. "I know Jonathan has a real nice rig. Contact him. Tell him you'll need to borrow it for a while, and that I'll make sure he gets whatever credits he needs to loan it to us. He's always fair."

"What if he says no?" asked Victor.

"He won't," said Dan. "I already know what he'll say. He'll tell you he won't let you have it unless he goes with it. When he does, let him. I know he really wants to get into ArcPoint, but he refuses to fly in a chopper. Can you do that?"

"Sure. What if he insists on doing the driving?"

"I wouldn't let him if I were you," warned Dan, "he hasn't driven in years. That's why I know he won't mind us using his rig. Now, do you know how to operate heavy machinery, like trackhoes and such?"

"I know how," said Victor. "I'm not very good at it."

"Doesn't matter," said Dan. "I still want to keep outsiders out of ArcPoint until they're ready. I'd like you to train someone from there to operate the equipment. Do you think you'd be up for that? Just so they can build the road from the ArcPoint side."

"I'll do my best."

"Good enough. Now, Sambo—I'll need you and Victor to talk to Jarden and Petra and work out the details. Can you two handle that?"

"Will I still be able to work on the utility building?" asked Victor.

"Sure. Once you train Jarden's people to work on the road, let them have at it. Just check on them once in a while. Oh, and if it works out for Jonathan to get there, make sure and introduce him to Jarden."

"And make sure and tell Jonathan I said hi," said Arcon.

"I'll do that," said Victor.

"Anything else?" asked Dan.

"No, I think we're fine," said Sam. "Enjoy your trip."

"Let me know if you need me. Otherwise, I'll check back with you when we get settled in Israel."

"Sounds like a plan, Ranger Dan. Nice meeting you all. Sam Boardman, signing off."

Sam's face disappeared from the screen, and Dan said, "It looks like things are moving smoothly without us there. Do you think that means we should stay away longer, or do we need to cut our trip short and get back?"

Roberto's eyes got big. "You wouldn't cancel the meeting in Jerusalem, would you?"

"No, no—never. That meeting is set up at a particular time and place, but we can adjust our travel before or after it. Let me think about it. We'll spend the night here, and let's get up an hour earlier than planned to go to Greenland, so we'll leave here about seven o'clock. We'll take some time in Greenland. Then we'll discuss it. Sound fair?"

"Sounds like a plan," said Roberto.

"Then let's get our rooms and get some sleep."

◆

Victor turned off his computer and sat-link and leaned back in his chair. It'd felt good to pull a fast one on all four of them at once. And it'd given him a bonus. Now he knew they really wanted him here. In the outside world, he was just another person. Everyone liked him well enough, but if he didn't show up at a get-together, nobody called to find out why. Other than his parents, he had nothing to keep him from moving. Besides, he had at least one family member here. He got up from his chair and headed for the dining area to find Jarden.

Downstairs, as Victor rounded the corner, he saw Jarden sitting at one of the tables with Brina. Victor stopped in his tracks, not emotionally prepared to talk to them. But just as he hesitated, Brina looked up, and they made eye contact. She quickly nodded at him, and he froze. He thought for a second and then remembered … that was the ArcPoint signal to engage in conversation. Then Jarden turned and nodded at him too. Visiting wasn't what Victor had planned, but he was certainly okay with it. He nodded and went over to join them.

"Jarden tells me you're going to move here," said Brina smiling as he settled into a chair at their table.

"Yeah, it just makes sense," said Victor, feeling a little more relaxed. "It looks like I have at least two months' worth of work lined up and nothing real important to go back to. Besides, I'd like to have some of my own tools to work with. You know how mechanics are."

"Not really, but I'll take your word for it," said Brina.

"Are you going to leave tomorrow?" asked Jarden.

"Yeah, in the morning," said Victor. "The helicopter is bringing in the supplies you want, and then they'll take me back to Base Camp in Baker. Then I'll hitch a ride to Vegas and take the tube train home."

Brina's brow furrowed, "Okay, I'll take your word for it."

"Oh, right. Well, someday, you'll get to ride in a tube train, and you'll know what I'm talking about. Arcon and Elaina are on one now, so they'll probably tell you all about it."

Jarden shook his head. "I still can't figure out how they're traveling across the ocean on a train."

"It wasn't easy for the engineers to figure out. Because the tubes are hollow, they float. So they anchored the tubes to the sea floor just below where ships travel. They only completed the stretch over Greenland and Iceland about ten years ago, even though they built the first tube trains a hundred years ago."

"I don't think I'd care to do it."

"I'd like to," said Brina. "It's probably safer than a helicopter, and I've done that."

"It's a lot safer than a helicopter," said Victor. "But not near as interesting. You travel inside a solid tube, so there's nothing to look at. But it gets you from one place to another very fast."

"When will you be back?" asked Jarden.

"In two or three days, but you need to know something. The construction crew finished the last bridge section on the I-15, so people will now be able to drive right in here. They plan to bring some heavy equipment in to help rebuild the road from here to the freeway. They want me to teach some of your people how to run the equipment, so we have no more strangers coming in here until you're ready. You and Petra will need to approve all this. If you have any questions, Sam Boardman is going to contact you tomorrow. He may even come in on the helicopter to talk to you in person."

"That'd be better. Can you tell him I'll arrange a meeting in the morning for him to talk to our leaders?"

"What time?"

"Whatever works best for him. We're not going anywhere."

"I'll talk to him tonight and let you know," said Victor. "I suggest we meet when the helicopter first arrives. Then I can stay for the meeting and leave after."

"I agree to your terms," said Jarden.

"Are you still going to work on the tractor?" asked Brina.

"Absolutely. I sure don't plan on working on the road building."

"Jarden says I can help you work on it."

"Oh, he did, did he? Well, just be warned that I can be hard to work with."

"And I'm a hard worker, so it's a perfect match."

Victor gave her a big smile and said, "I agree to your terms."

CHAPTER TWENTY

As he sat at a table with Elaina in the Nuuk, Greenland, tube train terminal, Arcon carefully laid the wheat stalks he'd collected for Lars on some paper. With a bit of info-net research the night before, they'd found a farm only fifteen minutes from the terminal. With time to spare, he arranged the stalks just like he wanted, then put more paper on top of them. He slid the sheets into the center of a book and closed it.

"Is that all you're going to get?" asked Elaina.

"This is good enough for Lars, although he'd have loved talking to the farm owner."

As the other two approached the table, Roberto asked him, "What did you end up with?"

Arcon opened the book to show them. "Since the grain wasn't ripe yet, I got a few stalks of buckwheat and a few of durum wheat. Now I'm pressing them in this book."

"Why did you choose those?" asked Dan.

"It says in this book that buckwheat was the first grain they planted here in Greenland. It had a short growing season and didn't mind the poor soil."

Elaina poked him. "Tell them why you decided to go with durum wheat."

"Uhh, it's because it's what they use that to make flour for spaghetti noodles."

Dan laughed. "That makes sense. What's the book about?"

"I found it in the gift shop. It's called *The Greening of Greenland*, and talks about the history of agriculture here. It even talks about the Vikings growing barley and corn around the year one thousand. I think the Ashfords will enjoy reading it."

"Sounds like it," said Dan as he sat down at the table. "Roberto and I bought food for the trip—packaged stuff, so we don't need to eat it now. You know, like sandwiches, bags of chips, that sort of thing."

Roberto added, "And, of course, pepperoni sticks and chocolate chip cookies."

Elaina laughed. "You found those here?"

"It wasn't easy," said Dan. He leaned forward. "We need to discuss how we handle the rest of the trip. It takes about an hour and a half to get to the other side of Greenland. After that, there is a terminal about every half hour. One on each side of Iceland, one on the Faroe Islands, and then one when we first hit the U.K. I arranged no more overnight stops between here and Jerusalem. This isn't a sight-seeing trip, so I planned to go pretty non-stop the rest of the way."

"No stops at all?" asked Elaina.

"Even I can't do that," said Dan. "We can stop at any terminal we want to, but if we want to stay more than a half hour, we'll have to unload our luggage so they can move out the pod. I'd prefer if we could just make a quick stop and keep going. We'll need to do our sleeping on the tube train. Does anyone have any objections?"

"None from me," said Elaina.

"How about you, Arcon?"

"I got what I came for," he said. "Hopefully, I'll get better at sleeping."

"If you can sleep, it'll help keep your internal clock from getting all messed up with the time changes. How about you, Roberto?"

"I like the schedule. We should try to push to get to the Faroe Islands before we stop. I looked it up, and the view from the observation area is spectacular. It's about three hours, but I think we can make it. It'll put us there at about, oh, between six and seven at night, their time. Still light enough to see the islands and the ocean, and maybe a sunset."

"Sounds like a plan," said Dan. "We can always stop earlier if we need to. Let's gather up our belongings and head down to the departure area."

Victor led Sam Boardman into the Franklin meeting room, and there were already a few people waiting. "I thought I was early," he said to Jarden.

"I told everyone to come meet here when they heard the helicopter landing."

"Oh. That makes sense." Victor looked around the room. "Everyone, I'd like you to meet Samuel Boardman. Ranger Dan has him in charge of making the I-15 freeway drivable again. He wants to help us build a road into here from the I-15 intersection where your people parked some of their cars. I've just been talking with him about how it needs to happen. I'll let him explain it to you. Sam?"

"Thanks, Victor. You all can call me Sambo. Ranger Dan does. There's a lot of vegetation between your facility here and the freeway. As you're aware, there used to be a road at one time, but now it's hard to see where it was. We have machinery that can make a road anywhere we want it. If you don't object, it'll rip a hole right through those sticker bushes and small trees. We'll want to avoid all the large trees if we can. It looks like we can roughly follow the way you've marked it, but not exactly."

"How long will it take to do that?" asked Petra.

"It depends on how much of a mess we can make," said Sambo. "We want to make a path as quick as we can that's large enough to get a vehicle through. Victor wants to drive back in here in two or three days, so we'd like to get the equipment on site tomorrow and get started. Then hopefully we'll be done the next day."

"Are you serious? That's about four miles."

"Uhh, yeah, about seven kilometers. Some of it isn't very dense, so it'll go fast. It might take us longer than that, but we'll do our best. We just need your okay to get started."

"If I might say something," said Victor. "Our goal is to keep outsiders away from disrupting your lives. As soon as we can get some kind of road to get the machinery down, everyone will go away except me. Hopefully, you don't want me to go away."

"We don't, do we, Jarden?" asked Petra.

"Not yet," said Jarden, smiling. "But couldn't you fly in a smaller machine?"

"No, a smaller machine won't make a dent in those sticker bushes," said Petra. "The machines that are powerful enough are too heavy to bring in on the helicopters we have. We'll have to plow our way in from the I-15 side. But we'll just poke a hole through and then send in the small machine for you folks to finish the job."

"So, these big machines are just making a path for the ones that we'll use here?" asked Jarden.

"And a way to get back in here myself," said Victor. "Oh, and there's one more person I'll be bringing in, and he may want to stay for a while. His name is Jonathan Greywolf, and his father was a friend of your Founders."

"You say his father knew the Founders?" asked Petra.

"Yes," said Victor. "He says he has proof of that and would like to show it to you."

"Let me say on behalf of all of us, if his father was a friend of the Founders, he's welcome here."

"I'm glad to hear that because it's his truck that I need to drive in here, and he goes with it. Does anyone have questions for Sam?"

"I do," said Jarden. "You're just going to leave the machinery for us to work with? You won't have an operator for them?"

"Right. They'll be smaller machines than what we start with. That way, you won't do as much damage while you're learning. There will be a bulldozer and a trackhoe. We'll let you decide how you want the road to go through your trees and use these machines to clear a path. Victor will teach some of you how to run them and let you know what we need as far as a road."

"Is that wise, Victor?"

"Probably not. I mean, having me as the teacher. But everyone has to learn somehow, and I know the mechanics are itching to drive anything. And if they break it, they're going to have to fix it."

"But please don't break them if you can help it," added Sam. "It won't be easy to get parts in here for them."

"We'll try to be careful," said Petra. "Does anyone else have questions? If not, then I think you brought in some supplies we need to unload, and then you can take Victor away from us."

"I think we'll make it," yelled Roberto. "We're almost to the top of the hill."

"Sure wish this tram would go faster," said Arcon. "I still think I could've outrun it."

"I think you could have," said Dan, "until you got to the outskirts of Tjornuvik. Then we'd have passed you. Two kilometers over rocky ground? We'd be on our way back to the tube train station by the time you reached the viewpoint."

"We're here," said Roberto, as the tram slowed down. "Look out there! The sun's not quite touching the horizon."

Elaina bent down so she could see through the tram window. "Good call, daddy. Look at the colors of those clouds. And the ocean is so blue."

"And large," said Arcon, as he stepped out of the West Faroe Island tram. He slowly turned around, taking in the smell of the ocean air and looking at the rugged hills.

Elaina joined him, wrapping one arm around his waist. "That's right. You haven't really seen the ocean in all its glory yet. And to think, you just traveled over four hundred kilometers under it. That's the longest under-sea stretch we'll have." She zipped up her jacket, then grabbed his hand as they walked into the stiff wind to where Dan and Roberto were enjoying the view.

"I agree with Elaina," said Dan. "You picked the right spot to watch the sun set. I didn't know they had a tube train station on the west side of the Faroe Islands. Or a tram ride to the top of the hill overlooking the ocean."

"You can learn a lot on the info-net," said Roberto. "You probably didn't know the Faroe Islands had undersea tunnels over a century ago, or the first ever undersea round-a-bout."

They were silent as they watched the sun disappear, and with it, the line of dancing red spots on the waves. "Someday, I'd like to come back here and spend more time," said Arcon.

"When we do, how about you and I hike up here from Tjornuvik?" said Elaina.

"That would be perfect."

Dan and Roberto walked back toward the tram, but Arcon kept staring at the glowing orange sky. He reached into his pants pocket and pulled out a rock. Holding it out toward the ocean, he said, "Look at the view, grandma. Can you believe we're on an island in the middle of the Atlantic Ocean—on our way to Jerusalem?"

"Oh, that's sweet," said Elaina. "That's the rock you gave your grandma, right?"

"Yeah. I couldn't have her with me, so this was the next best thing." He turned and pointed the rock at Elaina. "Look, grandma, I have a girlfriend!"

"I think I'm more than just a girlfriend."

"Don't tell me," said Arcon. "Talk to the rock."

CHAPTER TWENTY-ONE

Arcon opened his eyes and saw the other three were still asleep. They were obviously more accustomed to riding in a tube train than he was. But after three days of traveling, he could now nod off pretty quick. He just couldn't stay out for long.

At least he wasn't grabbing the armrests every time the pod did a sudden shift. He no longer felt queasy when the train suddenly dropped into a valley. He even enjoyed it when they'd go around a sharp corner, and the g-force would press him into the seat. But he'd thought the ride would be a lot more interesting than it was.

He felt the slight lurch of another pod dropping off the back of the train and looked at the map view to see where in the world they were now. Just passing Cairo, it would only be another half-hour, and they'd be in Jerusalem. Just an hour ago, they traveled through the vast farmlands of the Sahara.

He changed the view on the virtual window to 'Highlights' and could see an image of the pyramids slowly moving past, up close and personal. The Sphinx was something he read about in the Room of Remembrance. He wanted to see it in real life, but it didn't show up on the screen because it no longer existed, crumbling into the ground over fifty years ago. He switched to 'Real View' just to check and could see the pyramids far off in the distance. Close objects were a blur as they flew by at over a thousand kilometers per hour.

He turned off the screen and rolled over to his other side. He'd try once more to nod off since Dan told them they would arrive in Jerusalem with very little time for sleep. There would be a lot to see and do, and he didn't want to miss any of it.

Elaina nudged him. "Wake up, Arcon. Separation in five minutes." He moved slightly, jerked his head around to look at her, then sat straight up in his seat. As he tightened his seat belt and shoulder harness, she said, "This one won't be as bad. We've slowed to about five hundred through Israel." She turned the viewscreen on to the map. "See how the tunnel splits in two, then ends at Jerusalem and Tel Aviv? And look, the one from the north does the same thing, and so does the one from the east. So, no matter which direction you come from, you have to stop in Israel."

Arcon stared at the map. "No one can stay in their pod and keep going?"

"Not here. This was one of the earliest international destinations. I guess at first, all the major cities were planned to be full stop. But then someone figured out how pods could keep going. By the way, we'll be shifting to the right for Jerusalem. Hang on." As she spoke, the pods began decoupling and there was a rapid deceleration, followed by a sudden jog to the right as the pod moved to an exit tube. Within minutes, they were stopped at a station. "Welcome to Jerusalem."

"Wow. I can't believe we're here already."

"Did you get much sleep?"

"I'm fine," he said groggily. "Well, not really enough."

"Don't worry, we're a day ahead of schedule. We're not due to meet the American Council until 10 AM tomorrow, so you'll be able to get some sleep tonight."

"How did that happen?"

"Somebody," she said as she pointed at Ranger Dan, "added an extra day and didn't tell us about it."

Arcon saw Dan raise his hand as he said, "I didn't know if we could ride straight through or not. Technically, we gained ourselves a day."

"Well, I'm glad we did. I'm tired."

"And I'm hungry," said Dan. "Let's get off this thing and find something to eat. Then we can go to our rooms."

One by one, they climbed out of the pod and headed back to the baggage compartment. As Roberto grabbed his luggage, he said to Dan, "It's six-thirty in the morning. I sure hope there's something open."

"If there isn't, I suppose we could eat the sand which is here."

Arcon asked, "We still have sandwiches?" and they laughed.

Dan handed Roberto and Elaina some papers. "Could you two find the hotel? These are the directions. I'm going to talk with my wife as we're walking." " He pulled out his shoulder phone, tapped it, and said, "Call Mery."

Elaina and Arcon studied the written directions. "It looks like we can walk there," said Elaina.

"We can," injected Dan. "That's why I chose that ..."

"Hello, Dan?" came a voice on his shoulder phone.

"Hi Mery, it's me. We just got to Jerusalem and are walking to the hotel." His voice softened as he settled into the call. "How are you? How's your sister?"

"We're fine. We're getting down to the nit-picking stuff. How was your trip?"

"Exciting as usual," groaned Dan.

"That bad, huh? Aren't you a little early?" asked Mery.

"We had a nice stop in Greenland and a few quick ones in the Faroes, Paris, and such. But we rode straight through, so that's why we're here early. It'll get more interesting now."

"Aren't you tired? What time is it there?"

"Breakfast time. I'm fine. I slept most of the way. Arcon had a lot of trouble sleeping, though. Isn't it about bedtime there?"

"It's a little early for that, about eight-forty. It sounds noisy where you are."

"We're just picking up our luggage, so I should probably let you go. I'll call you after you get up tomorrow, okay?"

"Okay, I'll be up by seven. Talk to you then. Love you."

"I love you too, Mery. Be sure to say 'hi' to Bronwyn for me. Goodbye."

When Arcon woke up, he slowly opened his eyes before he made a move. When he was convinced he'd been dreaming and not actually sleeping in a tree, he sat up and looked around the suite. "How long did I sleep?"

Roberto looked at his watch and said, "About an hour. We were going to give you two. Was the couch comfortable?"

"Better than a tree," he responded. "Where are the others?"

"I'm right here," said Dan as he walked out of his room. "Jane is in her studio, putting on her pretty face."

"Since you're awake," said Roberto, "you've got time to take a shower, but you'll need to hurry. We have a driver arranged to pick us up at ten o'clock."

"Where are we going?"

"That was your decision," said Dan. "You said you wanted to see the Gihon River and the Dead Sea, or the Sea of

Chayamayim, as it's called today. We have enough time to go all the way to Masada, and then we'll come back and drive around Jerusalem for a while. We'll see you after you take a shower."

Elaina watched Arcon as he stared at the fishing boats on the Sea of Chayamayim. "What's going through your head?" she asked.

"I was thinking about swimming," he said.

"I hope you don't want to do that here."

He turned to her and smiled. "Not without swimming trunks."

"Good," she responded. "But I'm sure that's not all you were thinking about."

He looked back at the vast expanse of deep blue water, littered with boats. "When I worked in aquaponics, they taught me how evaporation would cause minerals to build up in the water and kill the plants and fish. I grew up seeing pictures of the Dead Sea. It was so mineral-laden people could sit in it without sinking, but nothing lived in it. I told my Grandma I wanted to sit in the Dead Sea someday. She read to me where Ezekiel said fresh water would flow out of the ground near the Gihon Spring and run all the way to the Dead Sea. One day people would fish here again, and plants would thrive, but I wouldn't be able to float like that."

"Sounds like you were disappointed."

"Honestly, I was. But I can see now I was being selfish. This is obviously better for everyone than a dead sea."

Behind them, they heard Roberto say, "Are you two about ready to go?"

"I think so," said Elaina.

"Isn't this something to see?" said Dan. "It's hard to compare this scene to the pictures we have from the 20th century. Hey,

Arcon, here's a trivia question. What do you think the name Chayamayim means?"

"I don't know," said Arcon. "But it should probably be the opposite of dead. I'll guess it means living sea, or sea of life, or maybe living water."

Their driver, Philippe, spoke up. "That is correct, mister Arcon. When Jesus returned, so did the rains. Water burst forth from the hill near the Gihon Spring, and life returned to this area. They changed the name to the sea of living water to honor him who brought us the living water."

"Well," said Dan, "are we ready to see the opposite end of the spectrum?"

"Ah yes, mister Dan," said Philippe. "Masada. So much death. Sad story, sad story." As they walked toward the tour van, he continued. "Conflict was bad here before the peace of Jesus returned. The Masada horror happened soon after he died for us. It is a sad thing to remember. The authorities are discussing whether we should stop touring this place of death. Already the Roman camps are hard to locate in the vegetation. Maybe no one goes there in the future, but today we will visit."

"I think I ate too much," said Arcon, as he collapsed on the couch. "It was so good, I couldn't help myself."

"I say you certainly helped yourself," said Elaina from the kitchen as she was making everyone some coffee. "How many of those falafel balls did you eat?"

"Three more than I should have," he said, as he loosened his belt. "It's still hard for me to believe we're here."

"I'm with you," said Roberto. "I never thought I'd have a good enough reason to come here."

Arcon sat up from his slouched position. "Couldn't you just get on a tube train and come here whenever you wanted?"

"Well, yes and no," answered Roberto. "Under the authority of Jesus, we have freedom, but we also have responsibility, and we take them both seriously. The tube train requires a lot of resources to operate. We all contribute to that, so it's there if we need it."

"Here's an example," said Dan. "My wife, Mery, travels fifteen hundred kilometers to help her sister in Oregon decorate her house. That's a need her sister has that Mery is skilled at. But if Mery went there just for lunch, it'd be a waste of tube train resources."

"Not everyone gets to go to Jerusalem then?"

"We're encouraged to visit at some point in our life," said Roberto. "But out of respect for those who may have a greater need, we tend to reserve the tube train for them."

"Besides," said Elaina, "there isn't room for everyone here."

Arcon stroked his goatee. "Just so I understand—Ranger Dan and I *need* to be here, and you two don't, but you believe this is a good enough reason to come here?"

"It was good enough for me," interjected Dan. "I made the official request for these two to join us, but it certainly wasn't an issue. I needed them to keep you under control. Who knows where you might swing off to when my back is turned?"

"They have swings here too?" asked Arcon. When they all looked at him, he said, "Just kidding. I think my swinging days are over."

"Oh, no, you don't," said Elaina as she handed him a mug of coffee. "You need to show me the Sunset Outpost. Or do I have to get Tawny to do that?"

Arcon squinted his eyes at her while he took a sip of his coffee. "When we get back, we'll test you on the trainer again. Then we'll see."

"Fair enough. So, what's the best thing you've seen so far?"

"The Dead Sea, for sure. But Masada was interesting. I hadn't heard of it."

Roberto added, "I enjoyed seeing the well where Jesus talked to the Samaritan woman."

"Jacob's Well," said Dan.

"Right. I liked how Philippe explained how the culture has changed."

"I'm glad it did," said Elaina. "By tradition, Jesus shouldn't have been speaking to a woman—especially a Samaritan one—even though Jacob was their common ancestor."

"We have a meeting tomorrow," said Dan. "But the next day, we'll take a trip up to the Sea of Galilee. It's not as large as I thought it'd be. I guess when you hear the term 'sea,' and you read about terrific storms, you think 'ocean.' But it's much smaller than the Sea of Chayamayim we saw today."

"Speaking of the meeting tomorrow," said Roberto. "Do you think Jesus will be there?"

"That's for him to decide," said Dan. "We're here to find out officially the chain of authority for the ArcPoint people. They used to be solely under Jesus and Central Authority, so there's a good chance he may want to do the honors. But my experience is, he prefers to surprise."

They all laughed as they recalled the uneaten sandwich and the missing milk. And the tears flowed as they recalled the message Jesus gave to Dan.

CHAPTER TWENTY-TWO

Jonathan Greywolf watched from his front window as the young man crawled out of the neon green driverless taxi. When he glanced toward the house, Jonathan waved at him, so he'd know he was at the right place. The man pulled some luggage and a toolbox out of the back of the vehicle. Then he opened his comm-pad, tapped on it several times, pressed his thumb down on it, and the taxi backed slowly away from him.

He started walking toward the house, but stopped to stare at the garden. That always happened with visitors, just as Jonathan intended. Discussing the garden was his favorite place for a conversation to begin. He opened the front door and walked out to greet him. "I presume you are Victor Merrick, friend of Ranger Dan."

"And you are the famous Jonathan Greywolf, friend of mines," said Victor with a beaming smile.

Ranger Dan has coached Victor well. "I am not really famous," he said with a grin. "In this world, I have a 'miner' role."

Victor thrust his hand out. "I can see I'm in the right place."

"You are indeed," said Jonathan, clasping Victor's hand with his. Then he squeezed hard enough to drop Victor to his knees.

"Now I *feel* like I'm in the right place," Victor said as he grimaced. "Ranger Dan told me you'd do that."

"Then you should have been better prepared," he said as he let go. Then he added, "Do you like gardening?"

"I actually do," he responded. "But where I live, I don't have room to grow much."

"If you are moving to ArcPoint, you should have plenty of room and good people to teach you."

"Have you seen their gardens?" Victor asked.

"No, but my father told me many stories about them. He was especially close to Norm Ashford, their plant doctor. He taught my father many growing tricks, and my father taught me. But I was born after the days of evil and after the Rift divided the land. It was many years before my father attempted to visit ArcPoint again, but he was unsuccessful. I feel fortunate that I may now fulfill his quest."

"Well, the ArcPoint gardens are mostly greenhouses, since they need to grow produce year-round. What you have there is more than a garden. It's a work of art."

"Thank you. That is my intention. I locate every plant so it will make a statement when it is grown. But I have a problem."

"What's that?"

"When they are grown, I have no place to step."

Victor laughed. "I can see that." He looked the garden over carefully and then glanced back at the sun. "I see you put all the tall plants in the back so they won't block the sun from the shorter ones. And the viny ones you put on the edge of the garden so they grow out like, I don't know, a bad hair day?"

"I prefer to say it is like the rays of the sun."

"That does sound better," said Victor. "I see something there I really miss."

"What's that?"

Victor walked toward the garden and pointed at a plant. "Lettuce. I've been living at ArcPoint for a while, and they don't have lettuce."

"What do you mean, they don't have lettuce?" asked Jonathan. "They used to."

"Why do you say that?" asked Victor.

"This lettuce was given to my father by Norm Ashford. It is a hybrid of his own making. He called it Titanic lettuce, because it grows large and is similar to iceberg. We've been saving the seed and growing it every year."

"Well, something must've happened because they don't have any now."

"Then we must take them some seed and some plants. How can people enjoy life without lettuce? Do they have zucchini?"

"They definitely have zucchini. They even put it in their spaghetti."

"Somehow, that doesn't sound good. Do they have chocolate?"

"They do now because we've given them some. Coffee too. But they didn't have either before we got there."

"Then we need to take them all the ingredients they need to make a large batch of chocolate zucchini cake. I've had none since I lost my wife six years ago. I will pay for enough ingredients to make a piece for everyone. How many are there?"

"There are about a thousand living there now."

"Oh. Guess we'll need to stop at a store. Will you come in for a few minutes? I have the truck packed already, so I'm prepared to leave. But I wanted to show you something."

"Sure. I'm in no hurry," said Victor.

Jonathan led Victor into the house and then into the dining room. He grabbed a picture album off the table and handed it to him. "Here, look at this while I get us something to drink. Would you like some iced tea?"

"That'd be great," said Victor, opening the album. "What are these photos of?"

"When I heard someone had contacted the ArcPoint people again, I searched through all of my father's archived photos to find the ones he'd taken of the ArcPoint people. I made prints from the digital files and put them in that album. I made one for myself, and plan to give that album to the ArcPoint people."

Victor turned the pages, seeing portraits of groups and individuals, and a lot of desert scenery. "Wow, they're going to like this. They have something they call the Room of Remembrance—where they keep stuff to remind them of the days of the Founders—but I didn't see anything like this in there."

"I thought they might not, since they'd have no way to protect their digital history. I helped my father archive ours, or else we would've lost these pictures."

"Could you tell me what that was like? I've never met someone who went through that archival process. It must have been difficult."

Jonathan handed Victor his iced tea and then motioned him into the living room. "Have a seat," he said as he pointed to a glider rocker. He sat in a recliner facing Victor and said, "It was both a hard time and a good time." As he sipped his tea, he studied Victor's face. He saw a young man eager to learn, and his own greatest joy was to teach. "Forgive me if the years have stolen some thoughts. It has been a long time."

"I understand that. They'll be celebrating the hundred-year anniversary of the beginning of the archiving next year. How old were you when you went through that?"

"I was about eight-years-old when we started. It took a few years to gather information from all the sources. We had some very old computers, and my father was nostalgic. Do you understand the goal of the archiving?"

"It was to preserve the things that were good and forsake that which was evil."

"That is part of it," Jonathan replied. "When Jesus returned, all mankind received His Holy Spirit, and we once more had the knowledge of the good He intended for us. But our world was still filled with the knowledge of evil that He wanted us to avoid. My father had grown up with that evil nature and, like many others, wanted it purged from his memory. But the computers also had a memory that needed to be purged.

"The answer was a new computer language that had never been used during the evil days. With the help of the Holy Spirit, it was designed to be incorruptible. Then, if there was any digital information that needed to be saved for future generations, it had to be converted to the new language. There could be no archiving of someone else's information unless that person designated them. Whatever was not archived was lost as the old computers died."

"It sounds like a lot of work."

"The work was easy, but the memories were sometimes painful. The evil contained in his own life embarrassed my father many times. He asked forgiveness often from God and from my mother and me. But it was healing to us all, eventually. He was glad to have the evidence of his past disappear with the forgiveness."

"I'm sorry if my questions forced you to relive them," said Victor.

"Thankfully, what I relive are the good memories." Jonathan smiled as he recalled one of his favorites. "In the summers we'd spend months at a time, deep in the earth, just my parents and I. Although mining was hard work, we were close to each other and to the land. Those memories are available to me at any time, and I don't have to swim through a sea of regret to find them." He drank down the rest of his tea.

Victor chugged down his tea and said, "Now I am too, if you know what I mean."

Jonathan chuckled. "Down the hall, first door on your left."

CHAPTER TWENTY-THREE

From their vantage point on the tenth floor of the World Authority Headquarters, they could see the renowned City of David. To the east, the Gihon River cascaded down the hill where homes once stood. But the dominant feature, and the most moving, was the Temple of Yahuah below them. Arcon felt honored to be in this place, but he wasn't sure if he deserved it. He hung his head and leaned on the railing in front of the floor to ceiling glass.

"Is something troubling you, son?" asked Dan.

"I was just thinking about my grandma Mary," he said. "She talked often about Jesus ruling from Jerusalem. Nearly her entire life, all this was already here, and none of us knew it. She could've been the one standing here, seeing what I see."

As they stared down at the Temple, Dan remarked, "I'm sure Jesus had his reasons for withholding that information from your people."

Arcon looked at Dan. "Oh, I don't doubt that. I just wish Grandma was here to see this with me."

Elaina responded, "I'm sure she's enjoying her own view of God's majesty."

"Yeah, I know," he said. Then he reached into his pants pocket and pulled out a rock.

"What's that?" asked Dan.

"It's his grandma," said Elaina. "Oops, I mean, it's a rock to remind him of his grandma. Tell him the story, Arcon."

"This rock was one that Jarden found. He gave it to me, and I polished it and gave it to my Grandma. It was one of her favorites." He handed the stone to Dan.

"It's beautiful! What kind of rock is it?"

"It's an agate, which is why it polishes so nice. Those things sticking up are called plumes, this fuzzy-looking stuff here is sagenite, and those fine lines are called fortifications. Anyway, I brought it along to remember Grandma. I thought about bringing her Bible, but I was afraid of losing it. Besides, this was easier to carry."

Dan handed the rock back to Arcon, who put it in his pocket. Then he noticed Roberto staring off into the distance. "Roberto, what are you thinking?"

Roberto jumped a little. "What?"

"Sorry, I don't mean to interrupt your thoughts," said Dan. "But I'd like to know what they are."

Roberto stared at the panoramic view of Jerusalem as he tried to recall what he'd been thinking. "I'm overwhelmed to be in this place," he said. "You may be used to being a boss. But I'm at the bottom of any line of authority. There's no one under me."

"What about me?" asked Elaina. "As my dad, you certainly have authority over me—"

"And what about the people you rescued?" interjected Dan. "Didn't they have to take orders from you?"

"I guess you're right," said Roberto. "But we're standing in the Hall of the Americas. This is where all authority flows out to the entire western hemisphere. Within this complex of buildings, all the authorities in the world are represented. Right in front of us is the earthly home of our Creator." He paused as if collecting his thoughts. "I'm just honored to be here. Thanks for letting me join you."

"To be honest, I'm pretty overwhelmed myself," said Dan. "I know I've been given dominion over the Mojave, but I'm still not exactly sure what that entails, and I don't know who I answer to." He glanced at his watch. "We're about to find out. I think we're next to meet with Central Authority."

"Wow," said Roberto. "I've never met one of their kind."

Arcon blinked. "What do you mean, their kind?"

"A resurrected one," said Roberto. "Those who died for Jesus during the evil time—what the Bible calls the great tribulation. They were brought back to life with resurrected bodies, like Jesus has. I've been told they don't appear any different than we do, except their bodies will never die."

"Or get too heavy," added Dan, patting his belly. "Plus, they can appear wherever they need to, and disappear again."

"Like Jesus did in your kitchen?" asked Elaina.

"Exactly. The most important thing is they won't take bribes. Their decisions are always fair and just."

"Will they be the ones we meet with today?" asked Arcon.

"At least one of them should be," said Dan. He saw the door to the meeting room open. "It may be our turn."

They watched ten people walk out of the room, mostly middle-aged men and a few women. Soon after, a man with a comm-pad asked, "Wilson party?"

Dan replied, "That's us."

They headed toward a set of double-doors across the foyer. Inside the conference room, Arcon's eyes were drawn to a variety of stone pieces on display in various-sized niches set into the walls. Some stones were large enough to be displayed alone, while others were in a collection of dozens. Arcon got close to one group, and he could see each rock had some words written near it in small Hebrew letters. Then he turned and saw Dan pointing to the seat next to him at the conference table.

Seated near the head of the table were four men and two women, and another man was standing at a podium. Arcon saw a plaque on the podium that read 'Judge Ben Klein'. He felt a light tug on his shirt sleeve, and Elaina whispered in his ear, "See the scar on his neck?" When he nodded, she added, "He was beheaded."

He turned and stared at her. "Is he …?"

She nodded. "Yes. One of the first resurrected."

Judge Klein shuffled some papers in front of him and asked, "Ranger Dan Wilson and Arcon Franklin?"

The two stood, and Dan tipped his head. "That's us, Judge." He put his hand on Arcon's shoulder. "This is Arcon. These other two are Roberto and Elaina Gonzales."

"You can call me Ben," he responded. "You're here regarding authority and dominion of the Mojave restricted area?"

"That is correct," said Dan.

"Have the people of the area agreed on their future course?"

"They have, sir." Dan referenced the notes he'd brought. "They would like the area to remain semi-restricted, with access at one portal only, and outsiders welcomed as invited guests."

"That sounds like a wise choice, given the circumstances," said one of the other men at the table. One woman added, "Would this be permanent?"

Dan replied, "They'd like it to be until further notice, but they expect the area to open up, eventually."

"Understood," said Ben. "Mr. Franklin, has Ranger Wilson stated the conditions as you perceive the desires of your people?"

"He has, sir," answered Arcon nervously.

Ben looked Arcon in the eyes and said, "I sense some hesitation."

"Sorry, sir," said Arcon. "My concern is not with Ranger Dan's words. It's with my role as ambassador. I do not feel qualified for the job. I would like to recommend Jarden Merrick as my replacement."

When Arcon said that, Dan interjected, "Can I comment on that?"

"Certainly," said Ben.

"I've spoken with Mr. Merrick, and he'd prefer to remain on site. For an ambassador, I need someone with complete mobility. But I understand Arcon's argument as well. I believe an acceptable compromise would be for them to be ... co-ambassadors."

Ben looked around the room and asked, "Are there any objections to that arrangement?" When he saw none, he asked Arcon, "Is that acceptable to you?"

"Uhh, sure, if it's okay with Jarden."

"At this time, we'll accept your agreement to the proposal. One of us will contact Mr. Merrick to verify his position. Now, Ranger Wilson, regarding the chain of authority. You will continue to serve under Western Hemisphere, but you'll now answer directly to the Continental United States' authority."

"So, the Mojave area will be treated as a state-level entity?" asked Dan.

"That's correct," said Ben. "That area is considered separate to our Lord. It will have unique needs and commands." Then the man looked at the back of the room and said, "I'll have him speak on those subjects himself. Welcome, Lord Jesus."

Arcon turned quickly to see where the judge was looking. Elaina gasped and grabbed his arm, which only compounded his fear. Then he felt an indescribable peace, and remembered how Dan had described his first meeting with Jesus. Just as Dan told him, Jesus didn't have a glow as paintings had portrayed Him. It was in Arcon's soul that he felt recognition and, as Dan had said, he couldn't explain it.

Jesus scanned each face. "Thanks for coming such a long distance." Then he looked squarely at Arcon. "Your people are special to me. Their faith is great."

Arcon trembled as he answered, "Thank you, Yahusha."

"I see you know some Hebrew," Jesus responded.

"Just a few names, sir, and how to count."

"Tell me if you know what this says." As he said that, he walked over to one of the rock displays and pointed at a label in front of a stand with no rock on it.

Arcon walked over to the display and looked closely at the label. "I only recognize one word, sir." He pointed and said, "This one. It says 'rock.'"

"How do you know?"

"My grandma figured out how to write it in Hebrew and taught it to me."

"Very good. The label reads *Mojave Remnant Rock*." He paused, allowing Arcon time to consider His words. "She also taught you about rocks, correct?"

"Yes, sir, a lot. She showed me the beauty in rocks and that no matter how close I look at them, they only get more beautiful and intricate. I polish them so I can see the detail better. She told me you are the solid rock, and all we are is a piece of that rock. Put us all together, and we are but sand."

"She taught you well," said Jesus. "Small rocks can also be bound together to create a firm foundation."

"You mean like in concrete?"

"Yes. Your people in the Mojave were like that. Your ancestor, Lee Franklin, understood concrete. He knew impurities would weaken it. He asked me to remove the impurities and for my Spirit to bind your people together as one. It was a request I was pleased to grant. In these buildings are many rooms with displays like these, where I honor those whom I consider special. In this room, I use a rock to represent the beauty of their faith and their solid character. Just like a rainbow, many people may not see these tokens of honor, but I will."

Arcon glanced around the room and had a new appreciation for the rocks on display, and the story that must go with them. His thoughts were interrupted when Jesus said, "I believe you have something for me."

Arcon's eyes widened. "What do you mean?"

Jesus pointed at the empty stand behind the label. "You have a rock in your pocket. Your friend Jarden found it in the Mojave, and you polished it by hand. You gave it to your grandmother Mary as a gift, but she had to leave it behind when I took her. You brought it with you to remind you of her. If you would be willing to part with it now, I have reserved this place of honor for it. It will remind me of the faith of your people. They were a true remnant of my body on earth."

Arcon looked at Elaina and could see tears streaming down her face. He reached in his pocket and grabbed the rock, but when it was in his hand, memories of his grandmother—and his rebellion—flooded into his mind. He sobbed but couldn't let go of the rock. Then Jesus put his hand on Arcon's shoulder. "You've been forgiven, child. Let it go."

Arcon looked into the eyes of Jesus and knew He understood the desire of his heart. "Can I?" he asked. When Jesus nodded to him, Arcon carefully placed the rock behind the label, and whispered, "This is for you, Grandma."

The room was silent as Arcon wept. As he regained his composure, Jesus spoke again. "You still have more questions, son. Tell us what's on your heart."

Arcon took a deep breath, exhaled, and thought of the people of ArcPoint. Then he said, "My people would like to know why we were set apart from everyone else. Why weren't we informed when you returned to earth?"

"The answer to both questions is simple," said Jesus, as he walked over to the rock Arcon had just placed on the stand. "That is what your people wanted, and it is what I desired for them. But it's more complex than that. When I created this world, it was only good. I wanted the people to enjoy it and improve on it in every way they could imagine. But a desire for evil made them destructive rather than creative."

Jesus picked up the rock and held it out for all to see. "Those who plot terror would never seek the beauty you have discovered in this simple stone." He returned it to its stand.

"In the days before my return, I removed my protection from those who rejected me and gave it to those who sought my help. Your people, from the least to the greatest, sought my help and protection. They chose a place to dwell, and I placed my hedge of protection around it all. I removed all evil from the people and the land. I did the same for other people, but no group as large as yours."

"When I returned, I had to establish a government that was incorruptible. I called on those from the first resurrection to assist me in governing. It took many years to establish the hierarchy of authority that is in place today. But your people were incorruptible before I returned, so we did not need to interrupt your governance. That is why your people are special to me and have remained set apart. But now is the time to rejoin my creation."

"Thank you, Yahusha. Now I understand. I will explain it to my people."

"I will give you more understanding when you do. I only have one command that will be unique to your people. They are free to enjoy whatever they want, and go wherever their heart leads them. But once a year, they should gather again in the Mojave. When they do, I will join them." Then Jesus turned to Ranger Dan. "You as well will receive understanding to care for these people. I thank you for humbling yourself to be a servant to them. Roberto and Elaina, I thank you for listening to my Spirit as it guided you to Arcon. Allow him to be a blessing to your family." Then he turned to the man at the podium and nodded.

"Thank you all for coming," said Judge Ben Klein. As everyone turned their attention to him, he continued. "Arcon,

I believe you are already rethinking your ability to lead your people, but we will contact Jarden, anyway. Dan, we will have you report to the Continental United States authority when you are comfortable. Roberto, we have a task for you as well."

"You do?" he asked, touching a hand to his chest.

"Yes. Our Creator placed many treasures in the land for us to discover and enjoy. The area around the Mojave has been unavailable for exploration for too long. Under Dan's authority, we would like you to open up that land. Allow mankind to explore its wonders and beauty, both above and below the surface. Be wise with the resources. What you restrict will be restricted. Do you understand?"

"Not fully, sir. But I'll do my best to learn about the area."

The judge smiled. "Good answer. Now Elaina, you have the most important task. Our Lord said to be the greatest of all, you must serve. The success of these three men depends on your support. Are you agreeable to that task?"

"Completely."

"Then our business here is finished. Unless any of you have other questions, you are free to enjoy Mount Zion."

Dan looked at the others, who nodded. "I think we understand. Thanks for the opportunity to serve." He turned to thank Jesus as well, but he was gone. When he turned back around, so was Judge Klein. The other six just smiled at him.

"Are we *sure* we understand our roles?" asked Dan in a hushed voice as his group left the room.

Roberto thought about it. "I did while I was in there, but now I'm second-guessing it."

"I know what you mean," said Dan. "Let's find a place where we can talk about it. If we have questions, we should probably get them answered while we're here."

Roberto saw a small, unoccupied visitor's area near a large window. "There's a good spot."

As they walked that direction, Elaina said, "I kind of understand what they were telling you guys to do. Especially you, daddy."

Arcon stared out the window while the others sat down. "Should we call Elaina Goodness or Mercy?"

"What are you talking about?" asked Elaina.

Arcon walked over and sat down. "Psalm one hundred," he said, "you know, the one that says *the Lord is my Shepherd*. At the end, it says, *goodness and mercy shall follow me all the days of my life*. My grandma told me goodness and mercy were like two sheepdogs the Lord uses to shepherd us, to keep us in line. It sounds like Elaina is supposed to keep the three of us herded in the right direction."

Roberto laughed. "I like that. I feel like I've been doing the herding. Now it's her turn."

"I still prefer to be called Elaina," she said, "and don't expect me to be merciful in my herding."

Roberto smiled at her. "I'll just continue to call you *girl*."

"Sounds good, Big D. So, let me tell you guys what you're supposed to do. Dan, you'll be the man in the middle, which means Jarden, Arcon, and Daddy will tell you what they need to do their jobs and you'll go to the higher authorities to get it. Arcon, you'll work with Jarden to find out what the ArcPoint people need, and you help Dan get it for them."

"What about dear ol' dad?" asked Roberto. "What do you all think about me opening the Mojave area for exploration?"

"I have an idea about that," said Dan. "Jonathan's family got involved with the Mojave People way back when. His grandparents owned a gold mine in the eastern section of the Preserve before it was deemed off-limits." Dan muttered, "I'm pretty sure these days resources like gold have controls for how they get prospected," and then continued with, "but anyways, who knows what there is to discover out there—what beauty there is to see in the hills? Waterfalls, canyons, and who knows what else no one living has ever seen?"

"I understand," said Roberto. "All these years, that area has been closed, even for recreation. As search and rescue agents, Elaina and I ultimately do what we do because people are encouraged to explore God's creation. Some lose their way or get in over their heads."

"Which is why we also maintain trails and signs, so they're less likely to get lost," added Elaina. "It sounds like they've tasked my dad with developing another playground for God's children. You know—roads, trails, signs, that sort of thing."

"And I know how you can help me with that," said Roberto. "We can start by exploring the land with drones. I'm skilled with handling them, and you've got good eyes for spotting things."

"And for fixing the drones," said Elaina.

"Well, yeah, there's that, too. But you'd be stuck indoors. Wouldn't you and Arcon rather hike and explore all that untamed wilderness?"

"I know what I'd like," injected Arcon, drawing everyone's attention. "I'd like to find a good homesite first. I've always wanted to build my own home—to live someplace with a view beyond the trees."

"Here's an idea," said Dan, slapping his knee, "We could accomplish all these things from the area around Baker! That way, we could all stay close by and help each other."

"And I wouldn't have to work so hard to keep you all herded together," said Elaina with a grin.

CHAPTER TWENTY-FOUR

Elaina woke when the tube train made a hard jolt. Ranger Dan was still sound asleep, stretched out in front of her as usual. The viewscreen was off. She turned, expecting Arcon to be asleep because he usually had it on when he was awake. He was reclined as she was, but staring straight ahead. "Deep in thought?" she asked.

"What? Oh … yeah … I suppose."

"What about?"

"I don't know. A lot of things, I guess. Mostly about ArcPoint and how much it's going to change soon. I sort of feel responsible for that."

"Arcon, we've talked about that. It was God who set into motion what happened. The rest of us just followed along and did our part."

He rolled onto his side to face her. "I get that, but I'm talking about what happens now. I was thinking about that kibbutz we got to visit while we were near the Sea of Galilee. When we talked about it before, I really didn't understand. But now I think I get it. It's a teaching thing, like the dude ranch."

"Yeah, you're right. A kibbutz isn't a necessary way of life now, but many people like the experience. I think they don't want to forget how it used to be before Jesus returned."

"ArcPoint is going to be like that, sort of. I mean, a lot of people in the Community enjoy the way things work there.

They'll be thrilled to show outsiders how we do things. I was just thinking about different chores that might work and what jobs will be too difficult."

"Have you come up with any ideas?"

Arcon was quiet for a moment, then chuckled. "Outsiders *have* to spend time hacking at the needle-brush."

"Oh, absolutely," said Elaina.

"I don't know about swinging through the trees though. That takes some time to learn. We wouldn't want someone getting hurt." He drummed on the seat tray for a minute. "They'll have to pump water."

Elaina raised her eyebrows. "What?"

"Outsiders will have to spend time pumping water into the tank for the hydroponic gardens." Arcon's excitement grew, and he spoke more quickly. "Did you know that for almost a hundred years, someone has had to hand pump the water from the main storage tank to the upper feed tank every three hours, seven days a week? Victor installed electric pumps, so half of hydro is automatic now. But they're leaving the other half for the outsiders."

"What about pitching in at Madelyn's department?"

"That's obvious. Spinning the wool, dying it in different colors, knitting the garments. I think the outsiders could get their hands dirty doing any of those things. She also takes care of the hemp cloth, ropes, and such. We call Maddy our textile choreographer."

"How about shearing the wool off the goats?"

"That's a seasonal thing, but they could do it. On the other hand, milking the goats has to be done twice a day, every day. That can be interesting if you've never done it before. Trust me, I've tried. The goats hated the way I squeezed them. They'd kick over the milk bucket."

"Sounds like you don't miss that job."

"You got that right. But I do miss playing with the goats."

"How about the things that Brina does?"

"Well, her primary responsibility is caring for the hemp plants. Only her parents could help oversee that. But she'll need a lot of workers to plant and harvest them. Those jobs are seasonal, too." Arcon tipped his seat upright again. "Every outsider will work with the hemp in one way or another. I'll talk to Maddy's husband about it. He's in charge of turning the hemp into things we need, like paper and ink, soap, insulation, and the fibers that Maddy's team uses."

"What about the technical jobs, like the mechanics and electricians and chemists?"

"Hmmm. If the outsiders have some of those skills, why not? We'll just have to have a way of testing their knowledge— for safety reasons. What we may have to do is have people sign up for jobs that are familiar to them."

"True, but they may *want* to learn something new."

"If they want to float around to differing jobs, we can let them. That's what Brina does. She goes wherever she's needed, so she has a lot of different skills. When I was a child, I worked in hydroponics because I liked the plants. I'd check water levels, look for wilting plants, pump the water. But then I got bored with that and hung out with the electricians. They taught me how to fix all sorts of things, and I shared what I learned with Brina. Then when my parents died, I became a hunter. All those things are completely different. I just …"

Elaina waited for Arcon to continue, but he just stared into space. After a few moments, she asked, "What is it?"

Arcon took a deep breath and exhaled. "I was trying to do anything except work with my parents in the chemistry lab. If I would have, maybe they wouldn't have died."

"Or maybe you'd have died with them. But either way, we wouldn't be having this conversation while riding a tube train across Siberia. You can't change the past. What did Jesus tell you? You've been forgiven, so let it go. That's the whole point of forgiveness, to be able to move forward."

"But you should still learn from the past."

"Yes, you should."

"Then we probably won't let outsiders work in the chemistry lab. And if we need some alcohol, we'll buy it."

"It sounds like you're gaining some valuable wisdom, Mr. Ambassador."

Victor pulled the truck up in front of the construction headquarters at Baker Base Camp. "We're here," he said as he and Jonathan crawled out of their seats and stretched. He closed the driver's side door and started walking toward the building to get out of the heat.

"That was a long way to drive," said Jonathan as he followed Victor. "Thanks to the Rift, it takes eight hours instead of two."

"And it's bumpier."

"But not as bad as some places I've been to, right Rover?" He patted his big green truck on the hood. "This old beast and I have been in some wild places."

"Let's locate Sam and find out how bad the next stretch into ArcPoint will be."

Victor opened the door to the office and held it for Jonathan, then followed him in. He saw Sam get up from his seat and introduced his new friend. "We made it. Sam Boardman, I'd like you to meet Jonathan Greywolf, a great man with a miner story to tell."

Sam laughed. "Ranger Dan told me about you. You can call me Sambo."

"That will be easy to remember," said Jonathan. "I had a dog named Sambo." He tipped his head as he stared at him and said, "You are fortunate. No resemblance."

Victor laughed again. "So, Sambo, how far did you get building the road?"

"We were able to push it all the way through the sticker bushes. The road's a mess, so we may need to clean it up a bit for you. What are you driving?"

"Jonathan's Earth Rover. It's been beefed up to handle just about anything you can throw at it."

"Then you could probably go in there now if you'd like."

Victor looked at Jonathan and could see the fatigue on his face. "I think we'll plan to spend the night here and go in after breakfast in the morning."

"That'll work great because we haven't taken the little trackhoe in yet. We'll deliver that as close as we can get with the trailer, then one of you will need to drive it the rest of the way in. That way, if there's an obstacle the Rover can't handle, the trackhoe can deal with it."

"Does that sound okay with you, Jonathan?" asked Victor.

"As long as I get to drive the trackhoe," he replied.

Sam scratched his head, considering. "Do you know how?"

"What did you think I mined with? A pick and shovel?"

"How long has it been since you used one?"

"How long has it been since you rode a bicycle?"

"Well, it's not a bike, and it's not a big trackhoe either," said Sam. "It's at most five-ton, with a blade and a bucket, and has a claw attachment you can remove. Once we drop it off, it'll take whoever drives it two or three hours to get it in there. And the road we built is narrow, so the hoe will have to go in first. If anything stops the Rover, there won't be room to get the hoe past it."

"I wish I could've been here when they pushed the other machine through the needle-brush," said Victor. "What kind of reception did you get?"

"The driver told me there were probably two hundred people cheering him on. They were all yelling, 'hack them back, hack them back.' He said he got the impression they didn't like those sticker bushes very much. He was tempted to keep smashing them down, but we know their people want to do that. Are you going to let them know you're coming?"

Victor looked at Jonathan, who just shook his head. "No, I think we'll surprise them," said Victor. "I'll let Jonathan lead the way, and we'll drive right up to the main building. We'll be the first outsiders to do that in a hundred and thirty years." Victor shoved his hand into the pocket of his blue jeans. Looking pleased, he said, "Did you know his father visited that place way back then? He may have been one of the last outsiders to do that. How appropriate is it for Jonathan to be the first outsider to come back?"

"Did you say your *father* was there?" asked Sam. "When was that?"

"It was years before our Lord returned. I don't know what year exactly, but I have pictures. Would you like to see them?"

"You bet I would. That place must've looked a lot different."

"Sure did," said Victor. "No sticker bushes and no big trees."

"Can't wait to see it. By the way, I have bunks ready for you. Victor, you know where the bunkhouse is, right?"

"Yep."

"Dinner is being served in the mess hall. Breakfast starts at six in the morning, and food is available until nine. We'll be ready to haul the trackhoe down there by eight. I'm sure you'll want to tag along. I'll let you get set up in your bunks, and then you have to let me see those pictures."

"How about if we meet you in the lounge in an hour?" asked Victor.

"I'll be there," said Sam.

CHAPTER TWENTY-FIVE

Victor watched as the machine slowly made its way through the forest of ArcPoint trees. The clackety-clack of the tracks had been going on for nearly four hours. Victor stopped frequently for Jonathan to move big rocks, small saplings, and lumps of crumpled briers away from the path in front of his truck. Most of it should have been left for ArcPoint workers to deal with, but Jonathan was enjoying himself.

He heard a hiss from his shoulder phone and then Sam's voice saying, "You should be getting close. Could you point the camera forward again?"

"Okay," said Victor, as he pivoted the camera on the dash of the truck. "Sorry, this truck keeps shaking it loose. I'm afraid to tighten it down any harder."

"That's okay," said Sam. "Wait! Look ahead. Is that someone coming toward you on the road?"

Victor looked past the trackhoe and could see someone watching from a distance. "It looks like a little kid. I'll try to zoom in on him." Victor stopped the truck and watched on his monitor as he zoomed the camera. "Yes, it's a young boy. We must be getting close enough for them to hear us."

"Looks like he's running away," said Sam. "I bet you'll have a crowd coming down the road in a few minutes."

"I agree," said Victor. "I'll warn Jonathan to keep an eye out for them."

Victor jumped out of the truck and jogged toward the trackhoe. Just as he was approaching it, the cab swung around in his direction, startling him and its driver. Victor jumped back and heard the engine speed drop to an idle.

"Must you scare an old man so?" asked Jonathan.

"Sorry," said Victor. "I just saw someone down the road. I think he ran to tell people we're coming. Keep an eye open for them. As soon as we get to the clearing, I'll pass you and drive to the Facility. Then you can follow *me* for a change."

Jonathan slowly pivoted the cab and surveyed the distance. "The view looks brighter ahead. I believe we'll come to the clearing soon."

"Good, I agree. Remember, you don't have to clear the path perfectly. If the truck can get over the debris, just leave it."

"I think Rover can handle it all. I'll just drive over it and wait for you. If you get stuck, I'll come back and help."

"That works for me. I'll do my best not to hurt Rover."

Victor ran back and hopped in the truck, making sure the camera was situated correctly. Noreena Chan was upset that the first trackhoe operator hadn't gotten footage of the crowd when he entered ArcPoint last time. She told Victor to make sure he got plenty of video of the crowd as soon as they showed up.

"Sambo, are the cameras on the trackhoe still working?"

"Yes, both front and rear cameras are working great, so is the one watching Jonathan. The one on the cab just swung around and is facing down the road."

"Good. Jonathan plans to stay that direction unless I need him, which I don't think I will. Is the one on top of the truck still good?"

"It's looking good. I think you'd better catch up to Jonathan. I see movement through the trees ahead."

Victor put the truck in gear and drove toward the trackhoe, which was now making pretty good time down the road. As he got close, he could see the young boy had several men with him now. He thought he recognized one of the mechanics from the shop and waved to him but got no response. He grabbed the camera off the dash and zoomed in on their faces. The crowd was slowly growing, but keeping their distance. After a few minutes, he stopped the truck and got out so they could see him. He waved to Dietrich, the mechanic, and yelled, "Hey, Ditto! Where's the party?"

"Wherever you are!" Dietrich yelled back.

Victor saw the clearing coming and moved closer so he could pass the trackhoe. When he was alongside it, he yelled to Jonathan, "Follow me!" As he got close to Dietrich, he leaned out the window and said, "Get in." Victor had to chuckle as he tried to figure out how to open the passenger side door. He reached across, opened it for him, and said, "Show me the best path to get to the main Facility." Dietrich hopped in, and Victor waited a moment, then said, "Close the door."

"Oh, right." Dietrich pulled on the door.

"Try again, a little harder this time. Just pull up on that handle. Right—" The truck door slammed shut with a WHAM! "Oh! Not that hard." Victor automatically cringed but gave him a thumbs up and said, "That's okay."

Victor took his time driving as Dietrich showed him where to go. He made sure Jonathan and the ever-growing throng could keep up with him. He panned the crowd with the camera and zoomed in on a few faces. *This should satisfy Noreena.*

From the entryway of her home, Brina noticed Jonathan Greywolf walking her grandpa through the new photo album at the dining room table. Victor emerged from the kitchen and joined her. "I've never seen Grandpa so happy," she said. "Where did you find Mr. Greywolf?""He's a close friend of Ranger Dan Wilson," said Victor. "They brought him in as a mineral expert to help solve the, uhh, infertility problem."

"Oh—sounds interesting! What's that about?"

"Well, when they found heavy metals and rare earths in Arcon's blood tests, they were struggling to figure out how he got them in his system. Jonathan was a miner and knew this area had those things in the ground. Anyway, with his help, they figured it out. Those minerals are highly sought after now. Jonathan is working with some other people to try to extract them from those sticker bushes."

"He's the one that's doing that?"

"He's part of the team."

Brina took a step toward the table. "Let's go closer, I want to hear what they're saying." They stood behind the two centenarians for an over-the-shoulder view of the photo album.

When she rested her hand on her grandfather's shoulder, Lars said, "Brina, honey, have you seen these?"

"Only a few of them, then I ran to get you."

"Look how small the trees in the grove are in this one. That's Jonathan's father, Sundown, when he was just a boy. Guess who the man is standing with him."

"I can't even guess," said Brina. She glanced over at Victor and he shrugged as if to say, don't ask me. She snickered.

"That's my father," said Lars.

"Oh, my Great-grandpa Norm!" Brina leaned in to get a better look. "Are there any more of him with his trees?"

"No, because he was always the one who took the pictures. Jonathan says his grandfather took this picture for them."

"Did you say, Sundown? That's creative," said Brina.

"My father didn't get that name till he was eleven years old when the earthquakes were happening—and the Rift was forming," said Jonathan. "His parents had a gold mine near here before the area was restricted. They got trapped here just like your people did. They believed the sun was setting on all their hopes, so they named him Sundown. Before that, they called him Ashkii, which meant 'boy' in their native language."

"That's kind of a sad story," said Brina.

"Not really. After coming to this place, God restored their fortune. The name reminded them of how much their lives got turned around. Now Brina—that's a creative name."

"Only a little," said Lars, "she was named after my mother, Sabrina, my father's second wife."

"Somewhere in here there's a picture of Norm standing next to a woman," said Jonathan, "maybe it's her."

"Grandpa, let's find it," said Brina, reaching past him to turn pages.

"It will probably be Christine. She was his first wife. We have some pictures of her in the Room of Remembrance. There are only a few of Sabrina when she was very young, back when they first moved to this place. She was an Organic Chemist at the time. Wait—" Lars tapped the page with his index finger. "Right there. That's Sabrina standing with little Lee and Victoria inside the Facility building."

"The Franklins?" asked Brina, "They sure look young."

"Sure do. And look, it still had a gravel floor at that time." He turned the page. "Okay, here's my dad and Christine from when they were building the hydroponics greenhouse. Jonathan, is that young boy with them your father?"

Jonathan adjusted his glasses. "I believe it is. I can't make out his face, but he looks Navajo." Victor nodded.

"Father took a lot of pictures around that time, but they were all for a computer," said Brina. "He never got any paper copies made."

Lars patted Brina's hand. "Now *that* is sad, isn't it. Jonathan, thank you for bringing these to us. Can we borrow this book for a while?"

"That entire album will stay here at ArcPoint. I have my own copy. The next time I come by, I'll bring another just for your family. My father highly respected your father."

"Thank you," said Lars, as he wiped away a tear. "Are you staying for a while?"

"If I am allowed to," said Jonathan.

"What do you mean?"

"If I find a bed here, I will stay. But in one week, my garden will call me home."

Brina grinned. "Our family understands that completely."

"And our home has a spare bed," added Lars, "please make use of it."

Jonathan smiled at Victor, remembering a conversation they'd had about ArcPoint customs. He looked at Lars and said resolutely, "I accept your terms."

Ranger Dan stretched as the other three crawled out of the tube train pod. "I guess this is where we part company for a while," he said. "But before you go, I want you to meet my wife. She should be waiting in the observation room."

"I'm surprised you didn't bring her with you on this trip," said Roberto.

"I sure wanted to, but it just didn't work out." As he said that, he got an alert tone on the phone in his pocket.

"Is that your wife?" asked Elaina.

"No, that's the tone for Sambo. Wonder what he wants? Let's go up and see Meredith; then I'll contact him."

When they got to the observation room, they found Meredith staring out a window at the beautiful view of Mount Hood. "I'm not nearly as attractive," said Dan as he approached, "But I hug better."

Meredith spun around, then wrapped her arms around him. "I bet you're tired."

"We all are," said Dan. "Meredith, I'd like you to meet my traveling companions. You've heard me talk a lot about Roberto and Elaina."

"I sure have. It's nice to put faces to names." She shook Roberto's hand. "You can call me Mery. Dan does—usually." When she turned to Elaina, she got a big hug.

"And this here is the renegade that brought us all together. Be careful. He's a dangerous hugger."

"Hi, Arcon," she said with a big smile. Then she threw her arms wide and said, "Give me all you've got."

Arcon hesitated until Dan nodded at him, then wrapped his arms around Meredith and lifted her off her feet. "Glad to finally meet you, Mery."

When he set her down, she looked at Dan and said, "Naahh, Patty still has him beat."

As they all laughed, Mery said, "Welcome to Portland, Oregon. Sorry, I have to steal him from you, but my sister wants to see him."

"No problem," said Roberto.

"Yeah," agreed Elaina. "We've seen far too much of him lately, anyway."

"Speaking of visiting," said Dan. "Could you four do that for a few minutes? I should find out what Sambo wants. I hope it doesn't change my plans."

"It better not," said Meredith.

Dan walked away from them to some empty chairs and sat down. He pulled out his shoulder phone, tapped in a number, and then stuck it on his shoulder. Pretty soon, he heard a voice say, "Hello, Sam here."

"Hi, Sam here. What's up?"

"Funny. Not. I wanted to let you know we pushed the road all the way into the ArcPoint Community. Victor and Jonathan Greywolf drove a small trackhoe in there for the locals to use."

"That's fantastic!" *I'm impressed. Sam really made it happen.* "They're in there already?"

"That's affirmative. It was great. Mr. Greywolf drove the trackhoe, and Victor followed in a tricked-out Earth Rover."

"I know which one you mean. It belongs to Jonathan."

"I believe so. Anyway, they were able to get a bunch of film footage for the documentary. The villagers are pretty excited."

"That's great," said Dan. "I'll bet you two doughnuts that it's Jonathan that teaches the ArcPoint people how to run the trackhoe and not Victor."

"That's if he lets them run it at all. That old guy was in his element, that's for sure."

"Well, great. It does my heart good to make Jonathan happy. Thanks for the news. Do you need me down there at all?"

"No, take your time. I just wondered if there was anything special you wanted me to do, now that someone can drive all the way into that place."

"Good point. Can you put up some temporary barricades, maybe in front of the span? I doubt we'll need them, but if it's not much trouble, it might give us peace of mind."

"I know just the thing," said Sam. "Don't worry; I'll take care of it. How soon before I see you again?"

"I'd say about a week. Arcon may get there sooner. I don't know about the other two. I'll tell them to think it over and contact you. Okay?"

"Perfect," said Sam. "Have a nice rest of the trip."

"Thanks. Dan out."

CHAPTER TWENTY-SIX

Brina stopped to marvel at the new utility building. Victor had made quite a few changes to his original design. She could see him on the roof, showing Dietrich how to install the metal roofing. "Hey, Ditto," she yelled, getting their attention. "Shouldn't you be running that digging machine?"

Dietrich looked down and waved her away. "Naahh, I already had my turn today," he yelled back. "Shouldn't you be helping your grandpa?"

She stepped closer and said, "He doesn't need my help anymore. Him and Mr. Greywolf are getting around just fine. I thought I'd come up here and make sure Victor's getting this building done."

Dietrich smiled at Victor and said softly, "Go ahead and show her what we've got done. I can handle this."

"Are you sure?" asked Victor, wiping his brow with his sleeve.

Dietrich grabbed another piece of roofing. "You better hurry before I get down and show Brina myself."

"Okay, thanks," said Victor. He yelled, "Wait a second. I'll come down and show you what we've got done."

"I'm waiting," replied Brina. She had to smile at the conversation, since they hadn't talked soft enough to hide it from her. She was used to boys acting strange around her, and it often made her uncomfortable. But with Victor, it was different. Maybe because he was an outsider.

As Victor climbed down and got off the ladder, Brina said, "I like the new look."

"Yeah, me too," said Victor. "It looks rustic ArcPoint now, instead of flashy outsider. The boys did a great job making natural siding with the portable saw mill we brought in."

"I didn't know there were machines that could slice the logs like that."

"Well, it helps that the trackhoe can set the logs on it. What I think is impressive is the grain of the wood. That Arcacia wood looks so nice, I don't think I'll paint it."

Brina wandered to the doorway. "I see the lumber you brought was used in here."

"Yeah, for the walls. But when it's done, you won't see them." Victor pointed to the opposite end of the room. "The generators and pumps will be in there, and this'll be the shop where we work on the tractor. I put some extra roof supports here in the middle, where I plan to hang a hoist so we can lift the heavy pieces into place, like the new generator or the tractor engine. There'll be a beam running the full length of the building, so we can pick the stuff off the trailer and move it wherever we need it."

"It looks bigger now with some walls up."

"It'll start feeling smaller as I add things. I want to put a workbench over here, and in that corner, I'm going to build a small paint booth."

"You're going to paint the tractor too?"

"They gave me permission to completely restore it, so when I'm done, it'll be shiny and new. If you remind me, I'll show you a picture of what it looked like over two hundred years ago."

Brina smiled and quickly asked, "If you're not busy, why don't you have dinner with us tonight? Then you can bring the picture and show the whole family."

"I'll do that," said Victor.

Brina turned her head and said, "What's that noise?"

"Sounds like Jonathan's truck." Victor looked out the door and added, "It is. He's coming this way, and I think he has your grandpa with him."

Brina stepped outside with Victor and watched as the old truck turned and drove across the open ground right up to them and stopped. When the doors opened, she went around to help her grandpa get out of his seat. Jonathan slid out and greeted Victor. "What are you two up to?" Brina asked her grandpa.

"We were headed to hydro when we saw you two, so we stopped to see how this building was going. Looks like it's coming right along."

"We're trying to get the roof on quick since it might rain tomorrow. But the next day, it should be sunny, and we'll bring in the generator and all the electrical stuff."

"None too soon," said Jonathan. "Lars showed me the old generator this morning. It sounds terrible."

"Well, if all goes right, we can shut it down soon."

"As long as we're here, we wanted to tell you something," said Jonathan. "Monday, I'm going to take Lars for a ride."

Brina smiled. "He's going for a ride now."

"I mean a real ride," said Jonathan. He looked at Victor. "I'm taking him to the ghost town of Baker, and we'll have lunch at Base Camp."

"Really?" asked Victor. "Does Sambo know?"

"Oh yeah, he's excited about it. He said they may have a barricade up, but he'll have it open for us."

Brina put her hands on Lars' shoulders and looked him in the eyes. "Now, Grandpa. I thought you said you'd never leave this place."

"I'm not," he said to her. "Jonathan says Baker is inside the Restricted Area, so technically, it's still part of ArcPoint. It's just past the needle-brush, that's all."

"Sounds like fun," said Victor. "You'll get to see which buildings survived the earthquakes, such as the fire station we set up operations in."

"He wants to see the palm trees," said Jonathan.

"Anything besides Acacias and needle-brush," mumbled Lars.

"Tell Sambo to give you a sneak peek at some of the video footage we've put together. You'll get to see all the trouble we went to trying to get into this place."

Meredith was happy to once again be in their normal late-night routine, even though they weren't in their own home yet. Dan was as far over on her side of the bed as he could get, helping to warm it up for her. She was lying tight against him, head on his chest, soaking up the heat generated by his recently consumed bowl of ice cream. He had his head propped up on the headboard, making sure he didn't fall asleep before she did. On a normal night, she'd be out within minutes, but not tonight.

"Are you still awake?" he asked her softly.

"Wide," she answered back. "Are you thinking about ArcPoint?"

"It's kind of hard not to. As anxious as I am to get back to our own bed and my favorite recliner, I may be more excited to get back to work. I mean, no offense, this is a comfortable bed your sister has. But a lot has been happening, and I'm eager to get it all sorted out."

"Speaking of sorting things out, did you talk with the authorities about moving to the Baker area?"

"Hon, that's a wide-open door. It's been a part of the Restricted Area for so long, no one has claim to any part of it—not even the land. They said we could do whatever we wanted there. As far as wisdom, they suggested we use it as a stopping point before people enter ArcPoint."

"That's exactly what we were thinking."

"Honestly, they came up with that idea on their own. I never said a thing. To me, that's one more indicator the Holy Spirit is guiding all that's taking place."

Meredith could feel herself getting comfortable and her mind drifting. But she wasn't ready to fall asleep yet. Rolling over on her back, she said, "Do you think we should look into it? You've been there, but I haven't even seen pictures of it yet. The archived photos on SearchNet make it look like a wasteland."

"That's the way the entire area was over a hundred years ago. It was just a rocky desert when the ArcPoint people got there. It's amazing the change that a hundred years of rain will bring. But I won't sugarcoat it. It'll be more work than we've faced for years."

"It sounds like we should go there and look it over carefully—and do it together."

"We always have the option of simply incorporating it into part of a Ranger Station, as sort of an attached residence. Then it would just be a home away from home, and we could have the Park system build and maintain it."

There was something in the way Dan spoke that wasn't convincing. "That's not what you'd prefer to do, is it?"

Dan was quiet for a moment. Then he said, "You're going to laugh."

"About what?"

"I want to get my girlish figure back."

Mery smirked, but she couldn't help it. She burst out laughing, and so did he. "How do you expect to do that?"

"Well, I have two options. If you remember, I used to be like Arcon, tall and lean. But that was when I was roping steers and hoisting heavy garbage cans in the parks. And then Patty and I got that Survival camp, and we worked long days and every weekend to fix it up. We both worked hard and ate a lot. Then I got this job, and we finished the Camp. Patty and I have it easy. We've basically stopped working but never stopped eating. Now, look at us."

"I could beef up my honey-do chore list if that'd help."

Dan chuckled. "I either need to start working again, or I need to eat less. Neither one sound like any fun. I think I'd like to get a place near Baker and work to fix it up. Maybe Patty would like to join me, just like old times. I know it'd be a lot of work, but I kind of miss it."

"And you certainly don't want to eat less," she said, smiling at him.

"Believe it or not, I've thought about eating wiser. But I'm already eating less than I used to, and my weight just stays the same. I need more activity. But hon, that means I either take you with me and put you to work or leave you at home till it's done. I don't like the thought of either one of those choices."

"You're forgetting something. I'm a really great supervisor. All I need is a lounge chair and a good supply of ice tea." She laughed. "Actually, whenever my sister asks for help with her remodeling, I jump at the chance. I enjoy it, but I'd much rather work with you for a change."

Dan put his arm around her and pulled her close. "Sounds like I'm about to become less of a man," he said as he kissed her on top of the head.

"Perhaps, but you'll never be girlish."

CHAPTER TWENTY-SEVEN

They'd been back home from their round-the-world trip for three days, but Elaina still hadn't finished the laundry. With her dad called away to work, Arcon not much help, and bedsheets that hadn't been changed for weeks, she still had two more loads to do. Now her shoulder phone was ringing with a tone she didn't recognize. She said, "Identify," and a mechanical voice replied, [WILSON, MEREDITH]. She accepted the call, saying, "Okay," and added, "How are you, Meredith?"

"She's fine, last time I checked," answered Ranger Dan in his deep voice. "I'm still at home, so I'm using her phone. I'd like to talk to Arcon if I could."

"Uhh, sure, he's right here."

"It's okay if you put the phone on speaker. I can talk to you both."

"Sure, just a second." Elaina pulled the phone off her shoulder and tapped the volume button. Then she held it out and said, "Arcon, this is Ranger Dan. He needs to talk to us."

"I'm here," yelled Arcon, as he dumped an armload of clothes on the counter.

"Hi, Arcon," said Dan. "I've been thinking about a few things regarding your people. You know, if you and I are going to work together, we're going to have to start sometime. Are you available for the next few days?"

"I'm not doing anything. Roberto is at work trying to catch up on things. Elaina is doing laundry, and we did some shopping. But I can only help do what they tell me to. Do *you* need me for something?"

"As a matter of fact, I do. Things are coming together quicker than we thought they would, and you and I need to make some decisions. I was wondering if you could meet me at Base Camp in Baker."

"I'd be glad to, but I'd need to talk to Elaina. I don't know how I'd get there unless she drove."

"Don't worry about that," said Dan, "I can get you there, provided you travel on a Monday or Thursday. I know it's short notice, but tomorrow is Monday. It'd work well if you could do it then."

"Wow, that's fast, but okay."

"So, what's the plan?" asked Elaina.

"If you can get Arcon booked on the tube trains to arrive in Las Vegas by nine in the morning, he could hitch a ride with Sambo to base camp from there."

"I'd have to check the route," said Elaina.

"I already did," said Dan. "It's simple. Get him on the 15 by seven o'clock and schedule a transfer to the Sunset. He shouldn't need to switch pods to do that, but he'll need to get off in Yuma and take the 95 Connector to Las Vegas. That's it. Easy enough, right?"

"It sounds easy," said Elaina. "I'll double-check it myself, so I can show him, but he's a worldwide tube train traveler now. How many days should we pack for?"

"Well, *he* can pack for a week. I didn't plan on you coming. I thought you and your dad might have things you need to get squared away there."

"Well, we do, actually. If you don't need me, I should probably stay and help him."

"Try and make tomorrow work if you can? Sam won't be coming through again till Thursday, and I'd rather not wait that long. Meredith and I plan to leave early for base camp tomorrow morning, but we're driving all the way, so we won't get in there until about two in the afternoon. Arcon will beat us there if he takes the tube train. Anyway, I'll let you two talk it over."

Elaina looked at Arcon, who nodded his head. "No need, let's just do it."

"Great. I'll talk to Sambo right now and let him know to pick you up at the terminal, Arcon. You'll need to ping him when you're ready to get on the connector in Yuma. I just sent his contact info to your PID. If anything changes, let me know. Otherwise, we'll see you tomorrow."

"I'm looking forward to it," said Arcon.

There was silence over the speaker for a moment, then Dan asked, "Don't you agree to my terms?"

Elaina laughed, but Arcon was expressionless as he said, "Well, of course."

Victor thought he heard something, so he stopped the saw. When he heard the tone, he yelled, "Answer," then ran across the room where his shoulder phone was lying on a windowsill. "Hi, this is Victor."

"Hi, Victor. This is Ranger Dan. What are you up to?"

"We just finished the roof on the utility building yesterday, so I'm back working inside. How was your trip?"

"The middle part was fun. The tube train was a snooze. Now I'm back trying to get in the swing of things. Would you be available tomorrow for a meeting in Baker? Sambo wants to talk about the road project, and I'd like you there."

"Me? I didn't think I'd have much to do with the road."

"Maybe not, but you said you were planning to move to ArcPoint, correct?"

"Yeah, for at least a few months."

"Then you can be a big help to me while you're there. Roberto is still undecided about whether or not he'll move. Elaina will eventually because of Arcon, but when that'll happen, she's not sure. Anyway, I need someone from our side that I can work with, and you've been doing a good job so far. If you can, I'd like to have the meeting about three in the afternoon tomorrow. Do you think you can make it?"

"Who else will be there?"

"Arcon will arrive around eleven with Sambo, and I'll have my wife with me. Other than that, it's just the five of us. Think you could get Jarden to come with you?"

"I bet I could. I'll ask and see what he says. Do you need to know, or should I just show up with him?"

"Just bring him if you can. I understand he's a busy man."

"Understood. I may show up early if Arcon's going to be there."

"He'd like that. Well, see you tomorrow."

Victor walked into the dining area of the Facility and saw Jarden having lunch with Jonathan and Lars. He walked into the kitchen and made himself a rabbit meat sandwich, grabbed a glass of goat's milk, and went out to join them.

"Do you mind the company of a young mechanic?"

"I thought you were a carpenter today," said Jarden.

"I guess you're right," he said as he sat down. "You're just the people I needed to talk to. If I remember right, you two are taking a drive to Base Camp tomorrow."

"What are you boys doing?" asked Jarden.

Jonathan responded, "I'm taking Lars out to the Baker ghost town to see the palm trees. He's only seen them in books."

"I've never seen them either. Can I go along?"

Victor chimed in and said, "That's what I wanted to talk with you about, Jarden. Ranger Dan is having a meeting at Base Camp with Arcon and Sambo. They need to talk about the road construction. Dan wanted to know if you could join them in the discussion."

"Come along with us," said Lars. "Jonathan said he's going to buy us lunch."

"I have a better idea," said Jonathan. "We should all sit in on the meeting, and Ranger Dan can buy us lunch."

Victor liked the sounds of that. "I think I have a plan. Arcon is getting there around eleven, so we can go early enough to see him and have lunch. Dan and his wife won't show up until around two."

"Meredith will be there too?" asked Jonathan.

"That's what he said."

"You boys will like Meredith. She's a sweetie. By the way, she likes to be called Mery."

"Anyway, I know where the meeting will be. Dan will expect me to drive in with Jonathan's truck. How about if Jarden and I hide in another room, and you and Lars drive in with the truck? He won't be expecting that. What do you say?"

"I know what he'd expect even less," said Jarden.

"What would that be?"

"Lars driving."

CHAPTER TWENTY-EIGHT

"I see some buildings up ahead," said Meredith.

"Yep, that'd be what's left of the town of Baker." Dan checked the clock on the dash of his Ranger vehicle. "Wow, it's two-thirty already. It took longer than I thought. But I still have time to show you a couple of things before the meeting."

"It looks like some of these buildings are still in good shape," she said, as they passed an abandoned gas station.

"Some of them we've fixed up, but yeah, for being over a hundred years old, they're mostly intact." He slowed down and pointed. "The old fire station here on the right is where we'll be meeting."

"That's Base Camp?"

"Right. It was just what we needed, and had a big clearing behind it where we could land the helicopters. It was well preserved, but so are most of the buildings. The people had to leave this town fast, and there was no one left to rip it up. They boarded up most of the buildings expecting to come back someday, but never did."

"It certainly isn't a desert wasteland like a lot of the archived pictures show."

Dan turned a corner and headed down another street. "All of the things they planted kind of took over when the rains came. Okay, see this bunch of buildings on the right? They were schools and public buildings back when this was a town." Dan looked down each street as he passed it. "I don't see Jonathan's truck. Maybe Victor and Arcon are driving around."

Meredith spotted a building that looked new. "What was that little white building?"

"The one we just passed? That was a church at one time."

"A church? I thought they were big stone buildings."

"Wouldn't have been enough people for something like that out here."

Meredith looked back at the snow-white building with its tall spire on the roof. "Did you guys paint it?"

"Yeah, we felt sorry for it. You can see it in the archived photos, and, well, since they built it to honor God, we just had to clean it up. I have some ideas about what to use the building for that I'll discuss later." Dan slowed down again. "Now, here on the left is an airport."

"An actual airport?"

"Well, it'll take some work before airplanes can use it, but it could come in handy." He made a U-turn and said, "We should probably get back to Base Camp and find Sambo."

Sam Boardman watched out the window as Ranger Dan and his wife drove in and found a parking spot in front of the big garage bay doors. "They're here," he yelled to Victor and Arcon.

"I'll run tell the guys," said Victor, as he made a bee-line for the back door.

As Arcon found a place to hide, Sam walked toward the door, wanting to keep Dan and Meredith outside. As he opened it, he said, "Hey, I wondered if you were going to make it."

"Traffic was worse than I thought it'd be. Were you able to connect with Arcon?"

"I never heard from him. Thought maybe he'd changed his mind."

"Nooo. You're kidding me, right?"

"No. Last I heard, he was supposed to get a message to me, hopefully before eight. I waited until just after nine, but I needed to get going. We don't really need him anyway, do we?"

"Well ... no, but ... what about Victor? Has he shown up yet in Jonathan's truck?"

"No, but he's still planning to come for the meeting. I talked to him earlier and told him Arcon was a no-show, so he said he'd wait. Should be here any minute."

Just then, they heard a loud motor coming down the street. "That sounds like Jonathan's old truck," said Dan. "It's probably Victor. Hopefully, he's bringing Jarden."

"He didn't mention Jarden."

"Yeah, that's Rover, all right. And it looks like there's someone else with him." As it got closer, Dan added, "Wait, it looks like three people in that truck."

As it pulled into the parking area, he could finally see inside the cab. "What? Victor's not even in the truck. Mery, look. That's Jonathan driving the truck, and he has Jarden and Lars with him. Where's Victor?"

"Right behind you," said Arcon, with Victor at his side.

"Gotcha again," said Victor.

"Well, I'll be," said Dan. "And I thought everyone abandoned me." Then he looked at the three men crawling out of the old truck and said, "Isn't that just the way it goes?"

"What do you mean?" asked Sam.

"I bring in a pretty woman, and old geezers show up by the truckload."

They all laughed as Meredith walked over and gave Jonathan a hug. He looked across the hood at Lars. "Sorry, age before beauty."

"I'm older than *you*," said Lars. "One hundred twenty in two months."

"Yup, you're right," said Jonathan. "Got eleven on me. Oh well, I may not have the age, but I got the beauty."

Meredith blushed as she looked at Lars and said, "Sorry. Jonathan and I are old friends. I don't know you. Can you be trusted?"

"Don't know," said Lars. "Haven't been tested in years, except by family."

Meredith asked, "Dan, are you going to introduce these handsome men or not?"

"Right, sorry. That's Lars Ashford. He's Brina's grandfather and son of the famous Dr. Norman Ashford. And the young guy here is just plain old Jarden Merrick."

"I'm older than you are," said Jarden. "I'll be eighty in four more months."

"Got me by fifty…well, maybe closer to thirty. Anyway, let's go in, find us something to drink, and find out what's happening with the road—after you three finish flirting with my wife, that is."

After they got themselves various soft drinks—the only thing to drink in the refrigerator—they sat down at a large table in the mess hall. "So, Sambo," boomed Ranger Dan, "what have we got going here?"

"We've finished the first major hurdle—access into ArcPoint. We obviously have a lot of work to do to bring it up to road-worthy standards. And since I've had to drive the highway in from Vegas twice a week, I've gotten to know its ups and downs, literally."

"Is it worse than you thought?" asked Dan.

"That's not the real question," replied Sam. "The real question is, what's it worth to you and to ArcPoint? I mean, I'll build anything you want me to. But I've done some calculating. You know how the desert soil buried a lot of the original roadway? Then the rains came and allowed things to grow on top of that? We need to unbury all the original pavement, and we need to repair what the earthquakes destroyed."

"Yeah, I see your point," said Dan, recalling how little pavement was still showing. "Do you have a cost on all that?"

"Let's just say I came up with a cheaper alternative, in the long run anyway."

"What would that be? And don't tell me you want to revive the airport."

"Hmmm, hadn't thought of that," pondered Sam. "No, I was thinking of a connector tube train from Las Vegas."

Dan's eyes got big. "That'd be cheaper?"

"In the long run, yes. It's hard for me to confess because I'll be losing a lot of business. We don't build the tube trains. But honestly, by the time we fix the road the way it needs to be for safe travel, we'll have spent 80% of the cost of a connector. After that, there'll be more expense to maintain the road."

"Sounds like a toss-up so far."

"It won't be a toss-up for guests. If someone wants to visit here, they'll take the tube train to Vegas. Then what? They won't have their own vehicle, so that means they requisition one or take a driverless taxi. Do you want either of those driving into Baker? It'd make more sense to let them hop on a connector and get dropped off here. They won't need a vehicle, anyway. People could come here on the tube train from anywhere in the world and never have to drive. It'd be so much easier."

Dan squinted his eyes and said, "I see what you're saying. I just didn't think the authorities would go for a connector just for ArcPoint."

"Whether it's a road or a train, the Transportation Authority will have to approve it, because it'll have to be subsidized. Part of the wisdom in the decision regards future use. Will the Mojave area be developed and require more roads? Or will it remain a tourist destination for a few guests?"

Ranger Dan was nervous about carrying on this conversation in front of Jarden and Lars. "I'll tell you what I think," he finally said. "Then I'd like to get some thoughts from the ArcPoint boys."

"Before you do," interrupted Sam, "I've been talking with Arcon and Victor about an alternative plan, and they like it."

"Sure, go ahead."

"First, we run a Connector from Las Vegas to here at Baker."

Arcon turned to Jarden and Lars. "I've ridden in one of these. They're a small little cylinder that holds two people and travels very fast. How long would it take to get here from Las Vegas, Sam?"

"About twenty minutes," he said. "Anyway, the trip would be non-stop, with no connection except at each end. That'd make it cost far less to construct. It would travel down the median of the current I-15 freeway, buried so there would be no outside interference. Once it got past the barricade at Highway164, it would stay on top of the ground, further reducing construction costs. By this point, we'd no longer be competitive trying to rebuild the highway."

"But the highway would stay the mess it is?" asked Dan.

"Correct. No more work other than to keep it drivable for off-road vehicles. The current barricade at highway 164 would stay there. The Mojave Restricted area would be accessible to guests only. Plus, Worldwide Transportation would maintain the tube train."

"Hmmm. I like it," said Dan. "Jarden, do you understand what we're talking about?"

"Not completely. What does it all mean to the ArcPoint Community?"

"What I was originally thinking was to rebuild the old freeway all the way to this town. Then guests visiting ArcPoint would drive here, check-in, and be approved before they could enter your area. Problem is, anyone with a vehicle could drive in here. Right now, they are stopped at a barrier sixty kilometers away. With this arrangement—with the tube train—we could approve guests before they ever left home and they could come straight to this town—from anywhere in the world. I just assumed the freeway would be easier to make work, but I see Sambo's point. This'd be better for the guests and keep vehicles out of the Restricted Area as well." Dan looked at Meredith. "Now that I think about it, it'd be better for us, too. By tube train, it'd probably only take an hour or two to get here from where we live."

Jarden looked at Lars and asked, "What do you think?"

Lars shook his head. "I've never understood why people would want to come visit us, anyway. But if they are, the tube thing sounds like it'd be easier to control."

"Okay then," said Ranger Dan, rapping his knuckles once on the table like a judge. "As the authority in this area, I'll approach the Transportation Authorities with this new idea. We can't move forward until they approve something, anyway. At least we can get into ArcPoint now with supplies without using a helicopter. If no one objects, I'll adjourn this meeting."

"What about the church?" asked Meredith.

"Oh, right. A few blocks from here is a white church building that we fixed up a bit. I thought it'd be a suitable location for a visitor's center, where we check in guests. It has room for parking, but if we do the tube train thing, we won't need that. Okay, something else to think about. Oh, and a location for a tube train terminal. Arcon, you can help me with that."

"So," said Sambo, "should I work on a formal proposal for you to submit?"

"Will it take long?" asked Dan.

"I'll have it done when I come back on Thursday."

"Great. I plan to be here until then, and we'll go from there. I think we're done. Thanks, everyone. Meeting adjourned."

As they got up from the table, Jonathan asked Dan, "Did you say you'll be here for a few days?"

"Right. Mery and I are thinking we may want to move, and we wanted to see what was available around here for a homesite."

"Are you looking in town?"

"No, we'd like some land. This area is wide open, and it doesn't look like many people will move in here soon. I might want to have a horse or two."

"When my father would come to Baker with his dad, they'd visit a friend who had a ranch near here. I met that man many times, but not until after he'd abandoned the place. He pointed it out once on a map. I think I could find it again. It had a good well and a pond for his cattle and horses."

"We'll have to find an old map and look for it."

"Wait a minute," said Jonathan, as his mind recalled something. "Follow me."

He walked outside and looked around. "I think it's in those hills right there."

"You think so?" asked Dan.

"I remember it was west of town. Not much town here to be west of. I say we take Rover out there tomorrow morning and see if we can find it."

"Sounds like fun," said Dan.

CHAPTER TWENTY-NINE

"I hope that was the hard part," said Arcon, as he sat down to rest on a stool next to the tractor. "Sure glad we waited till after lunch to push this tractor up the hill. I was worn out after spending all morning pushing it here from the Griffin home."

"We didn't have to push it down the hill," said Brina. "But it didn't roll very fast."

"The wheel bearings are dry," said Victor. "But at least it turns. We never could have *carried* the tractor up here to the utility building."

"I didn't think it was hard at all," said Brina.

"Of course you didn't," said Dietrich. "You were pulling it with the ATV."

"But you have to admit, I was pulling hard."

"She's right, Ditto," said Victor. "The front of the ATV was hardly ever on the ground."

"What do we do now?" asked Arcon.

"We just start taking every piece apart, all the way to the ground. I'll take pictures as every part comes off, so we remember how to put it back together. I've got two screw guns, so Arcon and I can get started. Ditto, I left my other tools in the shop. Would you go get a socket set and some wrenches?"

"Sure," said Dietrich, "I'll bring my tool chest, too—be right back," and ran off.

Brina glanced around. "What can I do?"

"Uhhh, see that blue pan over there?" asked Victor, "we'll need to drain the fluids out of the engine if it has any. Bring it here and I'll show you what needs to happen." He waved Arcon over. "Let's you and I start at the front."

Arcon was excited to tear into machinery again. It'd been years since he worked with wrenches every day and even longer since he worked side by side with Brina. He wished Elaina were here too, because he knew she'd enjoy it. But it'd be days before she got there with Roberto. He found an adjustable wrench to remove the cowling and then posed as Victor took the first picture.

"Here's that pan," said Brina.

"Okay," said Victor, as he took it from her. "Now, see this plug right here, on the bottom of the engine? When Ditto gets back with the wrenches, you'll need to find one that fits this plug and unthread it. As you start to loosen it, it'll leak oil, so you'll want to have this pan under it, so it doesn't make a mess on my new floor." As he said that, he placed the pan in that spot. "Let me know if you have trouble breaking it loose. As soon as it starts to drip, I'll come over and help."

"I think I can handle that," said Brina, as Dietrich walked through the door. "Ditto, I need one of those wrenches—about a one inch."

As she went to grab the wrench from Dietrich, Victor walked around to where Arcon was removing the last bolt on the cowling. "Smile," said Victor, snapping the picture without waiting.

"What do you need me to do?" asked Dietrich.

"Let's get the muffler and breather off the engine, then we'll work on the radiator."

"This thing is stuck pretty good," said Brina from underneath the tractor.

Arcon knelt to take a look at what she was doing. "Need some help?"

"I can get it," snapped Brina. "I just need to get in a better position."

"Is this what you're talking about?" asked Dietrich, tapping a rusted tube sticking out the top of the engine.

"Right, both of these pieces sticking up here."

Brina moved the pan and got squarely under the bolt. She jerked as hard as she could on the wrench, and the bolt turned. "It broke loose."

"Great," said Victor. "Ditto, the nuts on that muffler are probably seized. I have some rust-buster on the bench. Just dribble a little on the threads, and we'll get to them later."

"The bolt is turning," said Brina, crawling under to move the wrench around. "And it's not dripping."

"They probably drained it dry when they parked it," said Victor. "Go ahead and unthread it all the way."

"Aaahhh!" screamed Brina.

Arcon jumped when Brina yelled, and looked just in time to see black oil dump on her head. He grabbed for the pan, but by the time he got it under the engine's carriage, it was barely dripping. He yelled, "We need some rags."

Victor, having already figured that out, rushed to bring them to her. "Did you get any in your eyes?"

"No, I turned my head just in time," she said as she crawled out from under the tractor.

Victor handed her one of the towels, but there was only a little oil on her face. Her hair was drenched, and the oil was now running down her clothes. "I don't think this will help much."

Brina looked at him with sorrowful eyes and grimaced. "Sorry about your floor."

"Oh, don't worry about the floor. It'll clean up. I'm more worried about your hair."

"Yeah, I should probably go home and clean up."

Then Victor looked at her with a furrowed brow and said, "If it makes you feel any better, I think you look good as a brunette, too."

Brina swatted him with the oily towel. "I bet you knew it was going to do that. If you wanted a brunette, you could have just told me."

"What? Honest, that's not what I meant. I swear I had nothing to do with that."

"I think it was his fault," said Arcon. "How about you, Ditto?"

"Completely."

"There it is," said Brina. "From the mouth of two or more witnesses, you're guilty. Because of that, you get to clean up my mess. I'm leaving."

"Oh, yeah?" said Victor as she walked out the door. "These two bore false witness. They get to clean up your mess."

Brina stopped in her tracks, turned, and gazed at him with a frown. Then she smiled and said, "I accept your terms," and hurried away.

Arcon pointed at the oil on the floor, and Dietrich nodded. He grabbed another towel as Dietrich left to get some soapy water. Arcon looked at Victor and could see his long face. "What's the matter, Victor?"

"I think I may have upset her."

"Who, Brina? Naahh. She was just kidding. Trust me. I've known her all my life."

"I sure hope she's not mad at me."

"Oh, she's not. You'll see. The next time you see her, she'll act like nothing happened." Arcon could see he wasn't comforting Victor. He took a guess at what was wrong. "Are you growing fond of her?"

Victor turned and looked him in the eyes. "I must be easy to read."

"Why do you say that?"

"Jarden asked me the same thing."

"Okay, then I'm right." He heard someone approaching. "Ditto's back. Let's talk about this after dinner, okay?"

"Yeah … well … okay."

Arcon felt bad for Victor. They only had a couple hours to work on the tractor, but they knocked off early, anyway. Victor said he was exhausted from moving the tractor into the building, but Arcon thought it was more than that. It didn't help that Brina never returned.

Since Victor went to his apartment to lie down, and Ditto went to play with the trackhoe some more, he decided he should track down Brina. He found her at home, helping her mom with dinner. Her hair was still wet, and she was wearing her stay-at-home clothes. "Sybil, can I steal Brina from you for a moment?"

She looked him up and down and said, "As long as you're not oily."

"You saw that, huh?"

"Yeah, what a mess. She finished scrubbing her clothes just a few minutes ago."

"I won't keep her long, I promise."

"No problem. I don't need her … at the moment."

"Thanks. Can I talk to you in private, Brina?"

"Sure," she said, setting a pan back on the stove.

As they both walked away from the house, he asked her, "Are you okay?"

She gave him a goofy look and asked, "Why shouldn't I be?"

"Oh, Victor is all worried that you're mad at him. I told him you're not, but I don't think he believes me."

"Why should he? You're who tried to get him in trouble with me before!"

"Did it work?"

Brina shook her head. "I'm afraid maybe he thinks it did. I thought he could tell I was just joking. We talk to each other like that all the time."

"Hmmm. I need to ask you something serious, and no joking around."

Brina smiled. "With you, that won't be easy."

"I understand." He was silent for a moment and then blurted out, "Would you marry Victor?" When her mouth dropped open, he added, "I don't mean like tomorrow. I mean, if he did the Request for the Daughter's Hand, would you consider it, or would you laugh at him?"

Brina stared at him with big eyes and said, "That sounds so strange coming from you."

Arcon laughed. "It does, doesn't it? Sorry, I didn't mean to be so abrupt, but another way of putting it just wasn't coming to me. Have you even considered such a thing?"

"I don't know. Maybe. Sort of. I know I'm very comfortable around him. I was glad when he decided to move here."

"To be honest, I think he moved here to be around you more."

"Really? I hadn't considered that."

"You know how things work here. The two of you won't have a chance to get to know each other unless you court, and you can't do that without the formal Request. You can always turn him down before he can give it to your dad. I know you did that when Raymo tried to give you the request. But I'm afraid Victor wouldn't understand. They don't do things that way in the outside world. What do you think?"

Brina was silent for a while. "If I knew he understood what the Request means, I'd accept it. I'd like to get to know him better, officially. But he needs to know the rules."

"I'll explain that it's not a wedding proposal, it's a courtship proposal. And I'll let him know your dad has a final say. So do you give me permission to talk to him about it?"

"Yes, you have my permission."

"Good. I should probably wait until he's less nervous around you. I told him the next time you see him, you'll act like nothing happened."

"I'll do better than that," she said. "I'll act normal."

Arcon decided Victor needed a little push toward reconciling with Brina. All through dinner he'd been trying to explain the need for a Request for the Daughter's Hand.

"I still don't understand," said Victor. "I have to ask her to marry me before I can date her? How can I do that? I'm not even sure if she likes me."

"It doesn't say a request for the daughter's hand in marriage." replied Arcon. "Look at it this way. A girl is walking along, holding her daddy's hand. You come along and say, 'Can I walk with her?' Her dad asks, 'Can I trust you to protect her like I do? If you can be trusted, you can take her hand.' That's all this says."

"But what if the girl doesn't want to hold my hand?"

"That would be embarrassing, so we ask the girl first. We fill out one of these requests, and then we ask the girl if she would consider marrying somebody as socially clumsy as you. Sorry, I couldn't resist. You're making more out of this than it is. Around here, we consider courting assumes an endpoint. If you'd never consider marrying a person, why date them?"

"I guess that makes sense. But what if she's still mad at me?" He leaned on his forearms and stared at the floor.

Arcon looked across the room of empty dinner tables and saw Brina walk in the South man-door. When their eyes met, he gave her a slight nod. As she started walking their direction, Arcon said, "I think you're about to find out."

"Find out what?" he said, still looking down.

"If she's still mad. Here she comes. Act natural."

Victor lurched in his seat. "Oh, man. Okay." He ran a hand through his hair.

When Brina got close, she said, "It looks like you two are planning something."

"Wha—What do you mean?" stammered Victor.

"I know Arcon loves to tear things to pieces, and I know you brought a bunch of those battery lights. You two are planning to work late on the tractor, aren't you?"

"Uhhh … no … we weren't …"

"What he's trying to say," interrupted Arcon, following her lead, "is that he's too tired. I'm trying to get him to put in just a couple more hours. I'll do the work. He can supervise and take pictures."

"Well, you're not going to do that without me. I was just starting to have fun when the fun was interrupted by some oil. Sorry about the floor, by the way. Did the boys clean it up okay?"

"There'll be a little stain, but it's a utility building. That's bound to happen," said Victor.

"Good, I'm glad you're not mad at me," said Brina. "Now, are we going to work on the tractor or not?"

Victor scratched his head. "Uhh … sure … a couple hours wouldn't hurt."

"Alright then, let's get moving," she said as she started walking toward the door.

Arcon looked at Victor and gave him a thumbs up. When Brina turned around and waved for them to hurry, he discreetly gave her a thumbs up, too.

CHAPTER THIRTY

Elaina leaned toward the dash of her dad's Search and Rescue vehicle as they drove down the new dirt road toward the Facility. "Do you think Arcon is waiting for me?"

"Nope," said Roberto. "He's probably with his other girlfriend."

"That relationship is toast," said Elaina with a wave of her arm. "Arcon tells me a certain someone is taking a liking to her."

"Anybody we know?"

"I'm not gonna tell you. You're no good at keeping secrets."

"Neither is Arcon," said Roberto. "I'll ask *him*."

"No, Daddy, please. You'll get me in trouble."

As they turned a corner, the Facility came into view, and Arcon was standing by the north man-door. "There he is now," said Roberto, as he pulled up alongside him and rolled down the window. "Hey Arcon, buddy. Got a question for you."

"Daaad!"

Roberto smiled and asked, "Where's the nearest bathroom? That was a long drive."

"Just go through this door," said Arcon. "There's a hallway halfway down on your left."

"Thanks, Bud." Roberto crawled out of the vehicle as Elaina did the same. "By the way, Girl was telling me some story about—" He looked at Elaina, then added, "Never mind, gotta go."

"Hey, thanks for bringing Elaina back to me."

"Glad to do it. I've been wanting an excuse to see this place."

"Jarden is sitting in there. Have him give you a tour."

"I'll do that."

As Roberto went inside, Elaina grabbed Arcon quick and gave him a hug. "Good to see you again, stranger."

"Yeah, it's been too long," he said, as he kissed the top of her head. "Almost a month, right? Felt kinda strange."

"But it feels good now, huh?"

"Sure does. So, what story were you telling your dad?"

She pushed him at arm's length. "Oh, you know, about Victor and Brina. Working on the tractor? Oil on the head?"

"Oh, that," said Arcon.

"Right. But you need to catch me up on the other Victor and Brina stuff. Can we go somewhere to talk? In private?"

"Sure. Uhh, maybe we shouldn't go to my apartment. How about if we—"

"I've got an idea you'll love," said Elaina. "Someplace with people around so we're not breaking with ArcPoint tradition, but where we can talk in private."

"Where would that be?"

Elaina glanced up. "How about in one of these trees."

Arcon smiled. *Clever.* "Which one would you like?"

"I don't know. Let's find a good one."

They walked around the building and past the south courtyard. Elaina waved at one girl she knew, but was careful not to stare. As they walked into the forest, she looked at various trees, but rejected all of Arcon's suggestions. Then she spotted just the tree she was looking for. "This one," she said, standing under a tall tree with numerous branches.

"You won't be able to reach the first branch," said Arcon.

"Can you?"

"If I jump."

"I can reach it if you boost me up." Elaina put her hands on her hips. "I won't take no for an answer. Come on, give me a boost."

"Okay," he said. "Come over here, closer to the trunk. He cupped his hand."

Elaina braced one hand on Arcon's shoulder and the other on the trunk of the tree. As her foot met his cupped hand she said, "Ready!" and stepped up.

Her breath caught as she felt herself sailing up to the first branch. He kept pushing her one foot as the other found the lowest branch and her arm grabbed for the next one. It was a reach, but she was soon standing on one branch, then another, and then a third. "Well, are you coming or not?"

"You're lucky," said Arcon.

"Why is that?"

"If I could've gotten Brina to do that, we wouldn't be having this conversation."

"Real funny, monkey boy. Now hurry up. I'm going higher."

Before long, they were halfway up the tree, where they'd found two comfortable branches to sit on. "So, has Victor given Brina the Request?" asked Elaina.

"I don't think so," said Arcon. "Poor kid's a bit smitten, I'd say. I don't think he's said much at all to her since you and I spoke last."

"Okay, well—" Elaina adjusted her position on the branch. "Can we talk about us?"

"Uhh, sure. What about us?"

"Don't tell me you haven't missed me."

Arcon stared at her. "I lost my best machete once."

"What?"

"My best machete. It had a custom-made handle and was razor sharp. It fell out of its scabbard when I was swinging through the trees. Took me weeks to find it."

"So?"

"I missed you more than that," he said with a grin. "Did you miss me?"

"Of course not," she said. "I had daddy." She smiled, then looked down at the ground. "To be honest, I'm just not comfortable without you. I don't think daddy is either, but he'd never admit it. I think he's struggling with losing me, because it reminds him too much about losing momma. He won't come out and say it, but I bet he'll move to Baker if we do."

"Are you still thinking you'd be okay with that? asked Arcon.

"That's something else I wanted to talk to you about. I've been thinking about what you said, about wanting to build your own house, uh, you know, a house for us. And you still want to do that near Baker, right?"

"Haven't decided exactly, but that makes the most sense to me. How about you?"

"How long will it take you to build it?"

"Well, around here, by the time we decide to, and decide where, and draw up some plans, gather materials, build some, get delayed by weather, and finally get it built—it usually takes about three years."

"And you don't want to get married until we can move in?"

"That's the tradition."

Elaina couldn't speak as she wrestled with what she was going to say. "I just—" She looked away from him and stared into the forest.

"What is it?"

She turned back to look at him. "I don't want to wait that long to get married."

"I don't either. We could maybe build a small one, but—"

"But it'll still take years. And I don't want a small one that we keep adding onto. I want to build rooms for our children at the beginning."

"Children?"

"Yes, Arcon. If we get married, we should plan on having children. I know that may be difficult for you to imagine with that fertility issue around here. But I don't accept that for us. We *will* have children." She saw his eyes get big and added, "I have an idea."

He stared at her. "What is it?"

"Let's build a real small house fast, and move into it."

"You mean like a tiny house? There already is one we can move into, you know."

"No, you decided against the Franklin tiny house, remember? I'm talking about a small tree house—in this tree. No one will bother us up here. What do you think?"

Arcon stood up and looked around. He walked a few branches, climbed down toward the ground, then looked back up. Looked at some other trees. Then climbed back to Elaina. "What would you think about building a small room in this area, big enough for a few guests, and then," he said, pointing at another tree. "We'll build another room just for us in that other tree, and build a swing over to it?"

"Wow, really? How long would that take?"

"Well, it'd be like building two outposts. With help from my friends, maybe two or three months."

"Then we can get married?"

"Any time after it's done. But I warn you, it'll be rustic."

"I think I can handle it until we get our big house built."

"There'll just be one problem. Brina will never come visit."

Elaina laughed. "Neither will Victor."

"You know what?" asked Arcon, stepping over to sit next to her. "I'll be okay if no one comes to visit." He glanced at the south courtyard and around the forest. Then he reached over and kissed her. "How about you?"

Elaina put her arms around his neck. "I don't know. What about Jarden?"

"I'll tell him to whistle first." He kissed her again and said, "Welcome to our new home."

CHAPTER THIRTY-ONE

Petra was waiting near the north man-door as Ranger Dan pulled his red SUV up in front of the Facility. *It's still bizarre to see shiny motorized vehicles in ArcPoint.* He could see a pretty woman with red hair in the passenger seat. He walked around and opened the door for her. "You must be the famous Noreena Chan."

"Do I need to take off my shoes?" she asked, not getting out of the SUV.

"What do you mean? Why would you have to do that?"

"I've done my research about ArcPoint," she responded. "Isn't this holy ground?" She looked at the ground. "The word 'holy' means 'set apart.' Jesus set this land apart from everywhere else in the world, so it's holy ground. Don't you have to take off your shoes when walking on holy ground?"

Petra held onto the car door and tried to understand what she was saying. "Uhhh, we … you … it's not holy ground to us."

"But I'm an outsider," said Noreena, lengthening her words in all seriousness. "Doesn't that make a difference?"

At a loss for words, Petra simply said, "Umm, no."

Dan cut loose with a belly laugh, and Noreena pointed a thumb at him. "Sorry, he put me up to this. He said you'd think it was funny."

"Okay, I get it," said Petra with a chuckle. "No, I'd recommend keeping your shoes on. Our ground is just as dirty as everyone else's."

"That's great," she said as she hopped out of the vehicle. "It may not be holy, but it's still exciting for me to walk on."

"Sounds like Ranger Dan has been exaggerating about us. Petra Valerio, by the way—nice to meet you, Noreena."

"Petra runs this joint," said Dan.

"I know that," said Noreena. "I've seen him on a lot of the video footage."

"And you have a picture of him on your wall, with his name under it, and—"

"And that's enough, Dan. Don't give away all my secrets. Yes, Petra, I have a file on all the important people in ArcPoint, and I'm excited to get to interview them in person. Mostly, I just can't wait to see this place with my own eyes." She scanned the area, the paths and structures. The sound of a car door opening drew her attention back. "Oh, and this man getting out of the back seat is my cameraman, BJ. He'll be pointing his camera at everyone, if you all don't mind."

"Hey BJ, nice to meet ya. We know you've got a job to do, but please let us treat you as a guest."

"Thanks," said BJ. "Honored to be here."

"The first person you'll get to meet on your tour is Jarden," said Petra, helping BJ with his gear. "You're probably quite familiar with him."

"I sure am," said Noreena. "He'd be the perfect one to start with. Will he be with me for the rest of the tour? We have video of him in just about every location here. It'd be great to do a walking interview as I get the tour."

"I don't know. He's having one of his off days," said Petra.

"What do you mean by that?" said Noreena, concern written across her face.

"Well, you know he's the one that invented swinging in the trees, right?"

"Yes. That's a real interesting subject for most people."

"Well, over the years, he's fallen out of the trees a lot. It's taken a toll on his body, something fierce."

"He seemed fine in most of the videos."

"He hides the pain well, but he has good days and bad days. With all the commotion of the new road, I think he's overdone it lately. Let's go inside. I'll get you set up at a table and have someone go fetch him."

As they walked inside the Facility, they ran into Arcon, and Petra introduced him to Noreena and BJ. "We've met already," said Arcon.

"Oh, yeah, that's right," Dan smiled at Arcon as Petra asked, "Have you seen Jarden?"

"He's in his office."

"Could you go get him? Let him know Noreena's here to interview him."

"Sure. I'll be right back."

They watched as Arcon darted up the stairs. "Have a seat here," said Petra. "He'll be coming down those stairs in a moment."

It took a while before they saw Jarden inching his way down the stairs, with Arcon helping to support him. He was two steps from the bottom when they heard him say to Arcon, "Fetch my cane, will you?"

"Sure, boss," said Arcon, jogging back up the stairs.

Jarden looked their direction. He took his hand off the handrail to wave, but lost his balance. As he stumbled forward, Noreena gasped and jumped to help him. Before she could get there, Jarden fell, heading face first toward the floor. Then, in a quick move, he tucked his head under, landed on his back, rolled toward them, and jumped to his feet.

"What!" Noreena shrieked.

"That's called a tuck and roll," said Petra calmly.

Arcon yelled from the top of the stairs, "That was a good one, Jarden." He gave him a thumbs up without showing any apparent need of a cane.

"Okay, we're even," said Noreena.

"Naaah, not really," said Petra, pointing at Ranger Dan. "We *both* owe *him* one."

Dan looked over at BJ and said, "Hey, did you get it?"

"You bet," said BJ, still pointing his camera at Jarden and Noreena.

Noreena put her hands on her hips. "Hilarious, guys. Now, can I get that interview?"

"Tell you what," said Jarden. "How about if I give you a tour around the place while we talk?"

Noreena shook her head as if she were trying to forget what had just occurred. Then she smiled brightly at the camera lens and said, "That'd be perfect."

Jarden swept an arm around the room. "As you can see, where we're standing is one big room. We call this the main meeting room. It's the only indoor space large enough for the entire Community to meet—provided some people stand on the balcony above that surrounds the room." He led her through a set of double doors. "Through here is the Lee Franklin meeting room, which can hold about eighty people."

"Wow, that's a big table," said Noreena. "Is that made from acacia wood?"

"No, that's redwood. One of the founders brought that in for us. When we have large meetings, we move it out to the big room and use it as a stage. Those chairs are all acacia wood though." Jarden walked back into the main room and around a corner. "Down this hall is a machine shop on the left where we make the metal and wood things we need. Straight ahead is our north entrance, and on the right are bathrooms if you need one." Halfway down the hall he opened a door on his right. "This is one of our most important rooms."

"Wow," said Noreena. "I never would've expected something like this. You don't mind if we film this, do you?"

"Not at all," said Jarden. "This is our chemistry lab where we make, well ... chemical things."

"Really? I heard this room exploded—oh, I *am* sorry Arcon. I heard your parents died in that explosion."

Arcon read the distress in her expression. *She really is a good person.* "That's okay, Noreena. And this isn't where that accident happened, anyway."

"Thankfully," said Jarden. "We used another small building for volatile chemicals. We wanted to keep the fumes out of our main building. The explosion caused a catastrophe that could have been much, much worse." Jarden put his hand on Arcon's shoulder before continuing on.

"Okay, in the beginning, this corner of the room is where our doctor would see patients, although she mostly made house calls. Eventually we built another building for her we now call the Med Shack." He waited as BJ walked around, capturing images with his camera equipment.

Arcon stepped toward the door and said, "Next is the room I think is most important—"

"It certainly gets the most use," agreed Jarden. "It's our kitchen. That's another reason we didn't want toxic fumes in this area."

In the kitchen Jarden put his hand on one of two doors on his left. "This used to be a freezer, but its refrigerating unit became irreparable over twenty years ago, so they turned it into another cooler. We plan to get it fixed before we have kibbutzniks come here."

Noreena glanced around. "This isn't large enough to feed everyone at ArcPoint."

"Oh no, we just feed those who live in the apartments upstairs," said Petra. "But a lot of other people use it to make snacks or lunches or what-have-you. Most people eat in their log homes or tiny houses. We do keep bulk supplies in the pantry here, though."

"Shall we head upstairs?" asked Jarden, as he walked toward the main room and past the rows of picnic tables. He led them up a set of switchback stairs to the second-floor balcony.

"On this upper floor, we have apartments running down both sides and a walkway in front of them." They stopped halfway down the walkway for BJ to get a panoramic shot of it all. Then Jarden said, "Let me show you one of the apartments." He grabbed the door handle of the nearest apartment, opened the door, and she saw a young man standing with nothing covering his lower half but a towel. The man yelped and stepped back.

Noreena quickly averted her eyes. "Shouldn't you have knocked first?"

"We never knock around here," said Jarden. "We've got nothing to hide, right Chad?"

"That's right, boss," said Chad, dropping his towel right when Noreena glanced his way. She looked away again, then turned back around and saw Chad was wearing a leather kilt. She eyed Jarden, then Ranger Dan.

"It wasn't my idea," said Dan, holding his hand up. "Did you get that too, BJ?"

BJ patted his shoulder camera. "Got it all."

"All right, you guys," scolded Noreena. "Where to next? Uhh, nice to meet you, Chad."

"You too, ma'am."

Jarden motioned them to the railing, and waved his arm over the large room below. "Now, picture this. When we first moved here, this entire space was gravel and covered with travel trailers, campers, and tents. None of this upper story existed, and neither did the kitchen or Franklin meeting room. This building was originally supposed to be a warehouse for processing bareroot trees and rootstock." Jarden waited while BJ filmed the area.

"To your right—above the kitchen—is our library, which has an extensive selection of electrical books once belonging to Clive Barrows. Can't begin to tell you how important that was to the Community. We have a lot of survival and how-to-books, story books, magazines, service manuals, things like that. Behind that room is the mechanical room with all the refrigeration and air-conditioning equipment. Above the Franklin meeting room is what we call the Room of Remembrance where we keep all our stuff to remind us of our lives before moving here. Behind that is an electrical fixit shop."

"Rumor has it Arcon spent a lot of time there," said Noreena. "Made himself a radio transmitter, if I recall correctly."

"To be fair," said Petra, "Arcon fixed a lot of things that others had given up on. And besides, the transmitter turned out to be a blessing in the end."

"I know it was for me," said Noreena.

"Well, that completes the tour of the Facility," said Petra. "Do you have any questions before we move to the outbuildings?"

Noreena checked her notes. "I understand there were over two hundred people who first moved here. They weren't all staying in this room, were they?"

"No, not even half of them. There were others camping outside as well. Plus, as you probably noticed when you drove in, there are twenty-two tiny houses that got moved in at the very beginning. Our Founders worked hard to make this place comfortable."

"It's amazing, isn't it?" said Ranger Dan. "All of this sure destroys my idea they lived in caves and cooked around a campfire."

"Six months ago, I didn't even know they existed," said Noreena. "I'm anxious to see the rest of it."

"Then let's go," said Dan. "Lead the way, Jarden."

"Let's not go up to the tiny houses," said Petra. "They're just places to live. We want you to see what we've done to survive in this place. Let's go out to the gardens and the shacks."

As they left the Facility building, they entered a large landscaped area. "This is what we call the South Courtyard," said Jarden. "That sundial in the middle is our official timepiece. Most people told time by looking at smart phones. Those things didn't stay smart for long." When they chuckled, he added, "Wristwatches had batteries that died. We have a pile of dead timepieces in the Room of Remembrance."

Looking at the sundial, Noreena asked, "So, everyone had to come here to know what time it was?"

"Not at all," said Arcon. "We could go to the source. We'd look at the sun."

"After a while, nobody cared what time it was," said Jarden.

"I did," said Arcon. "I had to know when Elaina was going to send me Morse code."

"Good thing you had your Grandma Victoria's cuckoo clock, huh?"

"Yeah, when it worked. When it didn't, I could look at the sun, or this sundial, or the tree shadows on the Facility—I could see that from my apartment." He pointed at a second story window jutting out from the Facility.

As BJ walked around, filming the courtyard, Noreena marveled at the surroundings. Most of the courtyard was covered with large flat stones, with rustic Adirondack style chairs scattered about. "I assume you made the chairs," she said. "Did you also quarry the stone?"

"No, we didn't have tools for that," said Petra.

"We picked these up from an abandoned property over by the Rift," said Jarden. "We got permission from the owners to take whatever building materials we needed. The owners were afraid it'd all end up in the canyon anyway. A lot of the buildings we're about to see were built with those materials."

CHAPTER THIRTY-TWO

They left the courtyard and headed toward a crudely built log building with a rock foundation. Jarden stopped. "Before we go there, let me show you the hemp field. It's on the way."

Noreena followed Jarden as he walked toward a tree-less area away from the main buildings. They came to a field of plants held up by wire nearly ten feet tall. "We almost didn't have these hemp plants," said Jarden.

"When the Founders moved here, people were growing something called marijuana. These are industrial hemp, with no hallucinogenic properties. But the Founders were afraid outsiders wouldn't know that and try to steal them. People were being killed to get at marijuana in those days. But from this hemp we get paper, rope, fabrics, oil, soap, shampoo, and lots of other things. It was a lifesaver for our Community and grew well when this area was still a desert."

Jarden ran a hand over the delicate leaves. "Let BJ get a shot of you standing by the plants so people can see how tall they are. Then we'll go to the hemp shack and you can see some of the things we make out of it."

Noreena walked up to the plants and posed for the camera. When she did, some water sprinklers hissed with pressurization and started to spray. Noreena got the shot and they ran out of the field before they got soaked.

"Sorry about that," said Jarden. "By the way, those sprinklers aren't original. Victor just installed those for us. We used to have to water all of these plants by hand. The other field is still set up that way."

"Why didn't we go to *that* field?"

"Good question. Did you have any more questions before we move on?"

"I think you did that on purpose!"

"Couldn't have. Don't know how to operate that sprinkler thing. Anyway, follow me."

Noreena wondered what was in store for her in the shacks. She kept a wary eye on those traveling with her and scanned for people hiding in the shadows. She thought she could trust BJ, but now she wasn't sure. He seemed to always have the camera trained on her when someone pulled a trick.

As they walked into the first log building, Jarden told her, "We originally only had one building for all of our field operations—a small pole building. Then, when we outgrew that, we built more buildings with the free materials I told you about. Even moved a couple complete houses. Eventually the trees got large enough to make log homes. This building was our first attempt at that."

Noreena noticed a pungent grassy smell she wasn't familiar with. There were several tables with glass and metal containers, wooden spoons, and other items. It reminded her of a laboratory.

"This is where we make the soap," said Jarden. "We make oil from seeds of the hemp plants. We add oil from the ArcPoint trees and olive trees, then lye that we get from tree ashes. Anyway, you probably have better soap in the outside world, but it works for us." He walked her to another bench. "Here we make shampoo for hair. This process requires glycerin, which we get from animal fat. That's scarce since we don't have cows or pigs and have to rely on rabbit and goat fat. If you eat meat here, it's going to be lean. We cut every bit of fat off of it we can. When we don't have enough, we use soap ingredients, but glycerin from fat is better for hair. Now let's go to the fiber shop."

"Fiber shop?" asked Noreena.

"Right. We get cloth fibers from two primary sources— goats and hemp plants. Both have to be processed before they can be used for clothes, blankets, curtains, and things like that. Wool from the goats mostly just needs to be cleaned." Jarden pointed to some fiberglass tanks. "We clean it in those tanks. You should be thankful we're not doing that right now, because wet goat hair is rather unpleasant."

"I can imagine. Is it like wet dog hair?"

Jarden looked at her. "Wouldn't know. I've never smelled a wet dog, or seen one, except in pictures."

"Oh, sorry. I didn't know."

"Anyway, here is where we break down the hemp," Jarden explained, as they entered another room. "It's a tedious process of beating and crushing of the stalks to get the fibers." He explained the spinning of the fibers into yarn, the looms for making cloth, and other processes to get what the Community needed from the hemp and the wool. Noreena kept expecting something to happen to her, but it never did. She'd have to watch the film footage to see if she missed something.

"Noreena, I think you've met Madelyn McCoy."

"Right. Hi Maddy. Haven't seen you since the cabins in Calico."

Madelyn shook her hand. "You remember Nola and Steph, don't you?"

"Sure do. How are you girls doing?"

"Doing fine, ma'am," said Steph.

"You're just in time to see one of our regular procedures," said Madelyn. "We just made another batch of dirty blue dye."

"Dirty blue?"

"Correct. We crush the berries from the tree rhizomes and make a dye for our cloth that isn't, well, a pretty blue. It's our easiest dye to make, so most people wear this color clothes, in case you haven't noticed." The girls posed so the camera could get a picture of the dirty blue clothes they were wearing. "Nola, would you like to test the dye to see if it's ready for the latest batch of cloth?"

"Sure, Maddy." Noreena's eyes got big as Nola stuck her finger in the vat of dye and then put it in her mouth.

"Stick out your tongue," said Madelyn. Nola stuck out her tongue so Noreena could see it was dark blue. "Yep, it's ready."

"Ewww," said Noreena. "Doesn't that taste bad?"

"Tastes better than bug larvae," said Nola. "That's where we get the green dye."

"Oh … ack! … no, don't say any more."

Arcon burst out laughing. "Do you need a chuck wagon?" he asked.

"What are you talking about?"

As the girls laughed, Ranger Dan said, "Ask Elaina the next time you see her."

"I suppose you put them up to this."

Dan laughed. "Wish I could take credit, but they surprised me, too."

"Yuck," said Noreena. "But I will say, you folks are very resourceful. You're kidding about the bug larvae, right?"

"You don't want to know," said Jarden. "We'll check out the tanning process now. If you're squeamish at all, don't ask us how we do that."

"Gotcha."

After checking operations at the tanning shack, they moved to a building full of large machines made mostly of wood. "This is the heart of our operations," said Madelyn. "Here we turn the fibers into cloth. We have spinning wheels here, looms over there, and one machine in the corner that I hope Ranger Dan gets us parts for. It hasn't worked in years."

"What is it?" asked Noreena.

"It's a long-arm quilting machine. We've had to make quilts completely by hand since that quit working."

"I've got Victor looking into it," said Dan. "Says he's found someone familiar with them."

"Did you hear that, Lavelle?" Madelyn yelled to a woman working at a loom. "We're gonna get your great-granny's long-arm working."

"Praise God!" shouted Lavelle with both hands raised to the sky.

After watching someone work a spinning wheel, and viewing a lot of partially assembled clothing, Noreena asked, "Where do we go now?"

"Our most critical operation—food. First, the henhouse." Jarden led the group toward a large wooden structure. "When the Founders first set up this area, our meat source was going to be chickens, ducks, rabbits, and goats. We had to give up on the ducks because they're really waterfowl and, well, this was a desert at the time. The chickens were a necessity for the eggs. They needed the rabbits and goats for their meat and leather."

Noreena saw a tall wall of upright logs in front of an area covered with netting. Jarden pulled a latch, opening a gate into the area. A flood of chickens raced toward them. She hid behind Jarden.

"Don't be afraid of them," he said. "They won't hurt you." He glanced down at her feet and saw she was wearing open-toed shoes. "Then again, they might peck at your toes. But I wouldn't worry. We keep them well fed. Here, let me show you. Petra, would you like to do the honors?"

"Sure," said Petra. He walked to the far end of the enclosure.

"This is quite a building," said Noreena.

"Yeah," said Jarden. "It's one of the first outbuildings we built when we moved here. The Founders called it a strip mall. None of us now know what that means, but we've seen pictures."

"It makes sense. It's built like strip malls we have in our cities. You have buildings on three sides. This fenced area in the middle would be a parking lot for cars." She looked up. "That's a lot of netting up there."

"It's an ongoing job for the hemp workers to maintain. We need it so the bunny birds can't get to the chickens. They need a place to run free rather than stay cooped up in a, you know, chicken coop. Originally, we used metal fencing for a cover, but we had no way of replacing it when it rusted away."

Noreena saw Petra walking back toward them, carrying a shovel. There was a flock of nearly a hundred chickens following him. "What's that?"

"That's some of the chicken feed. We grow it ourselves."

"Is it some kind of grain?"

"What? No, we eat the grain ourselves. This is something that's more nutritional for the chickens. We grow it from the waste products of our kitchen."

"What is it?"

"Soldier fly larvae." Just as Jarden said that, Petra dumped the contents of the shovel near their feet. Noreena got a glimpse of crawling maggots just before the pile disappeared under a flood of pecking chickens. She screamed and jumped behind Jarden again. "They love food that moves," said Jarden. Then he looked at BJ.

"Got it," said BJ.

Noreena scurried toward the gate, swatting BJ as she passed him. "Let me outta here!"

Jarden opened the gate. "Let's go look at the rabbit pens; then we'll go to the gardens."

"I like the sounds of that much better," said Noreena.

Petra led them to another building and opened the door for them. Noreena looked at a miniature version of where they'd just been, with stacked cages around three sides of a fenced-in area of ground. A sign read Californian Rabbits. "All I see is more chickens."

"Yeah, that's the problem," said Jarden. "The rabbits were real escape artists, but the biggest problem were the children. The rabbits became pets, and when they found out we were going to eat them, the children turned them loose. That happened when I was a young man. We tried to recover them, but by then, there was already dense needle-brush around to protect them. Besides, the children put up such a fuss, we gave up. That's when we started trapping them and dressing them in the forest, where the children couldn't watch. Now we use the old rabbit pens for raising baby chicks. Okay, on to the gardens."

Noreena was glad to get away from the chickens. The odor was something her city-dwelling nose wasn't accustomed to. And the sight of the maggots made her queasy. The aroma in the greenhouse was much better. She tapped BJ and pointed at some plants near them. "Get a shot of these," she whispered. "And those in the corner." Then she said to Jarden, "It's warmer in here."

"Yeah. We condition the building to keep it the way plants like it, not humans. We used to heat or cool these raised planting beds, too. Some plants like cool soil, some warm. We lost that capability when I was young. It's one more thing we plan to restore, although it's not as necessary now as when it was a desert. This is the building we call aquaponics. We raise fish in those large tanks and water the plants with the fish water. The water we use gets replenished from another large tank where we collect rainwater. We also filter the rainwater for use in the Facility."

"What if you don't get enough rain?"

"We have large wells to draw from. When the Founders first moved here, this area was a desert, and we had orchards to irrigate. The wells were all we had. If it was still like that, those pumps would have died years ago. With the rains, we rarely have to use them. Anyway, in this area, we have the plants that need soil. That works best for tuberous things like potatoes, radishes, carrots, and sweet potatoes. We have yams, too, and onions. We also use this area for things like corn, wheat, and rice."

"Wow. You've got more variety than I thought. What are those plants in the far corner?"

"We call those crawlers. Things like squash, zucchini, cucumbers, pumpkins, that sort of thing. Sorry to hurry you along. You can come back whenever you want and look closer at all this. It's really interesting. The next room is hydroponics."

"Different from aquaponics?"

"Quite a bit. We all call it Hydro." They walked into a room full of pipes and planters of all sorts. "In this room, the plants have no soil. We keep the roots wet all the time with nutrient-rich water. We were fortunate that Dr. Norman Ashford studied this technology extensively in college. There's quite a trick to balance water flow, aeration, and fertilization. We use this area for smaller plants like tomatoes, herbs, strawberries, stuff like that. We also had small tabletop hydroponic gardens in the tiny houses, but we lost them years ago. That's why we built this area."

"It looks complicated."

"It requires monitoring, but other than that, it's pretty simple. The hard part is keeping the plants watered. We mix the nutrient water in a large tank in the ground. Then every few hours, someone has to pedal an old bicycle to move water from that tank into overhead tanks. Then the nutrient water gravity feeds down through troughs to the plants."

"Someone has to pump it manually?"

"Yeah, after all of the pumps in here died," said Jarden. "Now Victor has restored half of hydro to automatic operation." He smiled and winked. "We left the other half for the kibbutzers."

"For a true ArcPoint experience?"

"Exactly."

"Noreena," said Petra. "Are you ready to go see ArcPoint's most prized possession?"

"What might that be?"

"Our oldest member—the only person left who still remembers all ten of our Founders. Brina's grandfather, Lars Ashford."

"Oh, good. I've heard stories about him. Are we going back to your Facility?"

"Nope. We're going up to his house. That's an adventure all its own."

"Where is it?"

They stepped out of the hydroponic garden, and Petra pointed at a hill. "See that log cabin up there?"

"Way up there? Looks like quite a hike."

"If he can do it—every day for nearly a hundred years—you can do it."

Noreena wasn't convinced. "Okay, you first."

After hiking for twenty minutes—plus a ten-minute break at a bench halfway up the hill—they entered the Ashford home with Noreena panting and wheezing. The others quickly grabbed seats in the living room, where Lars sat next to an empty hammock-looking chair. She asked, "Can I sit here?"

"Please do," said Jarden.

She worked her way into it and remarked, "This is quite comfortable,"

"Thank you," said Brina. "Grandpa Lars made the frame, and I did the macramé sling for the seat."

"They say you want to talk to me," said Lars in a gruff voice.

"Uhh, yes, sir," said Noreena, leaning forward in her chair. "I'd appreciate you telling me about the old days here at ArcPoint."

"Old, huh?" snapped Lars. "Is that all I'm good for? Old stuff?"

"Now, Grandpa," said Brina. "Be nice. Noreena is just doing her job."

"Does she have to do it here?"

"Will you walk all the way down the hill so she can do it there?"

"I don't know why she has to do it at all."

"Oh, go ahead, Noreena. Ask him what you want. That grumpy thing he does is just a front for his sweet-hearted nature."

"Phooey," said Lars.

"Uhh, okay," said Noreena hesitantly. "Can I ask you first how old you are?"

Lars puffed out his chest. "I'll be a hundred and twenty in one month."

"Wow, that's impressive. And they tell me you walk up and down this hill every day."

"Several times a day," said Lars. He looked at Brina, who frowned back at him. "Well, some days I do. But I do it at least once a day, right Brina?"

"He sure does. I should know. I'm with him every time."

"But she's not helping me. I do it myself."

Brina nodded. "I'm only there because I want to be."

"That's right," said Lars, giving Noreena a stern look. "Some people may look at me like I've got one foot in the grave. They may see this bent-over body and wrinkle-covered face and think I'm totally done with life. Well, little lady, I'm not as done as I look."

The room was silent for a second, then Ranger Dan burst out laughing. That made everybody laugh, even Noreena, once she figured it out. She looked at Lars and saw a slight smile creep across his face. "You enjoyed doing that, didn't you?"

"I've waited a lot of years to say that. Thanks for giving me the opportunity."

"My pleasure," said Noreena.

They all enjoyed another two hours of hearing Lars tell his tales of the early years of ArcPoint. Petra didn't know how many Noreena believed, and wasn't sure about some of them, himself. He hoped BJ had recorded a lot of them, but knew he'd shut the camera off at least an hour ago.

"I hate to say it," said Noreena, "but we really need to be going."

"It's been a pleasure letting you listen to me," said Lars. "It's too much work making up stories that the ArcPoint people haven't heard yet."

"I'll come back someday," said Noreena.

Everyone got up from their seat. Brina tapped BJ on the arm and whispered, "You may want to start filming Noreena." She winked at him, and he nodded. He covertly turned the camera on and pointed it in her direction.

Noreena scooted in the seat, but the nature of its shape pushed her back. She lurched forward to get out of it, but it tipped to the side, throwing her flat on her face. She rolled over onto her side just in time to see Arcon and Lars give each other a high-five. As everyone laughed, she buried her hands in her face and joined them.

"Got it," said BJ.

Noreena smiled at him, shook her finger, and said, "You're fired."

CHAPTER THIRTY-THREE

Victor couldn't wipe the smile off his face as he drove the tractor past the tiny houses and back toward the Facility. A dozen people whooped and hollered as they rode on a flatbed trailer behind it. When he stopped at the South roll-up door, eleven people got off, and eleven others jumped on—one of which was Brina, going for her third ride. "This has to be the last one," he yelled to Elaina, who was monitoring the line of wannabe riders at the Facility.

"I'll let them know," she yelled back.

When the riders were safely settled onto the trailer, Victor took off for one more trip around Lookout Mountain. "Is everything still working?" yelled Arcon, as he walked across the three-point hitch and grabbed the tractor seat.

Victor jerked his head around to look at him. "I wish you wouldn't scare me like that."

"Like what?"

"It's dangerous to walk across the hitch while the tractor's moving."

"You forget. I can walk on tree branches in a windstorm. This is only two feet off the ground."

"Maybe so," said Victor. "But the needle-brush won't drive over you when you fall out of the tree." He glanced down at the gauges. "Everything's working. Good oil pressure and temperature. I think Gertie is ready to go to work."

"Great," said Arcon. He patted Victor on the back and walked back across the hitch to sit on the trailer.

After they made it around the mountain for the last time, Victor marveled at the view. *The outsiders will love this entrance into ArcPoint.* Coming into fall, the Mojave River was dry this time of year, but the massive trees were still bound to impress. The road crew did a great job of meandering the road through the best of them. Especially impressive was the wall of needle-brush that came before the trees. *The tour for the outsiders will travel through a tunnel of thorns before the road erupts into a beautiful grove. It'll be awe-inspiring.*

After crossing the new Mojave River bridge, Victor headed straight for the tiny houses. People lined the hill and waved as the tractor and trailer drove by. The current state of the tractor embarrassed him. It was just a skeleton, with none of the newly painted body panels installed yet. They would do that as soon as they could get the tractor back to the utility building. After dropping the riders off at the Facility, he drove it near the greenhouse. Victor and Arcon disconnected the trailer while Brina hiked to the utility building and opened the bay doors. It wasn't long before Gertie, the 730, was parked inside, ready to work on.

"Can you two finish this without me?" asked Arcon. "Jarden wants me to swing to the South Outpost and see if Chad was able to get a few rabbits. The kitchen is running low with all these extra mouths to feed."

"We can handle it," said Brina. "Can't we, Victor?"

"Sure. There's not that much to do. As long as I have you to help guide the pieces. I don't want to scratch this new paint job."

"I can stay. Go ahead and leave, Arcon. We'll be fine."

"I'd send Elaina down to help you, but her dad's here. She's introducing him to Maddy and the cloth house."

"That's okay," said Victor. "This is the easy part. I could do it myself if I had to." He smiled at Brina. "But I don't want to."

"I understand," said Arcon. He winked at Victor when Brina wasn't looking. "I'll come back as soon as I return from the Outpost. I'm leaving now."

"Bye, Arcon," said Brina.

As Arcon walked out the door, Brina asked, "What shall we do first?"

"It looks like all of these engine covers need to go on first. It doesn't matter too much, as long as the cowling goes on last, since it covers everything." Victor glanced at his comm-pad at all the photos he'd taken of the tractor before they dismantled it.

"How about this belt and pulley cover?" asked Brina.

"Perfect. I'll grab the bolts for it and the socket wrench."

Piece by piece, more of the tractor got covered with green and yellow painted parts. After each one, Victor wanted to take a break for a few minutes, but Brina kept pushing on. They'd been working on it for nearly two hours when Victor put his tools down. He wiped his hands on a rag. "Do you mind if I say something?"

"Why? Did I do something wrong?" Brina stepped back and looked over what they'd done. "I don't think we've overlooked anything."

"No, nothing like that. I just wanted to stop for a minute."

"Why stop? I'd like to get this done before Arcon gets back." She picked up another part, then looked at the engine. "I want to prove to him we can get along without him."

"Brina, please. Can we just stop for a minute?"

"Don't tell me you're getting tired already. I'm not."

Victor looked at the floor and shook his head. "Now I know what Arcon went through."

Brina fisted a hand on her hip and frowned. "Just what is that supposed to mean?"

"Nothing. It just means ... I mean ..." Victor reached into his pocket and pulled out a piece of paper. "I need to give

your dad something, but I wanted you to comment on it first."
He handed her the paper.

Brina no more than glanced at it, then folded it back up.
"No way."

"What?"

She handed it back to him. "Do you have any idea what
this is?"

"Well, yeah. No. I think so. What's wrong?"

Brina walked away from him and stared out the window.
"This is going to completely change our relationship. You know
that, don't you?"

Panic flushed over Victor. "I hope it doesn't."

She spun around and stared at him. "What's that supposed
to mean? Why would you give something like this to my dad if
you didn't want something to change between us?"

"I'm sorry, I just—"

"Go ahead. Give this to Dad. Then see what happens. We'll
just see how he takes this. And then you'll see what I have in store
for you."

Victor stared at the floor. "I should probably get what I have
coming to me now."

"Oh, no, you won't. What you have coming from me is
a kiss. But you won't get that until Dad sees that Request, and
we get this tractor finished."

"What?"

"You heard me. I don't know how you outsiders do things,
but here there is an order to courtship. Right now, we need to
get back to work on this tractor before Arcon gets back. And
I don't want him to hear anything about this. He's heard too
much already."

Victor looked up at her and saw a frown change to a smile.
"He told you about this?"

"To be honest, I've been practicing that speech for weeks.
You played right into it, just like he said you would."

Victor frowned. "Is this whole thing just a joke with you two? Do you have any idea how much it hurts to be toyed with like that? When you mean more to me than anyone I've ever met?" Victor held the paper out in front of him. "I should just tear this up."

"Nooo!" Brina yelled. "I was just kidding."

Victor stopped, then put the paper back in his pocket. He smiled at her. "Gotcha."

Brina laughed. "Okay, we're even."

"No, we're not," said Victor. "I'd still like to know what you think about the Request. I honestly don't want our relationship to change unless it's for the better."

"I feel the same way. But you need to promise me one thing. If you're going to talk about us, don't do it with Arcon."

"I agree to your terms," he said. "How about Jarden?"

"I think I could live with that."

CHAPTER THIRTY-FOUR

Jarden leaned back in his chair as he watched the ArcPoint leaders file into the Franklin meeting room. It would be a full room today; not a single leader in the Community would miss this early morning meeting. He watched Petra, who was standing at the head of the conference table. He was still a humble servant, but he'd also become a confident leader. Nearly everyone shook his hand or saluted him in some manner before visiting and finding their seats. Jarden was proud of Petra today, as he was with all of ArcPoint.

"I believe everyone is here," announced Petra over the noise. "Please find a seat." Conversations tapered off to a low rumble, and he said, "Jarden, would you do the favors today?"

Jarden stood. "I'd be glad to. Father, we need your Spirit to guide our meeting today. It's important to us, and, we believe, to you as well. We invite you to join us, and ask that only your Spirit guide our conversations and decisions. Thank you for all you've done so far, and for these obedient souls who've worked so hard. In your name …"

"AMEN!" voiced everyone at once, a chorus of enthusiastic support.

As Jarden sat down, Petra stood again. "Well, everybody, the time has arrived. I'd first like to introduce Noreena Chan." Noreena stood and Petra continued. "As most of you know, she's been working hard on a documentary about the ArcPoint Community. But some of you may not be aware that, by the standards put forth by Central Authority, she is not allowed to publicly show such a documentary until those involved approve of it. She's here today with some of her crew to show all of us what she's produced. If there's any part of it we're not comfortable with, she'll make changes." Petra looked at Noreena, who nodded. "Is there anything you'd like to say to us, Noreena, before you reveal the documentary to us tonight?"

Noreena stood and scanned the crowd. "I just want to thank you all for this opportunity to capture your world, although I'm sorry we had to invade your privacy. Special thanks to Arcon, Jarden, and Petra for working with me on this. I ask that, if anyone doesn't like the direction we took with this, please go easy on me and blame them."

"That only seems fair," said Petra, laughing.

She continued. "Tonight, you'll get a chance to see your story as we've conceived it. We've kept it short, so you won't see everything that's happened in this place over the past hundred years. Our primary goal was to stop the rumors and focus the attention on God and His influence on your group. I'll let the documentary speak for itself and wait for your input afterwards."

"Thank you, Noreena," said Petra. "Now, Ranger Dan Wilson, would you like to give us a report on construction outside of ArcPoint? By the way, should we still call you Ranger, or has your title changed?"

"You can call me whatever you want," said Dan. "My title has changed, so now Becca White is the new Ranger at the CalNeva Rift Station. She gets to answer all the questions about you folks instead of me. Becca, stand so everyone can see you." Up stood a young petite woman, wearing an olive-green Ranger uniform. Dan gestured in greeting, sweeping a hand to her and the group. "Ranger Becca, everyone. She's not sure if she'll be happy or panicked when the documentary airs."

"Hi, everyone," said Becca, scanning the room. She saw many familiar faces, one in particular. "Hi, Arcon," she said, grinning.

"Now, regarding construction," continued Dan, "Thanks to Sam Boardman, the road into Baker is navigable but rough, and that's how it will stay for the near future. The Visitor's Center in Baker is mostly finished. The tube train terminal needs a couple more weeks at least, but the connector tube is in place. In other words, we can shoot the pods into Baker, but they just fall out on the ground."

As everyone laughed, Petra said, "We should make sure they complete the terminal before opening for business. Speaking of that, Noreena, has a time been set to air the documentary?"

"After this meeting, if it's approved, we'll want at least two weeks for pre-release publicity. If substantial changes need to be made, we'll need more time."

"Understood. So far, it sounds like a month from today before accepting visitors, as far as outside preparations. Jarden, you've been coordinating accommodations. Is all of that coming together?"

Jarden rose. "It's been a scramble. I need to thank Luther and his men for all their help. As you know, Luther is in charge of maintenance around here. His crew was running out of things to fix, thanks to all the new parts they got. So they've put in a lot of long hours, converting living space for outsiders. Let's give them a show of thanks."

As the crowd clapped, Petra said, "Thank you, Luther."

"As far as housing for the visitors," explained Luther, "we had to be creative. You know we had ten empty, dilapidated tiny houses. We were able to fix up five of them for families. We repaired two more, enough to be livable, but they still need work. Three are almost beyond repair. We felt the visitors should help fix up what's left as part of their duties."

"We were able to get the bunkhouse completed," added Jarden. "So, a lot of the single men will be moving out of their apartments in the Facility, making them available for married couples without children. Finally, we have ArcPoint people with spare bedrooms willing to take individuals into their homes. So, at this time, we can handle about … forty visitors. Building living quarters will be an ongoing kibbutz task for a while."

"Does everyone feel comfortable handling forty visitors to start with?" asked Petra, glancing around for signs of concern. "Remember, we're free to do whatever we want as far as connecting with the outside world." When he saw a general nodding of acceptance from the leaders, he moved the meeting along. "Jarden, did you have anything else?"

"I did want to thank Madelyn's crew for getting their areas set up for the visitors. That was a lot of work. They prepared hemp cloth so the visitors could go home with their own official ArcPoint clothing."

"How about the road through the needle-brush and the trees?" asked Petra. "It looks like it's done."

"That's ready to go," said Jarden. "We put in culverts and raised the road through the river so it won't get washed out. We left some of the needle-brush near the road so the visitors could get a close look at the thorns on their way in. I have to thank the mechanics for learning how to run the equipment so we could do it ourselves."

"And let's not forget the tractor," injected Petra.

"That's right, Petra, you were busy when they were giving people rides around ArcPoint. It was a successful test for hauling visitors. Dietrich worked on both the road and the tractor, and so did Arcon. But of course, it was Victor's project. It's been completely restored and looks great. Oh, and we can't forget Brina. She threw herself at the project every chance she could."

"Yes—Victor and Brina," agreed Madelyn McCoy. "They put in a lot of hours on that thing. They were a real team."

"In more ways than one," grumbled Lars, leaning toward Jarden.

"Be nice," whispered Jarden. "I know you like Victor."

"Yeah, he's a good kid," Lars whispered back. "But he should've given me a Request for the Granddaughter's Hand. I'm the one that's been holding it."

Jarden patted Lars' shoulder. "That just shows he's as wise as he is good-looking. You might have said no. He's definitely a Merrick."

Petra said, "I think that covers all the major items on the agenda. I'll adjourn this part, so anybody who needs to leave can do so. We have a lot of details to discuss, so please stay if you need to. But I think the consensus is that we should shoot for opening this place up to visitors in early October. We'll have another meeting in two weeks to make sure we're on schedule. But now, make sure everyone knows about the screening of the documentary tonight. We don't want anyone to miss it. This meeting is adjourned."

At Petra's direction, the meeting hall darkened and the crowd grew quiet. On the wall at one end of the room were twelve of what Arcon told him were roll-up monitors. They were arrayed three high and four wide, and at a distance looked like one piece. There was a loud gasp from the crowd as the monitors came to life as one single large screen. The ArcPoint people had never seen a picture that was ten feet tall and twice as wide, let alone one that rolled up in pieces. Noreena's crew had hung it from the second story above the kitchen, so everyone in the main hall could see it clearly. Splashed across the screen read the words: LOST IN AMERICA–Before America was Lost.

Sitting on the still lit conference table stage were Dan Wilson and Noreena Chan. Petra stepped to the front edge of the table. "Welcome, everyone," he said, as his voice boomed around the room. "Sorry. I guess I don't need to yell when I'm wearing a microphone. I'd like to introduce Noreena Chan, the inspiration behind the show you're about to watch. Noreena, could you explain what we're about to see?"

Noreena walked to the front. "Hi, everyone. I'd just like to say how honored I am to be among you and to be in this place. Your story has greatly inspired me, and it's been a joy to research as much as I could about you."

The crowd applauded as she pointed to them and patted her heart. "Thanks, everyone … Thanks. It's only been a few months since a young man wearing animal skins emerged from this side of the Rift and changed my life. I was just a small-time reporter at that time, and I thought it would be interesting to do a story about him. But after doing some research, I decided the world needed to know what God created in this one-time, God-forsaken area. And I agree with Ranger Dan here, as well as your leaders, that this needs to remain a very special place. To that end, I've tried to emphasize in this documentary how God separated you from the world and why. I'll turn the stage over to Ranger Dan to explain how he's working to maintain that separation. Dan Wilson, everybody."

"Thanks, Noreena," said Dan, as the people applauded. "Doesn't she just have the prettiest red hair?" Noreena waved him off as the crowd laughed. "For the record, I'm no longer a Ranger, even though people still call me that. I don't really have an official title yet. I'm just the guy who makes sure that no one bothers you folks. So, if you want, you can refer to me as the Supreme Ruler of the ArcPoint Universe. Arcon thinks I should be called the Big Head. Personally, I prefer Dan, the Man."

Petra jumped to his feet and said, "How many here choose Dan the Man?"

There was a thunderous applause, so Dan gave them a thumbs up and then motioned for them to quiet down. "Most of you may not realize how special this place is. Almost nobody in the outside world does. This documentary seeks to change all that. Out there, we have many people who would like to get in here to study you, to study your ways, and even to study your trees. You may not know that every year thousands of people flock around this area to watch your Acacia trees bloom and just maybe catch a whiff of their fragrance."

"As most of you agreed to, we are preparing to allow small groups in here to work alongside you and experience what life in ArcPoint was like. As the outside world has gotten more technical, you folks have gotten simpler. There are many out there who long to live a simpler life, even if it's only for a week or two. They don't know what they're asking for."

The crowd roared, and Dan let them as he drank some water. When they quieted down, he said, "At the end of the documentary, we'll give them instructions on whom to contact to make reservations for a stay here. At first, we'll work with a few small groups to see how the plan works. If all goes well, we may add accommodations for larger groups. But everyone will realize this is not a tourist destination; it is a work camp. They will be expected to work like you do and learn what it's like to be self-sufficient. We'd all like to thank those of you who have opened your homes or moved out of them in order to take these people in. We'll do our best to make sure they're worthy of your sacrifices."

"There is one last point I'd like to make, and then I'll let you watch the documentary. As Noreena said, God was a huge part of bringing you people to this area, to helping you survive, and even helping to unite with our world again. If for any reason you think she missed something important, get a message to your leaders so we can consider making a change before this goes public. We want God to be as important in their experience of ArcPoint as He was to your Founders. Before we start, Willem, could you come up here?"

As Willem climbed up onto the conference table, Dan said, "This may sound familiar to you, but it still moves me. I'd like once again to sing an old worship song, this time with words that Petra helped me change. I want you all to sing it with Willem. The words will be on the screen over my head. Willem?"

As Willem prepared to sing, beautiful orchestra music started filling the room. Then the words popped onto the screen, and the crowd joined Willem as they sang:

Oh Lord, our God, when we in awesome wonder,
Consider all the changes you have made.
With evil bound, we now can freely thunder,
All of the praises you deserve today.

Then sings our soul, our Savior God, to thee.
How great thou art, How great thou art.
Then sings our soul, our Savior God, to thee.
How great thou art, How great thou art.

Now Christ has come, our lands are righteous governed.
His peace envelops land and sea and air.
There's no more war, or selfish greed and squander.
We're free to love, to sing, to laugh, to share.

Then sings our soul, our Savior God, to thee.
How great thou art, How great thou art.
Then sings our soul, our Savior God, to thee.
How great thou art, How great thou art.

CHAPTER THIRTY-FIVE

One by one, the connector pods glided to a stop at the tube train station in Baker. With each one's arrival, Dan Wilson got more excited. Every one of these outsiders had impacted the project to restore the ArcPoint people to the rest of the world. But only he had worked with them all. Finally, they'd all be in one place and get to meet each other. With the final testing and dedication of this station, a gateway would exist to the outside world. For the time being, Dan would hold the keys to that gate. Today, he was holding the gate open.

He glanced at the official station clock on the wall. The next pod was due to arrive in fifteen seconds. He heard a faint rumble as he stood on the pod dock. It got loud, then changed to a whine as the pod slid into its parking space. *Three seconds to spare. Best one so far.* He waited while the station attendant stepped up to the pod.

"Who's on it?" asked Dolores Reid, one of the first to arrive.

"Don't know," said Dan. "I'm expecting Sam Boardman and the President of Redi-Span. I suppose you're hoping for more of the relatives."

"I am, yeah. We'll see who shows up. There were a few who helped me a lot with tracking down family. I'd like the chance to show my appreciation. But to be honest, I told most of the family members not to come if they were planning to kibbutz here later. I didn't think you wanted this to be too busy."

"Thanks. I did the same thing. I wanted the workers here, like the helicopter pilots and road crew. But I told them not to bring their families. There'll be time for that later. I don't want to overwhelm the ArcPoint people on the first day."

They watched two people step out of the pod. "Looks like we're both wrong," said Dan as he waved to them.

"We made it," yelled Becca, as she and Dr. Stone walked toward Dan.

"Dolores Reid," said Dan, resting his hand on her shoulder. "I'd like you to meet Ranger Becca White of the CalNeva Ranger Station."

"You can just call me Becca."

"Nice to meet you, Becca," said Dolores. "And you must be Dr. Alicia Stone."

"How did you know?" said Dr. Stone.

"It's on your name tag," said Dan in a loud whisper.

"Oh. Right. Sorry, I forgot I was wearing it." She reached to remove it.

"Leave it on," said Dan. "Saves me having to introduce you." He looked at Becca. "Where's your name tag? You're out of uniform."

"I'm off duty. Besides, you're not the boss of me anymore."

"Speaking of bosses, is Sir Nelson coming?"

"He may be a little late," said Becca. "But he said he'll be here for the ceremony."

"Great. How about Dwight?"

"He plans to meet Sir Nelson in Vegas and share his pod."

"Hope they're not too late. I want to show all of you my new office down here." Dan heard the rumble of the next pod approaching. "Who do you think that is?"

"David Bryzinski," said Dolores.

"I'll guess Sam Boardman again," responded Dan.

As they were waiting, Dolores asked, "What did this place used to be?"

"You can hardly tell now, but this was a school gymnasium. It worked out great because the administration offices are right next door, and those are my offices now. That's where Meredith is, by the way. Just a couple of blocks away is an old church we converted into guest registration." He looked at the pod and saw two men get out of it. "Sambo!"

"And that's David," said Dolores. "Looks like we were both right." She walked toward the pod to meet him.

"Well, I'm going to leave you girls," said Dan. "I've got some business to discuss with Sambo. Patty is in the little church I was telling you about. Why don't you get her to show you around? Just walk out that door and follow the signs to Guest Registration."

No sooner had Ranger Becca and Dr. Alicia Stone walked into the registration building than they heard a woman yell, "Boy, they'll let anyone walk into this place."

Becca turned toward the voice, saw Patty, and said, "Obviously. They let you in."

"Well, if it isn't life guarantor number two," said Alicia. "Patty, how are you doing?"

Patty walked toward them. "I think I twisted my clavicle. Care to look at it?"

"Sure. Make an appointment with my office."

"Okay, never mind. It's fine. So, what do you two think of my office?"

"They've got you greeting the campers, huh?" said Becca.

"I know, a little counterproductive, right? Folks will take one look at me and jump back in the connector pod."

Becca put her hands on her hips. "With you guarding the gate, they'll feel completely at ease." She saw other people milling around, looking at displays. "Is that Noreena and BJ over there? Excuse me, I'm going to go talk with them."

"Sure, go ahead." Patty turned to Alicia. "Do you know very many people here?"

Alicia looked around. "No, nobody here except you and Becca. Are Arcon and Elaina around someplace?"

"They're waiting down at the entrance. We'll start shuttling people down there in about fifteen minutes. There's a sign-up sheet on that table over there. If you hurry, you may be able to get on the first shuttle. It's about an hour's wait for the next one."

"How many shuttles will there be?"

"Two. We have two vans that hold fifteen passengers each, and we're expecting about fifty people. But don't worry, they're not taking anyone into ArcPoint until everyone gets to the entrance. So, you either wait here or there. Once everyone is officially where they ought to be, they'll have the ceremony and then take in the first Gertie wagon batch."

"What's a gurdy wagon?"

"You'll find out when you get there."

"Okay. I'll go sign in and see where I end up. Talk to you later."

Sir Nelson stepped out of the shuttle van onto the once restricted Mojave soil. This was the first time he'd seen the massive acacia trees up close. He would've preferred seeing them in bloom, but he wasn't about to wait until spring. Regardless, it was an honor to be invited to this opening ceremony. On either side of the road leading into the forest were two rows of logs, arranged like stadium seating. Behind him were the rusted carcasses of dozens of vintage automobiles.

"Now that you're all here, we can start." The voice of Ranger Dan bellowed over the conversations taking place around him. Nelson had never met any of these people before today, other than Dan and Becca. He'd met Dwight for the first time at the Las Vegas tube train station. But he recognized many of them from video conferencing, like Roberto and Jonathan sitting in the back row. He looked forward to talking with everyone, especially Arcon Franklin. There was no mistaking the young man wearing animal skins.

When all eyes were on him, Dan said, "Let me start by giving honor to those who gave their lives for what you are about to witness today." A murmur went through the crowd. "Let me explain. As we were building the road you see before you, we encountered some large obstacles—Acacia trees. Those trees gave their lives so we could move forward. Now they honor us as a place to sit." Dan pointed to the logs on the ground. "Please, have a seat, everyone."

The crowd laughed and then applauded. Some of them even thanked the trees for their service. Then Dan yelled, "Wait, everybody. Before you settle in, we're going to have a short demonstration. If you could all move away from the logs, please? No, you don't have to go far. That's it. That's good. Okay, now just stand where you are. There have been rumors circulating around that Arcon doesn't really run through the treetops. Arcon, would you like to show us how you do it?"

Sir Nelson watched Arcon run toward the logs, leap over the first row, and land on the second, then stop. Arcon looked around, ran down the second row to the outside end, hopped over two more rows, and stopped again. Then he ran full tilt down that row, leaped over the road, and landed on one of the logs on the opposite side. Then he hopped to the back row, started to lose his balance, and hopped backwards to the front row. Losing his balance again, he waved his arms around, thrust his hips left and right, then fell to the ground, making a graceful roll to his feet.

"Show off," yelled Elaina. The crowd roared with laughter and applause.

"Let's see you do it," said Arcon. The crowd applauded again, and Arcon got them chanting, "Jump that branch! Jump that branch!"

Elaina shrugged her shoulders. "If you say so." They all went quiet as Elaina crouched to begin her run. She ran full tilt at the first row, then abruptly stopped when she got to it. "I think Ranger Dan should go first."

"I agree," said Dan. "First, let me thank you all for coming. Yes, you can sit down now. I'm not going to subject those poor trees to any more torture."

Sir Nelson grabbed a seat in the second row, near the road that separated the rows of logs. "Mind if we sit next to you?" asked Becca.

"Not at all." He turned his legs so she and three other women could get past.

"Sir Nelson, I think you already know Meredith."

"Yes, Dan's wife. We met at the Regional last year."

"Well, this is Dr. Alicia Stone and Dolores Reid."

"Glad to finally meet you in person, Dr. Stone. Dolores, you're related to Arcon, correct?"

"That's right, by marriage. Very distant relative, but I still claim him."

"I don't blame you. He's an impressive young man."

They heard Dan clear his throat. "I'm not going to try to introduce everybody. You're all here because you played a role in this. If you haven't already, I'd like you to introduce yourselves one-on-one after we get inside the ArcPoint compound. But I'd like to introduce one man now you've probably heard of but haven't met. He's my boss, the Authority over Southern California. Sir Nelson Richards, everybody."

Sir Nelson stood up and waved at everyone as they clapped. "I'd just like to say one thing." He walked to where Arcon was while he waited for the clapping to stop. "This young man caused me a lot of grief when he walked out of this forest. He stretched the limits of my understanding of my role as an Authority." He looked intently at Arcon. "For that, I will be forever grateful."

"Amen to that," boomed Dan. The crowd thundered their applause, then rose to their feet. Sir Nelson turned to Arcon and embraced him. Then he faced the crowd and pumped them for more applause while he pointed at Arcon. Then he sat back down.

"Okay!" yelled Dan. "Enough of this formal blah, blah. Let's get some of you into ArcPoint. The trailer can only hold half of you, so we'll solve this diplomatically. You're split pretty even in the rows. Everyone on Sir Nelson's side goes first. You folks follow Patty. The rest of you get to walk in."

"He's kidding," yelled Patty Abrams. "We'll come back for you. Hey Dan, aren't you forgetting something?"

"Yes, yes. Please, everyone. Listen up. On this trip, with all of you important people, we felt we needed to use our most experienced operator. The one person who has driven our tractor—the beloved Dirty Gertie the 730—more than anyone else, is with us today. Please welcome the patriarch of the ArcPoint Community, the one and only, Lars Ashford!"

Sneaking out from behind the trunk of a large acacia tree, Lars slowly made his way toward Dan. The murmur from the crowd was nearly as loud as the applause. Dan asked, "Would you like to say something to the audience?"

Lars looked silently at all the people for an uncomfortably long time. Then he said, "I can't believe you made a hundred and twenty year old man stand alone in the forest." Dan shook his head and laughed. Lars added, "Let's get this show on the road."

303

"Literally," said Dan. "You heard the man. Let's load it up and move it out."

Sir Nelson stood and walked toward the tractor and trailer—which looked more like a tour bus, with windowed sides and rows of seats. As he climbed into the front seat, he looked ahead toward the forest. Two large acacia trees flanked the road, with yellow ribbon crisscrossed back and forth between them.

When everyone was seated, Lars fired up the tractor and let it idle for a few minutes. Then he worked a few levers with his hands and feet. After taking one more glance at the passengers, with the engine revved, he grabbed the wheel and let out the clutch. The tractor lurched forward. Then Lars unceremoniously drove through the yellow ribbons without slowing down. Everyone roared their approval.

The road snaked past one big tree, then another, with long branches occasionally passing over the transparent top of the trailer. They hadn't gone far when they came to a stone-walled bridge. It spanned a wide riverbed that wasn't much more than a creek at this time. Then he saw what he was waiting for—a wall of green vegetation.

Lars slowed down as he approached a hole not much larger than the tractor. As the trailer entered the tunnel into the dense needle-brush, everything went dark. Then there were gasps and cheers as lights lit up the underside of the vines and the wicked thorns popped into view. Sir Nelson elbowed Becca next to him. "Now I see why they couldn't leave this place."

"And why we couldn't get in," said Becca.

Lars sped up again just as they burst from the needle-brush. After meandering through more trees, they came to a clearing. In a couple minutes, they stopped at a large Quonset hut styled building. "The famous Facility," said Sir Nelson as he stood up. "I've been curious about this place ever since I saw Ranger Dan's drone footage."

"So have I," said Becca as she stepped out of the trailer.

Sir Nelson took a few steps, then gazed at the surroundings. "You haven't been here yet?"

"A couple times," replied Becca. "But I didn't have time to look around. The Ranger Station has kept me too busy since Dan got involved with this."

"Well then, let's check this place out."

Brina waited as her grandpa Lars climbed down from Dirty Gertie, then asked, "Are you ready to meet our visitors?"

"Already met 'em," said Lars.

"Yes, I suppose you have," said Brina. "But let's go in so I can meet them."

As they walked into the Facility, numerous people migrated to greet them. Arcon introduced them to David Bryzinski. Dan brought over Becca and Dwight. Elaina let Brina meet Malika again, her friend that was praying for Arcon. After a few more, Brina could tell her grandpa was getting fatigued. "Would you like to sit down for a while?" she asked.

"Can we go upstairs where it's warmer," said Lars. "It's kind of drafty with the big doors open."

"Sure. I'll set up a couple of chairs on the balcony."

"That would be fine. Go ahead. I'll work my way up there."

Brina walked with him to the base of the stairs, then darted up them to get the chairs set up. She glanced back to see her grandpa slowly walking one step at a time, but never stopping. As soon as the chairs were in place, she sat in one and waited. Before long, he was seated next to her. "I think everyone in ArcPoint showed up for this," she said, as they glanced around the meeting hall.

"They certainly are a unique group of people, aren't they?" came a man's voice from behind.

While continuing to look at the crowd, Brina asked casually, "Are you talking about the outsiders?"

"No," the person responded. "My ArcPoint children."

Brina turned to see who was speaking and gasped. She grabbed Lars' arm and said, "Grandpa, look!"

He turned, and she pointed behind him. He turned further and exclaimed, "My Lord!"

Jesus smiled and responded, "My friend."

Lars struggled to hurry his old bones out of the chair. He held onto Brina's arm and was bending to go onto his knees when Jesus rested a hand on his shoulder.

"Stay seated. What is in your heart is all the honor I need."

Lars began trembling. "Are you … have you come to take me?" Lars asked.

Jesus chuckled. "No, son. ArcPoint still needs your wisdom. I just came because, well, it was time. I've stayed away long enough."

Brina took note of other faces in the meeting hall. No one seemed to have noticed Jesus standing next to them. "Can I tell everyone you're here?"

"Yes, you may." As she got up from her chair, he added, "Actually, just tell Dan—let him announce my arrival. I'll stay here." He scanned the crowd of people and smiled.

Brina slipped past her grandpa to the aisle. She hesitated, then turned back to say in a somber, respectful tone, "I suppose ArcPoint will never be the same."

Jesus smiled at her and said, "That was my plan."

EPILOGUE

Patty Abrams stood in front of a room full of people at the ArcPoint Visitor's Center in Baker. She tried to imagine how this building once functioned as a church a hundred and fifty years ago. She'd read stories of people gathering in places like this to honor God, sing songs to Him, read stories from the Bible, and collect money for Him. *Now He walks among us in a resurrected body and appears unexpectedly when He chooses.*

Behind her was a picture projected on the wall that said 'Welcome to the Mojave Restricted Area–Home of ArcPoint.' She watched as a few stragglers found their seats, and she soon had everyone's attention. "Welcome to ArcPoint," she boomed. "Who came the farthest?"

Someone in the back yelled, "Switzerland!"

"Okay. Can anyone beat Switzerland? I didn't think so. How many hours on the tube train?"

"Twenty too many," he answered.

"Did you ride it straight through to Vegas?"

"No. We stayed overnight at Hudson Crossing and last night in Las Vegas."

"Well good, then you're not worn out before you got here. Welcome to America."

"Thanks. We plan to see a lot on our way back."

"Starting with the Grand Canyon, I'm sure."

"Yup."

Patty glanced around the room. "How many of you believe in a Creator?" she asked, and watched as nearly every hand raised, some faster than others. "That may seem like a strange question since Jesus is ruling everything on the planet. But I want you to think back to another time, back to the dawn of the 21st century. If I would've asked that question of the general public, I would've gotten about twenty percent of the hands raised, and maybe less." She let that thought sink in before she continued.

"How many of you have read the Bible?" When she saw most people raise their hands, she raised hers and added, "Every day?" Out of over fifty people, only four still had their hands up, and hers went down. "Interesting. You can put your hands down."

"The building we are meeting in is called a church. People used to gather here to listen to someone read the Bible and talk to them about God. Many read it themselves every day, and others studied it intensely. Why? Because they believed it would bring them closer to God. The Bible was God's autobiography, and it held the keys to eternal life with Him. For them, all of that was true. So, what changed?"

A woman in the second row raised her hand and put forward, "Jesus returned?"

"Exactly," said Patty. "No longer do we need someone to teach us about God. We all know Him because we all have His Spirit within us. We're fortunate to have been born in the era known as the Sabbath Rest. Now we need the Bible to remind us of the way we were so we never go back to that evil way. Does anybody remember from the documentary what all of this has to do with the ArcPoint People?"

The same woman answered, "They entered this era before we did."

"You're right," said Patty. "They beat us to it, more or less. God removed the evil spirits from them and from the Mojave area and put up a wall of protection around them. Jesus didn't appear until later, but by then, they had gained the wisdom from the Holy Spirit to govern themselves, so He let them continue to enjoy their peace. In a little while, you'll all get to disrupt that peace. But don't worry; they're prepared for it. Besides, they asked for it. As you can imagine, there's not a lot to do in a place as confined as the Mojave Restricted Area. You'll also find out there's a lot to do simply to survive. This won't be a vacation for you. They'll expect you to earn your place among them."

She grabbed the remote and changed the overhead picture to one of a large Quonset hut shaped building. "This is their main building that they all call the Facility. It will be the central gathering place for meetings and meals, just as it was for the ArcPoint people for over a hundred years. Here you'll first meet your ArcPoint guide. Each couple or family has their own guide; single people will share one.

"When you signed up for this adventure, you chose a category of jobs in either food, clothing, shelter, or technical. Your guide will be someone who has worked in that field and will discuss with you what work is available and can explain what's expected of you. If you have a change of heart at that point, tough. This is a dictatorship, and you'll do what you're told. If you don't like that, let me know now, and we'll put you in a tube and shoot you back to where you came from."

Patty kept a stern look as she eyed the crowd. Then she broke into a big smile and said, "Just kidding. We don't know where you came from, so we'll just send you back to Las Vegas, and you're on your own from there." After another hesitation, she said, "I'm sorry, folks; you'll have to get used to sarcastic humor. There's a lot of it in ArcPoint. In truth, we can accommodate some changes to job type. Just discuss any concerns you have with your guide."

She changed the picture to one of the garden areas. "As a practical matter, I'll show you some pictures of the various work areas, but only a few. Why, you might ask? Because ArcPoint didn't have cameras, pictures, and projectors, or televisions, radios, comm-pads, shoulder-phones, or any other way to communicate visually. So, I'll show you a few things, and your guide will explain the rest verbally. Oh, and by the way, they have rules about how to do that as well. Okay, continuing on, for those of you who chose 'Food,' this is a picture of the gardens. This next one is the hydroponics area, where they grow food year-round. And this is the kitchen where, well, you know what a kitchen is for."

She changed the picture to a field of tall plants. "Do any of you know what crop this plant produces?" When she got no response, she said, "Trick question. This is my transition into the 'Clothing' jobs. Or, I could have shown you this," she said, changing to a picture of a goat.

"The first picture was of hemp plants. ArcPoint uses the hemp fibers for clothing, paper, ropes, insulation, and even bedding for the goats. They also use the nuts and seeds from the trees for food like bread and salad oil. The goats, on the other hand, grow the wool they use for clothing and—unfortunately for some of them—also get used for food. ArcPoint didn't have the luxury of an abundance of plant proteins, so they relied mostly on chickens for that. But as they needed the chickens for eggs, they supplemented with goat meat as well as rabbits caught in the wild. They did everything humanely, so don't judge them too harshly. As you can see, there is some crossover of jobs, even in your primary choice. Your guide will explain that."

Patty continued with pictures of the various buildings and materials the guests would work with, even handing them some samples off a table. Then she said, "I have a short video for you to watch. It was taken while we were walking Noreena Chan through the work areas. I think you'll like it. You'll see how fun it is to work alongside the ArcPoint people."

When the video finished—and they quieted down—she asked, "How many of you knew this area as the home of the Mojave People?" She saw about half the hands go up. "You folks must have lived close around here at some point, since no one knew these people existed except the locals, and even they had their doubts. I'm assuming the rest of you heard about them through the documentary. Either way, I'd like to clear up a few rumors. For instance, how many of you are concerned about the food?"

Several people raised their hands, so Patty said, "You must have watched the documentary. Let me assure you that the ArcPoint food is safe to eat. The heavy metal issue that caused fertility problems was discovered to come from the large, older Acacia trees. They had taproots long enough to get down where the metals and rare earths were concentrated. No problem has been noticed in trees younger than fifty years old, and we limit harvest to those younger than twenty."

Someone in the front row raised their hand and asked, "What about the berries?"

"Good question. There are two types of berries. One type grows on the rhizomes that pop out of the base of the Acacia trees. Avoid those because they may or may not have heavy metals, and they don't taste that good, anyway. There is another type of berry that comes from the seeds of the first. They're much tastier."

"How can you tell the difference?"

"The first type, called rhizome berries, grow on a woody stalk like a tree sapling and have monster thorns. The suitable type, called free berries, grow on a flimsy stalk, and the thorns are smaller but still larger than a typical blackberry."

"Why do they call them free berries?"

"Because they aren't attached to the Acacia trees, but grow freely out of the ground wherever the seeds get planted. But you need to be aware of something. The locals tend to refer to both of them as needle-brush, especially when they grow together into a giant mass. You'll probably all get the pleasure of taking a machete and hacking back the needle-brush. It's a local tradition dating way back.

Patty returned to the front of the room. "Now, regarding another rumor. This one was circulated mostly through the locals—those who referred to these folks as the Mojave People. It was rumored that the evil spirits that once inhabited earth still lived in this area. Can any of you tell me why some people believed this?"

Someone in a middle pew asked, "The Bible verses?"

"Can you quote me the verses?"

"Well, not exactly, but it went something like, *'For this reason, I will block her way with thornbushes and a wall to make her lose her way.'* And there's another one that says, *'There are thorns in the paths of the wicked. If you value your soul, you'll stay far away from them.'* That's what I was taught."

"That's close enough. We can certainly see the thornbushes, and the Rift makes an effective wall. But as you learned from the documentary, those verses were taken out of context. God actually favored The Mojave People. So why do you think He allowed the rumors to continue?" Patty allowed them to offer suggestions for a while, and then she stated, "He didn't. Both the documentary and your presence here today prove he put an end to the rumors. He had His own timing and waited until the ArcPoint people desired an end to it. Then He put the plan in place that had been there for many decades."

Patty pointed at a poster on the wall of Arcon in his hunter clothes and Elaina in her Search and Rescue uniform. "Now, there's one more rumor to deal with, and that's the one that says Arcon didn't actually swing through the trees to get out of ArcPoint. When you get into the Facility, there is a board with numbered tags on it. Take a tag, and you get a spot in line for swing training. When your time comes, you can get out of your daily tasks to join Arcon and Elaina at the Sunset Trainer. If you're like me and don't have the nerve to swing through trees, you can at least go and watch. If you do well at training, you may get hired to go into the forest and trap rabbits. Sound like fun?"

The only nod she got was from a young boy in the front row. "I hate to disappoint you, kid, but I was joking." Then she walked over to the window and glanced out. "The shuttle vans should be here soon. They'll take you down to the freeway intersection. On the way, you'll cross a narrow bridge over a road crack that isolated ArcPoint on the east side. That happened about nine months after the Rift, so by then, the I-15 was already abandoned. The ArcPoint people parked the remains of almost forty vehicles near the intersection, and you can still see a lot of those carcasses today."

"Why did they park them so far away?" asked a man in the middle of the front row.

"For several reasons," said Patty. "They were an eyesore near the Facility, and there was no other good solid ground. They assumed they'd be stuck in this place for years, and the cars wouldn't run when they got to them. There was a better chance of getting them fixed near the freeway. And they wanted to keep car-strippers away from the Facility. They were all junk cars, anyway. They'd sold their good ones and used these just to get them here."

"That makes sense," said the man.

Patty checked out the window. "The vans will transfer you to a trailer being pulled by a tractor. This is how they used to gather car parts to use in various ways. Once they stripped the cars as far as they felt they needed to, they pulled rhizomes across the road from the ArcPoint trees that lined it."

"Why did they do that?" asked someone else.

"To keep us outsiders out," she replied. "Contrary to popular belief at the time, the ArcPoint people had no ammunition left to defend themselves. Thieves had been trying to steal car parts, and they assumed they were next. That's why they stripped the cars, so no one would want to enter the area."

Patty picked a thorny branch off the table. "Speaking of rhizomes, it's an intimidating sight when you go through this stuff while riding in the tour trailer. In some areas, they are so tall you'll travel under them. For safety, we've installed sides on the trailer and a transparent roof so you can see the thorns up close. But the sides have open windows, so beware. If you stick your arms out far enough, the thorns will rip them open. That's not a good way to start your stay. Here, pass this around." She handed the piece of rhizome to the young boy. "The shuttle vans should be here any minute. Do any of you have a question?"

A young woman in the middle raised her hand. "Did Arcon and Elaina ever get married?"

"They'll tell you themselves later, but I'll be happy to spoil it for them. Arcon wanted to build his own house before they got married. Elaina didn't want to wait, so they built a treehouse in the forest. Then yes, they got married according to ArcPoint tradition, nine years to the day after they first connected by Morse code. They eventually built a home in the hills outside of this town. Good thing they didn't wait—it took three years to build."

Patty heard the shuttle vans pull up. "It's time for you to go. Welcome to life in the Mojave Forest."

For I know the plans I have for you, says the Lord.
Plans for good and not for evil, to give you an expected end.

(ArcPoint translation of Jeremiah 29:11)

What's *next* by J.W. Gilbert?

MOJAVE LEE

The world began with one man—the world of ArcPoint, that is. And the man was Arcon's great-great-grandfather, Lee Franklin. He had the vision and the skills to make a thriving community happen—with the help of a few hundred others. Surviving in a desert could be tricky, but a wasteland of sand was guaranteed to be safer than trying to raise a family in lawless Los Angeles—or anywhere else, for that matter. The desert need only sustain 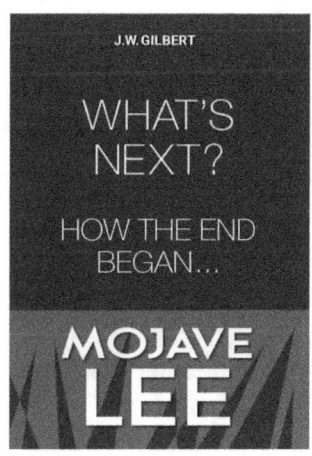 them until Jesus returned. And the way things were going in the world? That may only be a few years. Maybe a dozen.

Where MOJAVE ROCK tells how Arcon's adventure ends, MOJAVE LEE reveals how it all began.

MOJAVE LEE
FOR THE LOVE *of* ARCPOINT

JOHN WOZNIAK IS A CHRISTIAN FICTION WRITER with a knack for stories, research, and rock hunting. He and his wife are life-long Oregon residents with a passion for discovering the beauty in rocks and the One who created them. John's goal is to create rather than destroy, conserve rather than waste, hope rather than despair, and to laugh rather than weep. These goals have served him well, even when he was determined to remain an atheist.

Life altering experiences drove John to write his second book: Escaping Ignorance—Pursuing Wisdom: More Than 150 Stories Revealing God's Grace, Guidance, and Goodness in the Life of a Former Atheist. He's been writing ever since, honing his skills, and making headway with editing and self-publishing.

Before retiring, John worked as an international trouble-shooter for data-center cooling. He now draws readily from his years in research to shape realistic environments for his characters. Mojave Rift, the award-winning first book in his post-apocalyptic series, takes place many decades from now in the once desert regions of California. John has spent thousands of hours researching science trends and comparing them to Bible prophecy for this series. "I've sought expert advice in computers, energy, climatology, genetics, botany, geology, transportation, and other fields."

John is also having a lot of fun creating characters who are admirable without being super-human. He writes characters who lend a helping hand rather than a swift kick. He's met those kinds of people, and tries hard to emulate them. Many of their positive traits are portrayed in the characters of John's books. "In the Bible, I discovered predictions for a time when these attitudes would be normal, without being forced. My desire is for the reader to discover the same hope I did."

To learn more about J.W. and the saga of Arcon, please visit:

JWGilbertBooks.com

www.ingramcontent.com/pod-product-compliance
Lightning Source LLC
Chambersburg PA
CBHW071058250626
47159CB00002B/510